Out
of
Darkness

CLIFTON LABREE

© 2004 by Author, Clifton LaBree

Published by
Fading Shadows Imprint
New Boston, New Hampshire

Paperback ISBN-10: 194332915X
Paperback ISBN-13: 978-1-943329-15-1

Cover Design by Vivian LaBree

Dedicated to my wife Pauline, and my family, with thanks for all their support and encouragement.

Chapter One

Colonel Simon D. Hanley, United States Army, watched the bright lights of Paris through the airplane window. As far as the eye could see, glistening lights created a brilliant glow around the city as if it was wearing a halo of light. Most of the passengers on board the commercial flight were thrilled at the prospect of being in Paris, which was rapidly coming back to life after five long years of war and German occupation. Many of the passengers were anxious to make up for lost time. A festive air of anticipation filled the aircraft's cabin. Colonel Hanley's mood was in stark contrast to that of his fellow passengers.

The trip was one Colonel Hanley had hoped he would never have to make. Fresh from a stateside hospital where he had been recovering from bullet wounds and a severe bout of malaria, he had insisted on making the trip with the assistance of a cane. The tall broad-shouldered soldier with the serious demeanor and deep-set eyes reflected the inner turmoil that had been his daily lot since he was notified a year ago that his only son was killed in combat. It seemed an eternity.

***

He could remember the day his Division Commander, Major General Alex Grady, had called him to Division Operations on Okinawa. Hanley's regiment was conducting several complex maneuvers under heavy opposition from the Japanese and he was reluctant to leave the command post in such a fluid situation. His call to report to headquarters at such a crucial time worried him that something had gone wrong. He had caught a Jeep ride to Division Headquarters and ran inside the underground bunker, weakened and sweating profusely from the effort, a residual side effect of his bout with malaria.

1

"We're in a hot spot, General," declared Simon, apprehensively saluting General Grady.

"Sit down, Simon," requested Grady. The two men had served together off and on over the past twenty-five years. Grady was a crusty plain-talking man with a physique that looked as if he was undernourished. Tall and gaunt with prominent angular facial features, Grady had a pair of blue eyes that could look through a man at a glance. His thin appearance belied the fact that he was a bundle of energy and endurance. He was one of the Army's best division commanders, and Simon felt honored to serve under him.

"Yes, Sir. I hope this hasn't got anything to do with Keith," said Simon, studying Grady's facial countenance for some hint of what his visit was about.

"You and I go back a long ways, Simon. Yes, I'm afraid it is about Keith. Last night I received word that he was missing in action. I sent a priority communiqué to First Army for confirmation. An answer came in just an hour ago," the General replied in a calm voice. He never knew how to tell a person that their son had been killed without inflicting trauma. "Keith was killed in action..."

Simon heard the news. It was like a hard physical blow hurting all over. He had a sensation of wanting to run away and not hear that his son was gone forever. "I knew it was coming... I felt it on my way over here," Simon cursed in agony. Tears gushed from his eyes washing the battlefield grime from his cheeks. He cradled his head in both hands and wept uncontrollably. His world had collapsed.

General Grady let Simon vent his grief. He grasped Simon's shoulders to comfort his friend of many years. "I can't tell you how I hated to be the one to tell you the bad news. I've watched Keith grow from a chubby baby to a fine West Point graduate, and I loved him almost as much as you did, Simon."

"I always knew that, General," answered Simon. General Grady and his wife had been frequent visitors to the Hanley quarters. "Miriam and I were so happy the day he was born at Leavenworth. I remember you and Mrs. Grady helped us obtain more spacious quarters at the base. He was a chubby little guy then, wasn't he?" Simon wiped his face and blew his nose in a clean handkerchief Grady passed to him. The day he became a father was the proudest day of his life.

"I'm so sorry, Simon. We're losing our best young men at alarming rates here in the Pacific Theater. Losses are an integral part of what we do, and they're the biggest cross we have to bear, but you know that already. Keith's company commander will be forwarding a personal letter to you. As soon as it comes in I'll see that you get it. Is there anything I can do for you, Simon?"

"Thanks, General," responded Simon. He looked at his Division Commander with a stern set to his jaw. "I just want to return to my command post. My men need me, especially at this critical time of our offensive. Their welfare is my responsibility. It amazes me how every piece of real estate we fight over can cost so much."

"God be with you, Simon. Just as soon as the situation eases a little, I'm going to pull your regiment out of the line. You've done a great job. I often wonder if the folks back home appreciate the sacrifices made to keep them safe… but that's not for me to judge. Don't forget, Simon, your friends share your grief."

"Thanks, General," Simon had answered, leaving the dark bunker.

***

"Colonel, are you all right?" asked an airline stewardess, bending over him. She noticed that haunting far-away look in his eyes. "You should fasten your seat belt. We're in a landing pattern, Sir. May I get something for you?"

"Thanks for asking. I'll be fine."

The stewardess recognized two of the ribbons on his uniform, the Distinguished Service Cross and the Silver Star. She also recognized the yellowish tan caused by the Atabrine (quinine) tablets they took to help prevent malaria. Most of the veterans from the South Pacific looked the same. "My father was wounded on Saipan. He came home with a tan just like yours."

"You're observant, young lady. They say it takes a few months to wear off. Your father must be proud of a daughter

3

like you. I wish him luck in recovering from his wounds. Saipan was a hard fight."

"It's been nice talking with you, Colonel. Buckle up please."

Simon did as he was instructed and took a well-worn letter out of his pocket. He started to read it again while the plane circled above Paris, waiting for its turn to land:

Somewhere in France
November, 1944

Dear Colonel Hanley:

Army Headquarters has informed me that you have been notified of the death of your son, Lieutenant Keith Hanley.

I was his company commander and can assure you that he carried the traditions of West Point, Duty, Honor, Country, to the fullest degree. The men in his platoon respected and admired him. But there was more to him than that. He was first and foremost a gentleman. His quiet and calm demeanor inspired his men to extraordinary effort.

My interpretation of his courage and valor, above and beyond the call of duty, I believe, are worthy of the Medal of Honor and I am recommending it. His actions against multi machine gun nests blocking the advance of his platoon saved the lives of many men. He was killed conducting a successful assault with several satchel bombs against the well defended enemy positions. He threw the satchel charges like baseballs. I am proud to make the recommendation.

Your son personified the American soldier. His loss is an example of the high price we are paying for victory. The Army and the nation join you in mourning his loss.

Respectfully yours,
Captain Carl Langford, USA

4

Simon slowly started down the steps from the plane, one at a time, searching for a familiar face in the audience. The doctor at the Army's Walter Reed Hospital in Washington, DC insisted that he take the cane. A frown appeared on his face when he failed to recognize anyone in the crowd. He looked tired and was feeling more exhausted than he expected. His left leg had been shattered by a machine gun bullet on Okinawa and was more painful than usual. Now he was glad that he had taken the cane. The hospital had tried to keep him from making the trip, but he was determined to attend the commemoration of the cemetery on the coast of Normandy where Keith was buried. Keith's mother, Miriam, also wanted to attend the ceremony and had planned to meet him at the airport.

A staff sergeant met Simon at the foot of the stairs with a salute. "Excuse me, Colonel Hanley. I'm Sergeant Jones and have been instructed to escort you to the car waiting at the main entrance. May I help you with your luggage, Sir?"

"Thanks, Sergeant, I have only one bag," answered Simon, returning his salute.

"I'll pick it up when they sort them out, Colonel. Mrs. Miriam Carter is waiting for you in the car near the entrance. I'll be along as soon as I retrieve your bag."

***

"Thanks," Simon replied, heading for the main entrance of the terminal. Miriam had requested that she meet him at the airport and accompany him to the cemetery in Normandy.

Simon was still bitter about what had taken place between them. Their marriage of fourteen years had been tossed aside when she met a dashing higher ranking officer at Fort Benning, Georgia, where Simon was assigned to attend the world famous Infantry Course under the competent General George Marshall. Keith was twelve years old in 1933 and Simon was a newly commissioned captain anxious to do well in the course that prepared officers to command battalions and regiments. The school was difficult and demanded 110% of his time and energy. He never knew exactly why she left him for the handsome Colonel Carter. It was a bitter experience that had shattered his life.

5

Miriam and Simon had been childhood sweethearts through elementary and high school at Wilson River, a small town in northern Maine. He had returned unscathed from the crucible that was World War One. His twin brother, Samuel, was killed in action and buried in the soil of France. Simon and Miriam were married September 1, 1919 in Wilson River, two months after he returned from France. Remembering Miriam at their wedding day still sent chills down his spine. She was a beautiful bride, almost as tall as Simon. There was a softness and gentleness to her that defied description. Unpretentious and plain speaking, she was well-liked in the small community. They enjoyed hiking in the forest and walking along the river that bisected the town. Every summer they climbed mount Katadin together, a tradition they always looked forward to. She studied education at college while Simon studied forestry. She taught school during the war, then quit to marry Simon.

The six months at Benning was long enough for Colonel Carter, to win Miriam's heart. Within a year, the divorce was final. Keith went to live with his mother until Simon was posted to a station where he could attend school without interruptions. When he entered high school, Keith elected to stay at the Presidio in San Francisco with his father until he graduated. The separation was hard on Keith because he loved them both. He was fortunate in that neither of his parents used him as a means to attack each other. Keith was never close to Leroy Carter and disliked the man intensely.

Over the years since the divorce, Simon went out with other women, for he had frequent offers, yet the memories of Miriam were deeply ingrained. He had developed a seething hatred for General Carter and a deep resentment toward Miriam. It helped him get through each day. She left without a word of explanation. He never forgave her for the betrayal and shabby way she treated his devotion to her. The fact that such a strong and long-standing bond of trust had been broken so easily, shattered his trust in women and in his own self-worth. That soon led to a problem with alcohol that severely jeopardized his career in the Army.

One day, shortly after being promoted to a captain commanding a company, he was heavily inebriated and staggering at an evening parade attended by several outraged senior officers who demanded an immediate resignation of his commission. He would have voluntarily resigned if it had not been for Colonel Grady, his regimental commander. Never in his life had he been so severely insulted and berated as he was by Grady at that time. The scuttlebutt circulating through the troops had it that Grady did everything except physically attack Simon. Grady told Simon that he was putting his own career on the line in supporting him, and that Keith would look upon his father with disgust and shame if he was washed out of the Army. It was a powerful incentive to stop the destructive conduct. The intense chewing out had its intended effect. Simon never used alcohol to excess after the confrontation.

***

Simon walked through the Paris Airport terminal entrance looking for the Army sedan. He spotted it off to the right with Miriam standing beside it. She was watching the busy entrance for Simon and failed to recognize him until he stepped directly in front of her. Four long years had passed since they had seen each other. She was dressed in black and was as attractive as ever. Gray strands shown through her short brown hair. The small hat sat off to the side of her head with a black veil hanging over her eyes. Simon noticed a first lieutenant bar attached to the cap. She was never showy or sultry, but she always turned heads. It was the proud, confident way she looked at the world that made people take a second glance. She gave the impression of being intimidating, but Simon knew from experience that she was the opposite, a very warm understanding individual, and that made the mystery of her attraction to Grady that much more baffling.

"Simon," she exclaimed. "I hardly recognized you. You didn't tell me that you were wounded." His deep-set eyes alarmed her. She reached out to take him in her arms.

It was impossible for Simon to resist. For a moment he forgot the long years of bitterness and loneliness, and remembered how it used to be. It was as natural for them to embrace upon meeting as it was to breathe, but he had to be careful and not carry it too far.

7

"You're as lovely as ever, Miriam. It's been a long time."

"What happened to you, Simon?" she asked in a desperate tone. She noticed the Silver Star and the Distinguished Service Cross in his ribbons. Keith had looked a lot like his father. Even though Simon limped with a cane and possessed that empty thousand-yard stare common to men who have seen too much combat, he was a handsome man. His broad shoulders and confident air projected a strong sense of presence that made people take notice. The well-trimmed sideburns showing beneath his cap were completely gray.

"I was hit by a Japanese machine gun on Okinawa. The doctors wanted me to stay in the hospital, but when I received word from you about the ceremony, nothing could have kept me from coming," Simon explained, trying to calm the knots forming in his stomach. "I hope this trip will help. I see Keith everywhere. I can't sleep, and I don't know where I'm going. Nothing seems to matter now. I keep asking why, but I know there's no answer to the question. I've lost hundreds of young men in my commands over the past few years, so I know what death is, but I just can't accept it happening to Keith. It probably doesn't make much sense, but there are a lot of things that defy logic."

"I understand," answered Miriam, biting her lip. She knew what Simon was referring to and did not blame him. "Come, Simon, let's sit in the car. Sergeant Jones will be along shortly."

"He's getting my bag," Simon added, holding the door for Miriam to enter before he climbed into the back seat of the 1942 Ford sedan. He placed the cane on the floor and reached into his pants pocket. "Keith's company commander sent me his West Point ring. I thought you might want to have it. I'm sure he would agree."

Miriam took the ring, slowly turning it over in her hand. She kissed it and started to cry. Simon held her hand until Sergeant Jones returned with his bag.

"Sergeant, you may take Colonel Hanley to his hotel now." Miriam instructed in a wavering voice.

"It was thoughtful of you to make all the preparations for me, Miriam. I appreciate it."

"Leroy has been stationed in Paris at Allied Headquarters for a few months. We can drive in the morning to the Normandy coast. Sergeant Jones has been assigned to us for as long as we need him. I'm sorry that you've been wounded. I didn't know. You and Keith have always been in my daily prayers. I hope you can forgive me for what I put you through. I really am sorry, Simon. If I had it to do over again, I'd handle it differently…"

"I don't want to get into recriminating discussions, Miriam. However, I do want to tell you that a lot of hurt and grief rubbed off on Keith. What took place was devastating and the hurt lingers. You made the choice without any consideration of Keith or me. I would have climbed any mountain for you, and I can truthfully tell you that deep down beneath all the layers of bitterness and anger, I still love you, but the trust and respect that we shared for so many years has been destroyed, probably forever," he confessed.

"Yes, you're right, I made the choice for selfish reasons," admitted Miriam. She laid her head back against the seat and remained silent until Sergeant Jones pulled the Ford into the hotel carport. A porter opened the car door for Simon. Jones took his bag out of the trunk and placed it beside the entrance door.

"Thank you, Sergeant," said Simon, saluting him.

"You're welcome, Sir."

"I hope that you rest well," Miriam told him, rolling the car window down. He looked exhausted, and she was concerned for him. "Leroy suggested that you stay with us. I thought it would be awkward for everyone, so I made reservations here at the hotel for you."

"I think you did the right thing."

"Sergeant Jones and I will pick you up at eight o'clock in the morning. It'll take about two hours to drive to Normandy," declared Miriam.

"I'll be ready when you get here."

"No matter what you may think of me," whispered Miriam, hanging onto his arm. "I never stopped caring about you, Simon." Tears blurred her vision as the car pulled away from the portico.

9

Chapter Two

Throughout the night, Simon could not get Miriam's last statement out of his mind. What was she trying to tell him? He attributed the confession to the trauma of revisiting Keith's death and the guilt she probably carried for breaking up a family. Once he had arrived at a logical explanation, he went to bed and slept soundly the rest of the night, knowing that the next day was going to demand all of his strength. The noisy streets of Paris filtered through his open window.

The deep sleep helped to revive him. It was still a new and pleasant experience to wake up to silence even though he had not been in combat for the past four months. The rumble of gunfire had been a large part of his daily life for four years. Sometimes the silence between salvoes would wake him quicker than the thundering echoes. Those were the times when he came face to face with the divorce, admitting angrily that he was no closer to understanding it now than he was in 1934.

He had been in the Army for twenty-eight years. Now he was considering the possibility of retiring his commission. He was almost fifty years old, too young to stop working. Maybe he could find work as a forester in Maine. The logic of retiring in 1945 or 1946 touched his desire for a change in his life.

He searched for peace of mind. Happiness would be nice, but at this stage of his life, he would settle for contentment and satisfaction. For too long he had been filling each day with activity without any specific goal to guide him. He had lived his life for Miriam and Keith and never regretted a day, but now he was on his own. The possibility of regaining control of his life excited his imagination, but he was at a loss of how to accomplish that goal.

Simon ate breakfast and was waiting in the lobby when Sergeant Jones came through the door at exactly 8:00 AM.

10

"Good morning, Sergeant."

"Good morning, Colonel," replied the young enlisted man. "The car is right outside, Sir."

"How are the roads between here and the coast, Sergeant? I served in the Pacific Theater."

"I've been told by my quartermaster that the roads are good most of the way. Some villages were badly damaged, but the bulk of the destroyed infrastructure occurred farther to the north. My mess sergeant sent along a basket of food and drinks in case you and Mrs. Carter wanted refreshment on the trip. I also have two thermos bottles of coffee. I'm a coffee addict," grinned the young sergeant.

"Then we have that in common, Sergeant. I'm ready to leave. Are you going to bring me back here tonight?"

"Yes, Sir. I'm ordered to stay with you for as long as you need me. I want to say how sorry I am about your son. I lost a brother in the battle for Bastogne. I visited his grave the other day in Belgium. It was rough. I just wanted to let you know that I understand what you and Mrs. Grady are going through. I should add, Colonel Hanley, that whatever I see or hear on this trip stays with me. I give you my word on that."

"That's good enough for me. Thanks for letting me know. Our country has paid a terrible price for freedom. Citizen-soldiers, like you and your brother, have shown the world what courage and valor is capable of doing. Hold your head high, son. That uniform you wear represents the best the world has ever seen."

"Yes, Sir."

Miriam was again dressed in black for the solemn occasion. The small hat with the first lieutenant bar attached to the front of it sat at a more rakish angle than the day before. She also wore Keith's West Point ring on a gold chain around her neck. A more refreshed Simon walked towards the automobile. She was concerned about the words she had whispered in his ear upon leaving last night, determined to not lose control like that again.

"Good morning, Miriam."

"Good morning, Simon. You look a lot more refreshed than you did last night. I guess we both needed that for the day ahead of us."

11

They started on the road toward Arromanches on the English Channel in Normandy. A few miles from the Paris metropolitan area, Sergeant Jones asked them if they would like a cup of coffee.

"Is it your own brew, Sergeant," asked Simon. "Or is it regulation issue?"

"I made it myself, Sir. It has cream and sugar added," hailed the driver, handing a thermos to them. "I hope you like it."

"Would you like some, Miriam?" asked Simon.

"Yes, there's a chill in the air, and a hot cup would be nice," she replied.

Simon poured Miriam a cup and one for himself. He tasted it and found it to be delicious. "Your recipe for coffee is right on target, Sergeant. Thanks, it hits the spot."

"You're welcome, Sir," responded Sergeant Jones, smiling in the rear view mirror. Miriam listened to the small discourse between the two men with a smile on her face. It was typical of Simon's gentle courtesy. She had always liked that common touch he had with people. Her husband, General Leroy Carter, would never have entered into the exchange even if he wanted a cup of coffee.

"Have you heard anything about the recommendation for Keith's Medal of Honor?" asked Simon.

"No, Leroy mentioned that they are investigated thoroughly, and that takes time. I read Captain Langford's recommendation. I was not surprised that Keith would think of his men's safety first. I spent a few hours last night going over some family photographs. The last one I took of him after graduation from West Point is one of his best. I should have brought it along for you, but I forgot. He was so proud of his commission. He loved life. It's difficult to imagine how fleeting our time really is here on earth. I have the last letter he sent to me in my purse. Would you like to read it?"

"Oh, yes, I would." Simon eagerly accepted the letter, and slowly read each word:

Somewhere on the
English Channel
October, 1944

Dear Mom,

A few words tonight before I hit the sack to let you know how much I love you and Dad. In a day or two my unit will go into the line of combat for the first time. I'm mindful of what that means.

I want you to know that I'm scared like everybody else. Dad said he was always afraid in combat and I can relate to that now. My greatest fear is that I may not live up to the standards my platoon has a right to expect from their commander. I've always admired the quiet courage that was such a large part of Dad. He didn't talk about what he was going to do: he just went ahead and did it. I always respected that about him.

There is a chance that this may be my last letter, and I want you to know what my true feelings are about the divorce. It doesn't matter now who was to blame. People make choices. I frequently prayed that the two of you would get back together, but that was the optimism of a child who loved both parents equally. Our home on Army bases scattered all over the country before Benning, Georgia, was exciting and a model of harmony and security. I felt loved and protected. Both of you made me feel special and that whatever I did was important. I loved you dearly for that, and I missed that warm atmosphere after the divorce.

I hope you are happy, Mom. You put on a good act for my benefit, and at times you seemed to be discontented. Kids can be quite perceptive you know, and I saw tears in your eyes more than you'll ever know. I'm not sure if you knew it, but Dad was lost for quite a long time after you left him. He was bitter and hurt, but he never mentioned the cause of his anguish to me. As a matter of fact, he reprimanded

13

me sharply several times when I blamed you for the divorce. His often repeated words went something like this: "Your Mother deserves your love and respect. Whatever happened between the two of us has nothing to do with you. Nobody loves you any more than your Mother and I don't want to hear you bad-mouth her again. Is that understood?"

I hope that I can find the right girl to love the way Dad loved you.

Don't take offense, Mom. I'm not placing blame, I just wanted to let you know what is in my heart before they announce lights out on the ship. I honor you not because Dad has told me that it is the right thing to do. I love and respect you because you have been the best Mom this kid could ever ask for. And you won that love by being your wonderful self.

Lights out... I love you Mom.

Keith

PS: If it is my time to go, I want you and Dad to remember that I give my life freely for the defense of freedom. Maybe I will be greeted by Uncle Samuel who must know his way around in the Great Beyond...

Don't mourn for me. Live life to the fullest without regrets.

Simon finished the letter and carefully placed it back in the envelope. He looked out the window and stared into space, not wanting Miriam to see the tears blurring his vision. He had a strong desire to cry out in protest. He loved their son more than life itself. Now that he was gone, he didn't know where to turn for comfort and direction.

Miriam saw the tenseness in his facial muscles and the set of his jaw. She knew what he was going through. He began to cry, and she pulled him into her arms. Grief overwhelmed him, even as he tried to hold it back. He held Miriam too, for she was also caught up in despair and could no longer deny the need for relief. They embraced for a long time, sharing their grief and sense of loss. Simon composed himself first.

"I never knew that it could hurt so much and last for so long. Right after Pearl Harbor I received warning orders to be shipped to the Pacific area, so I drove to West Point before I left for California. We ate lunch at the Thayer Hotel, talking about things like he wrote in the letter. It was the first time he ever mentioned having those thoughts. I knew that he was worried about me going into combat so soon. It was the first time I saw him shed a tear as we parted. Even then, I had a terrible premonition that that might be the last time I see our son alive. His first posting would normally have been to a platoon which is the tip of the spear in combat. He stood in the hotel parking lot waving until I pulled out of sight. I almost went back to steal him away somewhere safe until the war was over."

"That's strange, I had similar feelings too," Miriam recalled in a soft voice. "I remember how we used to be able to read each other's thoughts. You may not believe it, but I think often of those days."

"For the past eleven years, I've thought of little else," Simon answered truthfully. "On the flight to France I promised myself that I was going to be positive and look forward to the future. I know that there are heartaches in looking backward. Yet, at this stage of life, memories are a large part of who we are, and they just happen to be centered around you. There were a lot of good times. It was so typical of Keith to mention Sam. I plan to visit his grave in Montfaucon before I return to the states. I've thought of him more lately than I had in ages."

"You two were so close. Did I ever tell you about the time Sam stopped by the house to ask me if I would go to a church picnic with him? He said he was you. My mother and father believed him. I did at first until I noticed a pack of cigars in his shirt pocket; you never smoked them. I joked with him, and we laughed about the attempted deception. He laughed as he left the yard. You remember how he was."

"He never told me about that incident. We had a standing bet of five dollars if he could go on a date with you without being caught. I'm not surprised that he tried. He did like those small cigars. I tried them, but they were too strong for me. I settled for a pipe and still enjoy it. Sam was a lot of fun to be around. We were identical twins, but we had different dispositions. He was a lot more outgoing and could laugh easier, too.

"I was in the trenches near Bouresches when I received word of his death. I couldn't acknowledge the fact that he was gone, until I came home to familiar surroundings where I expected to see him come through the door and ask for a cup of coffee. Sometimes I'd wake from a sound sleep and hear his voice calling to me. It would have been much more difficult for me if it had not been for you, Miriam. Your presence and support during those difficult times gave meaning to the future. I don't know if I ever told you that, but it's true."

"Life was simpler then, Simon. As we grow older it's comforting to look back to see where we've been. What was that old saying? 'Once a man twice a boy.' There's some validity to it," she sighed, looking out the window.

"Are you saying that your enthusiasm for the future is waning, Miriam?" asked Simon, regretting it as soon as he said it. "No, don't answer that. I have no right to ask such a question. I've wanted to visit Keith's grave since I learned of his death, and I don't want to get into a conversation filled with recriminations that could spoil it for either of us. I want to say good-bye to our son, hoping that he can help me find the future. Right now I don't know where I'm going, and I admit to needing some help. It was good of you to suggest that we put aside our differences for his sake. I also thank General Carter for his courtesy to both of us. This is not the beginning of the end for me. It has to be the beginning of a new life. Hopefully, it will be a time of discovery of new challenges and meaningful opportunities. I believe Keith would want that for both of us."

Simon was alarmed at the ease he was able to express himself to Miriam after such a long absence. Her presence was making the trip easier for him. She knew what was in his heart, and was thankful that, in some small way, she could help him find his way to the future. He deserved to be happy. Simon was an uncomplicated man of strong character, and she loved his gentle and unpretentious ways.

16

They rode in silence across agricultural fields being harvested of sugar beets, grapes, and wheat. It brought back memories of the land as he saw it through the eyes of a young officer in 1918. The most memorable day was the eleventh hour of the eleventh day of the eleventh month.

***

The ravaged land began its renewal the moment the guns fell silent. The four years of upheaval and destruction were grim reminders of the vicious struggle that had spread across the land like the plague. Abandoned farmhouses stood in mute disarray from artillery bombardment. Once the roofs were violated, the rest of the structure soon crumbled back to the soil from whence it came. Impenetrable formations of rusted barbed wire twisted in grotesque shapes hung on the crests of miles and miles of trenches and dug-outs partially filled with water. Crumbled walls of masonry and plaster was all that was left of once stately buildings and modest homes.

The killing fields of Verdun and other battlefields soon began filling in with poppies and clover, the first stage of ultimate reclamation. Nature was healing its wounds. Shattered stubs of trees had stood as mute witnesses to the ferocity of the contest for the land. Black burned shards sprouted from the dark pulverized soil. A few trees had started to sprout new leaves, but most of them died shortly thereafter, mute testimony to the community of death that visited the land and its occupants. The first living things to return to the battlefields were songbirds, and for the first time in four long years, they announced the rebirth of the land with their songs.

***

"We'll be coming into Arromanches soon," announced Sergeant Jones. "A museum is being constructed there near the Normandy cemeteries. Omaha Beach has over nine thousand graves. The memorial ceremony will start at twelve-thirty. It's now nine-thirty. What would you like to do?"

"If you can find a suitable café I'd like to make a rest stop, Sergeant," requested Miriam.

"I agree. I'd like to stretch my legs," added Simon.

17

"Where did you get the Silver Star?" requested Miriam. She knew that he would never mention such a decoration on his own.

"That was early in the war on New Guinea," Simon answered modestly. "That place was a putrid hell hole. I never want to see another tropical jungle as long as I live. I had sent a night patrol to check on Japanese positions. They became disoriented, and it was my responsibility to open a safe corridor so they could return to our lines."

"Here's a nice looking Café with plenty of parking space and room to move about," interrupted Sergeant Jones.

"It looks good to me," Miriam said, pleased with his choice. It was a large Inn constructed of stone and mortar with an attached café overlooking a lake. Jones parked the Ford sedan and jumped out to open both rear doors.

"Ah, it feels good to stretch my leg," claimed Simon.

The café was half-filled with local French villagers and a small number of British and American soldiers. The interior was constructed of large hand-hewn wooden beams spanning the length of the great room. On the opposite end of the room large logs were burning over a wrought iron grill in the fireplace. They were escorted to a table near the fireplace with a view of the water.

"I'll leave you two in private for now," declared Sergeant Jones. "I'll be in the car whenever you're ready."

"You're welcome to share our table, Sergeant," said Simon.

"Thanks just the same, Sir, but I'm looking forward to what my mess Sarge made up for the road. You two enjoy the stop. We're about twenty minutes from the ceremony location, so take as long a rest stop as you want."

"Thanks, Sergeant," Miriam replied, searching for a woman's restroom.

The waiter took their order, refusing payment, and presented a bottle of wine as a token of appreciation for the sacrifices of the American Army in the name of freedom. Simon poured two long-stemmed wine glasses and placed one in front of Miriam.

"Shall we have a toast to the memory of our Son?" asked Simon.

She lifted her eyes to meet his across the table, shaking her head in compliance. "To the precious memories of a little boy who grew up to be a soldier like his father. We are thankful for the memories and ask for the courage to face the future the way he would want us to do. To Keith, who was all that a mother and father could ever ask for in a child."

"In remembrance, Son." They touched glasses and drank in salute and thanksgiving for the memories of happier days.

Chapter Three

After the toast, they ordered French onion soup, bread, and cheese. Miriam also ordered a cup of tea. The small café was comfortable and cultivated a warm feeling of intimacy. Being with each other after a long, tenuous absence was a new experience for them, yet it was almost as if they had not gone their separate ways. Simon and Miriam recognized the danger signs of letting this tragic period of their lives represent anything beyond what it actually was — a temporary gathering to honor their son. A lot of hurt and acrimonious feelings had passed between them.

"Are you going to stay in the Army, Simon?" asked Miriam, studying the lines on his face. She thought he had aged beyond his years. There was a severity to his eyes that she had never noticed before the war. His sensitive and generous disposition conditioned his vulnerability to the losses in his command. It would have been impossible for him to be a detached observer.

"The doctors have told me that the leg wound will heal and should not be a factor if I decide to remain in the Army. I don't know, Miriam. Lately I've been thinking about returning to Maine to take a job that's been a standing offer for years from the Great Northern Paper Company. It has some appeal to me right now."

"Maybe it would be good for you. I miss Maine a lot. Leroy wants to retire to Hawaii. I'll probably give in, but it would not be my first choice."

Simon detected reluctance on her part. It was fortunate that she brought up Leroy's name. His imagination was starting to work overtime, and the mention of her husband's name brought him back to reality. At one time the attractive lady sitting across from him was his best friend, his lover, and his wife. Now, she was Mrs. Leroy Carter, and that reality

20

should not be lost in the fog of nostalgic dreams. The rest stop was a comforting interlude preparing them for their journey's destination. Thoughts beyond that fact were dangerous and speculatory.

A half-hour later, Sergeant Jones parked the sedan in a large parking lot adjacent to the cemetery and memorial, which was still under construction. Thousands of people were attending the commissioning ceremony. Jones accompanied Simon and Miriam to empty seats near the front of the outdoor amphitheater, telling them that he would be available to guide them to the car after the proceedings were over. They planned to visit Keith's grave site after the ceremony.

A temporary stage had been constructed to accommodate speakers from England, France, United States, and Canada. One by one the delegates from each nation paid tribute to the nobility of the cause that took so many lives. Valor, courage, and charity were common themes for each of the speakers.

***

General Henri Lamontagne, a French Army General, addressed the large audience in a booming voice and perfect English: "I requested the distinction of addressing this audience. In the name of France, I want the privilege of expressing our profound thanks for the sacrifice you have made. Twice in my lifetime I have seen the country I love more than life itself bow in shame to the occupation of enemy forces. As long as I live I'll never forget 1918. It was late in the summer. The German forces were steadily advancing southward deeper and deeper into France. They were pushing aside French troops and those of our brave allies, Canada, Australia, and England, with relative ease. Despair and gloom filled the air. Four years of horrendous losses on all sides had left the French and her allies in a state of near collapse, emotionally and physically. Exhaustion and fear ran rampant through the ranks. Paris was the objective of the powerful, unstoppable German thrust to our beloved capital. France was doomed. Then, in the midst of widespread defeatism, an American Army positioned itself between Paris and the spearhead of the German attack. The defeated French and allied troops were marching away from the advancing enemy. At the same time the independent and cocky American

21

doughboys were marching towards the sound of the guns into the German advance.

"The retreating troops begged the Americans to turn around and leave the area. The answer from the Americans was a simple declaration, symbolic of the pride and determination our American friends possessed. 'Why?' they asked with surprise. 'Hell, we just got here.'

"They were young and lacked experience, but they made up for it with courage, valor, and tenacity. They fixed bayonets and stopped the Germans all the way across the line where American doughboys entered combat. The French and allied armies took note of their success, and in a span of hours a new spirit gripped their hearts and souls. Hope was rekindled, and a new meaning was given to the nobility of their cause. Not only were the Germans stopped in their tracks, they were methodically being pushed back with such ferocity that the Germans soon lost their desire to continue with the struggle. Peace came to the land.

"I lived to see the sad day when German occupation forces pounded the pavement beneath our beloved Arch de Triumph and the Eiffel Tower. It was the ultimate in shame and degradation that this old soldier has ever witnessed.

"Once again France and the free world looked to the United States of America for assistance. American soldiers answered the call of the beleaguered French people and pierced the impenetrable fortress of Europe, pushing the invaders from French soil back to Germany. The campaign started here on the coast of Normandy. Once again, the American soldier lifted the yoke of tyranny from the shoulders of Frenchmen, and gave us back our beloved France. The price was high as evidenced by the thousands of new graves in which we honor. They entered the fray championing liberty and freedom, and asked for nothing in return except that the world honor their sacrifice. What a noble legacy for generations to come to study and think about.

"The cost of victory can be measured by the tears wrenched from the hearts of fallen soldiers' mothers. A generation of young men have been lost to the world in defense of freedom. Words are so inadequate to describe the debt we proud Frenchmen owe for the sacrifice and valor of the American soldiers we honor today. *Viva-la-France* cries out from our heart accompanied by a tear-filled thank you to the United States of America for sending us your beloved sons. We pledge to always honor them."

***

"The general is right." Simon whispered to himself. "It was something that needed to be said."

A silence hung over the audience for several seconds before they responded with a standing ovation. Simon and Miriam joined in, too. There was not a dry eye in the crowd. An hour later, the official ceremonies ended. Simon and Miriam stood up to stretch their legs. Simon searched the crowd, checking for familiar faces and found none. His long years of service in the Army had allowed him, at one time or another, to meet many members of the officer corps. It was a close-knit brotherhood of individuals dedicated to serving their country.

Sergeant Jones approached them with a bottle of water in case they needed it. Miriam accepted the water, relieving her dry mouth and throat. "Are you ready to visit the grave site?" he asked.

"Yes, I'm ready if you are, Miriam," answered Simon. She shook her head in agreement, and they followed Jones back toward the sedan.

"I'll hurry ahead to bring the automobile down to the gate where we entered the reception area. You wait there for me. I won't be long."

"I was gratified to hear a French General acknowledge what our soldiers have given to France. I realize that France suffered a lot during the war, but the world should never forget that our son and thousands of comrades-in-arms like him paid the ultimate price. They damn well better be worthy of that sacrifice," Simon exclaimed.

"Here comes Sergeant Jones."

He drove the sedan along the outer perimeter of the vast field of crosses spaced in precise rows as far as the eye could see. They were silent testaments to the magnitude and severity of the battle that had taken place. Sergeant Jones entered the lane closest to Keith's grave, for he had scouted its location previous to their coming, and parked the sedan in a parking area.

Simon stepped out of the sedan and viewed the cemetery as a whole. His first thought was what a beautiful place. Located on a high bluff overlooking the Omaha Beach, peace and serenity emanated from the area. A soft breeze from the English Channel swept through the scattered trees in the cemetery. Simon and Miriam walked slowly among the graves and stood in front of the cross they had been searching for. Their flesh and blood was in his final resting place. "First Lieutenant Keith Samuel Hanley, USA", leaped from the white cross and was seared on their memories, leaving an emptiness in their hearts.

The feeling of reverence and respect that emanates from the sacred ground was in stark contrast to the violence that consumed Keith and his comrades, like a giant scythe harvesting wheat for the winter. Simon had the sinking feeling as he stood at the cemetery that their sacrifice would cease to be honored or even remembered by generations yet unborn. The solitude and peacefulness of the cemetery surprisingly left them strengthened by the visit instead of weakened by despair and sorrow. It was as if Keith wanted them to know that he was at peace, and that they should no longer mourn his passing. Both of them felt his presence and were comforted by the feeling of serenity that rained upon them. The large number of crosses representing young men joined in the brotherhood of death assured Miriam and Simon that their journey through eternity would be shared in good fellowship. Keith was not alone.

"I wish that I could take you in my arms just one more time, dear Keith," yearned Miriam, kneeling beside the white cross, running her fingers over his name. "There are so many things I would like to say to you. We don't know for sure, but maybe you're listening to my words now. If that is so, I beg your forgiveness for the sorrow I brought to your young life. I'm sorry, dear Son. You will always be in my heart." Miriam embraced the cross and took a gold crucifix from her blazer pocket and, with shaking fingers, carefully placed it at the base of the grave marker. The emptiness she felt the first day she learned of his death still lingered.

Simon knelt beside Miriam holding his injured leg straight. "Your Mother and I will carry your memory in our hearts until we join you, beloved Son. As for me, I'll especially

24

remember you when I go fishing in the river back home in Maine. I recall the first time we went, and I showed you how to fish. At the end of the day, you caught your legal limit, and all I had was a couple of nibbles on the line. You laughed all the way home. The day I decided to stay in the Army to become a professional soldier was a commitment to a way of life that had to have been difficult on you and your mother. I wish that I had done better for both of you. When you chose to attend West Point, you made this old soldier a happy dad. The Hanleys have been a family of soldiers. Now, I'm all that's left of four generations of soldiering. Link up with your Uncle Samuel, and be ready for that day when I cross the divide to join the two of you. Good-by, Son. Rest in peace..."

Simon took Miriam's hand and squeezed it firmly. She returned the pressure. He helped Miriam stand. There were no more tears. The trip to the cemetery had given them a chance to say good-bye and to let go. It did not erase the emptiness, but it did give them courage and resolve to face a future without their son.

Sergeant Jones kept his eye on the couple approaching them as soon as they started to leave the grave site. He efficiently shepherded them into the sedan and started on the road back towards Paris. Simon was able to leave with a new hope for the days ahead. He looked at Miriam beside him. She was quiet and lost in her private thoughts. She had aged some, but he still saw that familiar flash of fire in the gray depths of her eyes. She glanced at him and gave him a wistfully sad smile.

The sedan pulled into the same café they had stopped at earlier. "While you two are in the café, I'm going to relax in the car. That way I'll be rested for the drive to Paris after dark. Take as long as you need."

"Sergeant Jones, you've been wonderful on this trip. You've helped make this a very special day that I'll always remember. Thank you," said Miriam, kissing him on the cheek.

"You're welcome, Ma'am," answered a surprised Jones.

"She's right. I thank you too, Sergeant. If there's any way that I can repay the consideration you've shown, please let me know."

"I'll keep it in mind, Sir."

Simon directed Miriam to the café, opening the door for her. The host recognized them and took them to the same table they had used a few hours ago next to the crackling fireplace. There was a full moon just beginning to lift above the surrounding hills. The moonlight on the sparkling lake accentuated the movement of the water as if it was dancing.

Miriam softly commented, "What a beautiful night with the moon on the water."

"Back home we'd call it a harvest moon."

"Yes, how well I remember…"

Simon watched the shadows from the flickering flames of the fireplace fall across her face. Sadness filled Miriam's eyes. She had been quiet and reflective since they left Keith's grave. He came away from the grave with a new feeling of strength and sense of purpose. Miriam seemed trapped and was reluctant to think of the future. They ordered grilled Atlantic salmon with an orange sauce over a bed of rice. Miriam asked for tea again, and, predictably, Simon chose coffee.

"Would you like some wine?" asked Simon.

"I'm not much of a drinker as you know, but if you want I'll share a glass with you. I knew that you had a problem."

"Yes, I went over the edge with alcohol at one time. I still have a beer now and then. I took control of myself," explained Simon, ordering a glass of wine for them. "Seriously though, I rarely have a drink. I really didn't like it even when I was abusing it."

Simon suggested a toast to the future. "Being with you these past two days have been special for me. I had visions of angry outbursts and rancorous comments that would have spoiled the occasion for both of us. I propose a toast to the future and whatever it brings." Simon touched his glass against hers with a small clink.

Miriam looked at him and said in a sober voice: "To the future. I pray that it will be better for you than it has been for the past twelve years." She sipped from the glass and put it down on the table. "How soon are you going to Montfaucon?"

"Probably tomorrow. I feel a certain urgency about visiting Sam's grave. I can't explain why it has become so compelling all of a sudden, but it's there."

"Then this is good-bye for us?"

"You could say that," acknowledged Simon. "The memories we share make good-byes less final than they would be to a lot of people. We share so many memories that we can tap into anytime we want to revisit the past. I confess that I've frequently found comfort in that same place. Now, I've told you about my plans, what are you doing tomorrow?"

"Probably the same thing I usually do," she paused to look out the window. "I'm not involved in any of the civic affairs Leroy is working on. He's busy most of the time. I read and study a lot. I had been working as a substitute teacher in Virginia for years. I've never told you, but I've always had the desire to write. They say that in order to do so you must have something to say. Well, I've been carrying a lot of guilt for too long, and writing helps take the sting from my tarnished past."

"That sounds wonderful, Miriam. I'm proud of you."

"I started the manuscript at first to pass the idle time on my hands, but as I became more involved I found that I looked forward to it. All writing is biographical. I confess that I've utilized a lot of situations you and I have shared over the years. You mention old memories; well, I can tell you that I've been there more than you'll ever know. It has been not only a comfort but an inspiration to me."

"Are you telling me that this thing with Leroy is not working out?" asked Simon at last. He had wanted to ask that question all day but didn't find the appropriate moment until now. "If I'm out of line, just tell me so. I don't mean to pry and I don't want to make you feel uncomfortable. It's just that here and there over the past twenty-four hours I've picked up comments and seen that wistful look on your face that has made me wonder. Is he good to you, Miriam?"

"Yes and no," Miriam answered, not daring to look into his eyes. She was thankful for the interruption of the waiter bringing their meals to them. "Would you mind if I don't answer anymore than I already have, Simon? Regardless of what is going on in my life, it was a choice that I made, and I don't have the courage or the right to complain that it could be better. I don't think too much about the future. I just take one day at a time and do the best I can with what I've got."

"I'm sorry that I asked." All of a sudden he was not as hungry as he thought.

They completed the meal in silence and returned to the waiting sedan prepared for the final leg of their journey. Sergeant Jones had placed a couple of pillows on the seat for their use. Miriam laid her head against the back of the seat and tried to rest. She dozed off and woke with a start when the car made a sudden turn.

"Miriam, why don't you stretch out across the seat? I'll place the two pillows against the door and on my lap. Take off your shoes and try to get comfortable."

"You don't mind?" she whispered in his ear.

"Of course not."

She laid her head on the pillow and rested against his chest. He cradled her in his strong arms so that she would not fall on the floor if they had to stop quickly. Within minutes she fell asleep. Holding her the way he was brought back a lot of memories. She felt good in his arms. Her breathing was soft and steady. On one stretch of the road moonlight streamed through the windows illuminating her face against his jacket. He fought the urge to kiss her.

A little later, she woke up and touched his face. "I'd forgotten how it felt to be in your arms." She touched his face again and raised her head to kiss him. No power on earth could have stopped him from responding to the softness of her lips. Every nerve in his body was alive. He too remembered how it had been...

"If you were to ask me, I'd stay with you tonight," she whispered in his ear. It would have been easy for Simon to accept the offer, but he thought of tomorrow and passion dissipated.

"You know what's in my heart, Miriam. I don't want you just for a one night stand. There could be devastating consequences for everybody concerned. Remember you're married to a general officer, I'm only a colonel. He could put me in jail and destroy you in the process. You know how the system works. Is one night worth that?"

She was slow to answer. "You're right, the consequences could be severe, but I'd take the chance if you were willing. I never forgot you, Simon, never. The thought of saying good-bye to you tonight is painful to me. The questions you asked at the café can be answered with a simple honest statement. I'm

28

not happy, and I haven't been for a long time. I knew that you'd figure that out without my having to tell you."

"I'm sorry, Miriam. We may not be lovers now, but I'm always your friend. We should let some time pass. A lot of our emotions are tied up with Keith. If it's all right with you, I'll be in touch after I make the trip to Montfaucon before I leave for the States. Things may look different a few days from now."

"I'll be waiting for your call," she said, lifting her head to kiss him one more time.

Chapter Four

Simon awoke in the middle of the night from a nervous, fitful sleep. He lay on his bed with hands behind his head, staring at the ornately decorated ceiling. The warmth of Miriam in his arms had haunted him for much of the night. He knew that she was crying when the Army sedan left the hotel portico. The fact that she would have risked all to stay with him for one night brought up a lot of memories and unanswered questions.

The next morning, he showered and changed into a clean uniform in preparation for an appointment with an Army medical unit attached to Allied Headquarters, Paris. Simon's doctor at Walter Reed Hospital in Washington, DC, had made him promise to check in at the Paris center for a checkup shortly after his arrival. He had to admit that his leg did hurt more than usual, and realized that it would be unwise to continue on to Montfaucon without being sure about the cause of the pain.

He saw a familiar face as soon as he entered the medical center. Army nurse, Captain Lee Rogers, was working with some files behind a reception desk. They had met twice over several years of their careers in the Army. The first time was at the Presidio Army Base in San Francisco prior to Pearl Harbor. They had a date and went to a dance at an Officer's Club. The next time they crossed paths was at Guadalcanal where she treated him for a severe case of malaria that had hospitalized him for several weeks.

Lee was filled with energy and high spirits. Everyone liked her outgoing personality. She had a low tolerance for people who did not do their share and had a reputation as a tireless worker, treating every person in her care with compassion and competence. She was an attractive woman in her late forties. Gray streaks filled her long black hair pulled back behind her ears, falling loose about her shoulders. She smiled a lot and rarely took herself seriously. If the occasion warranted she could be caustic and sarcastic to those whom she perceived as deceptive or false. Simon liked her direct approach. Her husband of twenty years had left her for a younger woman. Shortly after the divorce was final, she had accepted an offer to join the Army Nurse Corps in the late thirties.

"Captain Lee Rogers, I presume," he announced with mock formality. She was absorbed in something at the file cabinets and had not noticed him. As soon as he spoke she looked up, recognizing him instantly.

"Colonel Simon Hanley, of course," she cried, getting up to salute him. "We seem to be bumping into each other in strange places all over the globe." She was more cute than beautiful. Her bubbly personality and quick intellect endeared her to all who knew her.

"It's nice to see a familiar face. When did you leave the Pacific theater for Europe?" Simon returned her salute.

"I requested it. I've been in France for a few months. They consolidated several of the field operations we had on Guadalcanal. I hated it there and was glad to leave."

"I don't blame you. It was a stink hole."

"What's with the cane, Colonel?" she inquired with concern.

"That's what I came to see you about. I was wounded on Okinawa. Three of the bullets were flesh wounds. The fourth one broke my leg bone. It had partially healed when I received word that the Normandy cemetery, where my son is buried, was going to be officially commissioned. I wanted to attend the ceremony. The doctor in the states at Walter Reed Hospital made me promise to check in with a Doctor Colonel Connors in this allied complex."

"Yes, his office is just down the hall," added Lee. Simon looked distressed. "Does the leg hurt you?"

"I hate to admit it but, yes, it's more painful than it was yesterday. I was planning to go to Montfaucon today to visit my twin brother's grave."

"Why don't you take a seat, Colonel. Can I get you anything?"

31

"I'm really fine. I just want to make sure that I'm not going to get myself in trouble by ignoring the leg."

"You wait a minute. Let me see if the doctor is free."

Five minutes later, Lee returned with a doctor dressed in a long white coat. "Doctor Connors, this is Colonel Simon Hanley."

"I'm glad to meet you, Colonel. My old friend, Doctor Goodwin, had the audacity to send me a wire warning me that you may show up in my office. He threatened dire consequences if I failed you in any way," Doctor Connors laughed.

"It's a pleasure to meet you, Sir. Dr. Goodwin had glowing things to say about you," smiled Simon. He was going to like this Army doctor. They were part of the fraternity of professionals that bound its members into a close family that looked after each other. Simon liked that part of the Army. It seemed that no matter where you went in the world you could probably meet someone you had met before.

"Follow me, Simon. Lee, would you please have the receptionist hold my calls until I'm finished?" They walked side by side down the corridor to an examination room. "How long has the pain been as intense as it is now?"

"Twenty-four hours. I can handle the pain, Doctor, I just don't want to develop any complications."

"I can appreciate that. You're thinking smart. Here let me remove your shoes."

Simon took off his tunic and pants and climbed on the examination table. Dr. Connors cut off the old dressing covering the wound around the bone fracture. Simon watched his facial expression for some indication of what was wrong, but the Doctor remained focused on the wound, registering nothing except an appreciation for the work of his colleague in Washington.

"You're problem is not a big one now, Colonel. It had the potential of becoming one if you had not followed common sense. The wound has become infected. I'm going to clean and sterilize it and apply a new dressing. You should also have an antibiotic injection just in case." Simon was relieved to hear the news.

"Would I throw a monkey wrench in your plans if I asked you to report back to me tomorrow afternoon, Colonel? I'll give you a prescription to take, but I want to be certain that our treatment is on the right track."

"Another day won't matter much, Sir."

"I'm about done for now, Colonel Hanley," said Doctor Connors after dressing the wound. "If you see Captain Rogers on your way out, would you please tell her to sign out and take some time off?"

"I'd be glad to, Doctor. I've known her since before Pearl Harbor. She's a part of what makes our Army Nurse Corps the best in the world."

"I don't know how I managed before she reported to our center. If she's not careful though, she's going to burn herself out. The patients adore her. She's hard on them, but they love her just the same. If you're an old friend, advise her to slow down. We've won the war, so it's time to breathe easier."

"I'll try, Sir. I would not bet on success though." Simon left the examination room.

A young lieutenant was at the reception desk as Simon walked by. "Excuse me lieutenant, has Captain Rogers left?"

"No, Sir, not yet. She's just around the corner to your right in the records room."

"Thank you."

"You're welcome, Colonel."

Simon knocked on the door and pushed it open. "Hello, is Captain Rogers here?"

"Come in, Colonel," answered a voice from behind a large battery of filing cabinets. "How did you make out?"

"I'm fine. I just need some antibiotics to clear up a small infection. Doctor Connors authorized me to order you off duty. How long have you been here today?"

"Twelve hours."

"Surely, Captain, you can find someone to assist you so that you can save your time and energy for those things that only you can do. I wouldn't tolerate a captain doing filing chores that a corporal should be doing."

"Are you congratulating me or lecturing me?" she asked, smiling impishly.

"You haven't changed, Lee. Listen, I've got to hang around Paris for another day so that the Doc can check me again. I'm ready for a cup of coffee and a donut. Would you like to join me in a late breakfast, or is this dinner for you?"

"You're being critical of me," she teased closing a file drawer. "I could use something to eat. How about the Officers' Club? It's right down the street."

"Sounds good to me."

Lee pinned a nurse cap to her head and followed him out the door. "I'm glad to see you again. I worried about you when you left Guadalcanal. You were a very sick man. Listen, can we drop the rank stuff. I can remember when we were both captains. I'm going to call you Simon unless you've become one of those rank-conscious ladder-climbers."

Simon laughed with her. She had a way of making everybody around her feel good. If anyone had an inflated ego, she went out of her way to burst their bubble. "Does that mean we're getting old, or that time flies by rapidly?"

"Sometimes I feel my age."

"Lee, you're timeless. At seventy you'll be younger at heart than a lot of twenty-year-olds."

"How was your visit to the cemetery? I remember you talking about your son at West Point. I'm sorry for you. So many young men have been lost to the world."

"He was killed during the breakout from the Normandy beachhead. He's buried in Arromanches. Yesterday was rough. At the day's end I was able to deal with the reality of his death for the first time. It was as if Keith's spirit was speaking to me and his mother from the grave."

"Your ex-wife?" asked Lee surprised. She knew about Simon's divorce years before the war. Lee and Simon had that in common. The sting of rejection was deeply felt and lasted for a long time.

"Yes, Miriam went to the ceremony with me, or to be correct I went with her. She arranged everything for us. It was the first time I'd seen her in over five years." Simon continued: "Lee, I know that people including myself talk about the brass. What do the people at HQ think about General Leroy Carter?"

"Oh, my. You're not asking for much," feigned Lee, rolling her eyes. "Come, let's get settled at the Club first, and then I'll fill you in on the latest scuttlebutt."

"Okay, don't walk too fast. I may have trouble keeping up."

"Then I'll hold onto your arm, and you can set the pace," said Lee, linking her arm with his. "You're a good-looking

34

man, Simon, and have the reputation of being a good officer with common sense. How come some beauty hasn't taken you under her wing by now?"

Simon laughed. "One can't fight a war and court a lady at the same time. You're being a little speculative to a superior officer. If you're not careful, I may ask you for another date. Now let's see, that would be a date every five years..."

"If you ask, I'll say yes," she said seriously. "The Club is just around the corner. The Paris headquarters is being dispersed to Germany and Belgium in the near future. Right now, it's overcrowded with too much brass trying to look and act important. They're not representative of the Army I know. Ones like you are the genuine article. Your Distinguished Service Cross and Silver Star were not awarded for efficiency; they were awarded for leadership and courage under fire on the battlefield." She had a healthy skepticism of high-ranking officers who never commanded troops in combat.

"Flattery will get you anything," he grinned. It was easy to laugh and joke with Lee. She was fun to be with.

The Officers' Club was established in a large stone and masonry house that had once been the home of a wealthy businessman at the turn of the century. The large rooms on the first floor were turned into dining rooms with high sculptured ceilings and walls filled with reproduction paintings of masters such as Monet and Michelangelo.

They were seated in what had once been the ballroom, a large room of thirty or more tables. Lunch was served cafeteria-style. The moment they entered the building, tempting aromas whetted their appetites. They chose lasagna, a fresh salad, and coffee.

"The food looks and smells good. Most of the Officer Clubs I've attended have been top rate in the food department," described Simon. "Now that we're here, I'm going to ask you again about Carter."

"You know how things can get out of control once something out of the ordinary is discovered?"

"Sure, we see it everyday."

"Well, the word around HQ is that Grady has been seeing a wealthy French widow in Paris."

"Wow," interrupted Simon. If the rumors were true, he mused, then Miriam's moody behavior was understandable.

"We speak of angels and we hear the flutter of their wings," replied Lee. "Don't turn around, Simon. Our most elevated General just took a seat with his court of sycophants." The level of her displeasure was not lost on Simon.

"I've hated him for a long time."

Lee studied his response. She was an astute student of human behavior. "Are you still in love with your ex-wife, Miriam?" she asked casually. "You don't have to answer. I know what it's like to be in that situation. I can truthfully tell you that if my ex-husband was available again, I'd consider giving it another try. I hated him for a long time, but we shared so many memories that they've overshadowed my hatred. In a way, I suppose that's why I've remained single all the years since."

"You're a very perceptive lady, Lee. Your husband must have been crazy to have given you up. I've had thoughts along the line you described. Let me put it this way. I still think enough of her that I'd hate to see her get hurt by a good-time-Charlie like Grady."

"Miriam is a lucky woman to earn your loyalty. Now, to change the subject. Do we have a date tonight? What do you suggest?"

"Sure, I haven't given it much thought, Lee. Anything with you would be fun. I've heard that a ride along the Seine River on one of those boats that look like barges could be interesting. I've never visited the Tomb of the Unknown Soldier at the Arc de Triomphe. I'd like to see that."

"I'd like that too. Do you mind if I dress in civilian clothes?"

"That would be nice. I only have my uniform."

"That uniform belongs on you, Colonel Hanley. It deserves a real soldier like you and your son, not the power brokers across the room."

They left the Club, walking back to the medical center. Lee planned to return to her apartment building to change and rest. She gave Simon her address.

"I'll be at your apartment at about six o'clock. Rest well, Lee. I'll be looking forward to our date tonight. Au revoir, Mademoiselle."

"Au revoir, m'sieur," she smiled, kissing him softly on the lips. "Don't forget the address now."

"Never," he answered.

The Allied Headquarters complex was scattered among several buildings in the city block around the medical center. Simon decided to check on the possibility of transport to Montfaucon. The sidewalk was crowded, and Simon kept close to the buildings to avoid holding up pedestrian traffic when he saw Miriam approaching him.

"Hello, Simon. What a surprise to see you here."

"Hi, Miriam. I had to have my leg checked. It's slightly infected. The doctor wants me to stop by again tomorrow before I head north. I just had lunch at the Officer Club with an old acquaintance."

"I saw her in front of the Medical Center."

"Yes, she treated me for malaria on Guadalcanal."

"I was on my way to the Officer Club. Headquarters told me that Leroy was there."

"Yes, we saw him in the dining room."

"Did he recognize you?"

"I don't believe so. Did you sleep well last night?" he asked, looking at the dark shadows around her eyes.

"I don't complain," she shrugged her shoulders. There was a sullen, indifferent attitude about her that was out of character.

"Is there anything I can do to help you, Miriam? I'm going to be in Paris for another twenty-four hours at least."

"Leroy is busy with appointments even into the evenings. I'm sure I'll be alone tonight if you want to stop by."

"I'm sorry, Miriam. I would stop by except that Lee Rogers and I have a date tonight. How about tomorrow or tomorrow evening if you're free?"

"I'm not sure," she said, sounding disappointed and let down. "You seem to have a busy schedule. I could leave word at your hotel."

"You look terrible. What's wrong, Miriam?" demanded Simon, concerned about the distraught look on her face. "I know when you're upset about something. I can't just walk away and leave you like this."

"There are too many people on the street to talk right now. I'll tell you the next time we're together. Please, Simon, don't let Leroy see us together. He could be coming out any minute, and he's been in a nasty mood lately."

Simon took her arm and started walking with her towards the Club. "We haven't violated any honor or behavioral codes or breached any protocols that should upset him. I'm not afraid of General officers when I know that I haven't done anything wrong."

"We had a terrible fight last night. The worst yet," she cried. He could feel the tenseness in her.

"Are you physically afraid of him?" asked Simon firmly.

"Sometimes," she admitted, getting upset. "You should leave, Simon. Please do it now, for me."

"Do you promise to call the hotel if you need me?"

"I will."

"Do you want me to break my date with Lee?"

"Of course not. You need to get out and enjoy yourself more. I do want to see you before you go to Montefaucon. Oh, no, here comes Leroy, and he's seen us."

"I can't and won't run away from him."

"Miriam," exclaimed General Leroy Carter, approaching them with a smug sneer on his lips. "I see you've found Colonel Hanley again."

Simon saluted and held it until Carter returned it. "We just met here on the street, General. I want to thank you for helping to make yesterday's trip possible. It was a difficult time for both of us."

"I'm glad to have been of assistance," said Leroy Carter. He was a small man with dark complexion and a protruding Adam's apple on a skinny neck. He talked as if he was on a stage making a speech. There was nothing warm or natural about him. Simon pegged him for a phony. He came off as a pompous jerk. If he wasn't in the Army, Simon would have told him so to his face.

"Well," Leroy said, clearing his throat as if he was going to make an important announcement. "I'm glad to see that your wounds are not holding you down, Colonel Hanley. It's been a pleasure meeting you. I won't be home this evening, Miriam. I'll call you. Good day, Colonel."

"Goodbye, General," said Simon, giving another very proper salute. After the General and his court left, Simon turned to Miriam, who was near tears, and demanded: "What in the world did you ever see in that cold pompous ass?"

Chapter Five

"I ask myself that same question every day. If you had not been with me, he would not have been so courtly or so proper, the damn hypocrite," she swore sarcastically.

Simon was worried about her. She was on the verge of collapse right there on the sidewalk. He quickly hailed an approaching taxi cab.

"Come on, Miriam," he said, taking her arm.

"I don't know where I want to go except to wake up and find that it has all been a bad dream." Simon helped her into the back seat and told the driver to take them to his hotel.

"Do you remember what you said about going to your hotel last night?" she reminded him.

"That was last night. This is today, and a few things have changed. I understand the situation much better now. When was the last time you ate?"

"Last night with you at the café."

"If I had the hotel room service send up something, would you try to eat?"

"I'd like some hot tea," she cried, holding her head in her hands. "Here in the midst of the wreckage of my marriage you come along and are concerned for me after the terrible ordeal I put you through. Choosing Leroy over you was a monstrous failure on my part. I don't deserve your thoughtfulness. I hate myself for the cheapness of the act and deserve anything I get. You and Keith were blameless." She wept continuously until they arrived at the portico of the hotel. Simon looked on helplessly.

"Come on, Miriam, we'll go to the room."

She wiped the tears from her face. To hide her red eyes, she took a pair of sunglasses from her pocketbook and put them on. The lobby was almost empty as they walked quickly to the elevators. Simon's room was on the twelfth floor with

39

an excellent view of the Eiffel Tower. He opened the door and directed her towards the large sofa in the sitting room.

"What should I have room service bring up besides tea?" asked Simon, getting a couple of pillows from the bedroom and placing them on the sofa. "I've already eaten, but I'll join you for coffee."

"Some toast would be nice with tea," she suggested.

"You should be able to rest here on the sofa. You look drained, Miriam. I'll order tea and toast. Don't worry about Leroy, he's not going to bother you here."

"He'll probably call the apartment."

"Let him... you're not his slave," Simon replied. He removed his cap and tunic and loosened his necktie. It was the first time Miriam had seen him in the daylight without his hat on. His hair was completely gray with scattered white streaks. It made him look more distinguished instead of older.

"Is that nurse captain someone special? I saw her kiss you."

"She's a wonderful person. I first met her before Pearl Harbor. We went to a dance together at the Presidio. I saw her again in 1944 on Guadalcanal where she treated me for malaria. We lost touch until we met again at the Medical Center today. We're good friends. She was divorced before the war when her husband left her for a younger woman."

"What time is your date tonight?" Miriam checked her watch.

"About six o'clock. Should I postpone it?"

"Would you do that for me?"

"That's not fair, Miriam. My relationship with you will always be different than anyone else. We shared fourteen years of our lives together, and you're the mother of our son. The divorce severed my obligation to you, but it never dissolved the way I feel towards you."

"I apologize for the nagging questions. Imagine, here I am a little jealous of another woman it's bizarre. I don't deserve your kindness and decency. Keith inherited those characteristics from you. I admit that it makes me feel warm all over to be the object of your concern, but I'm unworthy... I don't even care about myself anymore."

Room service rang the door bell, breaking the intimacy of the conversation. A waiter wheeled a small table into the emotion-filled room. Simon paid him and closed the door.

"If I remember correctly, you take your tea with cream and one sugar. Here, you help yourself to the toast. I see they sent up some sweet rolls, too."

"I was h than I thought. I'm not used to this kind of treatment. I want you to promise me one thing, Simon."

"I will if it's possible."

"Keep your date with Lee. She sounds like a nice person."

"If that's the way you feel, I will. You're welcome to stay for the night. You take the bedroom, and I'll use the couch; that way I won't disturb you when I return. Promise me that you'll try to sleep this afternoon before I leave. Things always look different when we're rested."

"I will, Simon. Sometimes I wish I'd never wake up," she confessed.

"None of that kind of talk, Miriam. I've never seen you like this, and we go way back to the first grade together," Simon scolded her.

She smiled at him, placing an empty tea cup on the table. She was tired and laid her head on the back of the sofa. Minutes later, she felt Simon remove her shoes, and lay her on the pillows placing a light blanket over her. She felt the softness of his lips against hers. How comforting it was! Soon, her body relaxed, and she succumbed to a deep sleep.

Simon rested quietly for a few hours and changed into a clean uniform for the evening. He checked on Miriam who was still fast asleep, and placed a note on the table beside the sofa before leaving for Lee's apartment.

Dear Miriam,

You are sleeping soundly and that pleases me. I'm taking a chance that you might wake up to read this note. Please take the bedroom so that you may rest better.

I don't know what the answer is for your situation, but the solution has to come from you if it is to be successful. I just wanted you to know that regardless of what the future holds, I will always be

41

available to help you in any way possible if I'm needed.

Sleep well, Miriam.

Simon

Simon asked the taxi driver to stop at a sidewalk florist shop to purchase a bouquet of roses for Lee. Street lights were being turned on all over Paris. Lee's apartment was on the ground floor, making it easy for Simon to negotiate with the cane. He rang the door bell and waited.

"You're right on time," Lee greeted him with excitement in her bright eyes.

"Pretty flowers for a pretty lady," Simon graciously presented the bouquet to her.

He saw a different Lee Rogers from the one he had talked to that morning. She looked rested, and her eyes shined with high expectations for the evening. Her black hair with streaks of gray was pulled on top of her head, making her look taller. She wore a rose colored dress with white lace covering her neck and red shoes with a low heel.

"Thank you, Simon," she responded nervously, accepting the flowers and kissing him. "I've been looking forward to tonight. The flowers are pretty. Let me put them in a vase of water before we leave."

"Do you have any place in mind for a good dinner for starters? You know Paris better than I do."

"There's a small place near the Arc de Triomphe. We could stop to see the Tomb of the Unknown Soldier of France first. I'm ready," she said, putting on a dark maroon blazer. "The evenings can be cool at this time of year."

"Your apartment is smaller than I expected. I'm sure it beats living in barracks."

They took a cab to the Arc de Triomphe. It was a revelation to drive through the streets without a blackout. The city of lights had been dark for five years under German occupation. It was slowly coming back to its normal pace, which could be hectic and boisterous. Automobiles were driven on the streets of Paris with a proud disregard of traffic lights or warning signs. The worst culprits were the cab drivers who worked diligently to maintain their international reputation of being the most fearless of drivers.

Simon and Lee got off at the broad Champs Elysees leading east toward the Arc de Triomphe, home of the Tomb of the Unknown Soldier. The Tomb is located beneath the arch next to a circular brazier which feeds an eternal flame, symbolic of the unquenchable spirit of the dead soldiers it honors. It is the most holy shrine in France, where people talk in whispers and reflect on the price of their freedom. The flame silently draws people to the sanctity of the memorial in admiration of the valor of those fallen heroes who remain forever young. Most leave the tomb with a feeling of peace and thanksgiving.

Lee held tight to Simon's arm as they watched the eternal flame. There were several older people under the archway. One elderly lady saw Simon standing respectfully over the Tomb, and approached him speaking in broken English: "M'sieur Colonel, I thank you and all the brave young Americans who have made it possible for us to stand in this holy place. Just a few months ago the German swines held us hostage in our own city. You removed the beasts from our beloved Paris. Thank you. May God be with you."

"Thank you, Ma'am," answered Simon, touched by her sincerity. "My country remembers when a great Frenchman, Lafayette, helped us win our freedom from England. All mankind should be the enemy of oppression. Thank you for appreciating what has been done."

"I've had similar encounters on the streets when I've been in uniform. At least the Germans spared Paris from heavy destruction," added Lee.

"It's good that the people are thankful, but they should be... I'm hungry for a steak if such a thing is available in Paris. I'm not much on French cuisine with a lot of sauces and gravies. I guess I'm a meat and potatoes kind of country boy."

"You're that and more," said Lee, laying her head affectionately against his shoulder. "The place I had in mind is just around the corner. We can walk there if your leg is up to the exercise. Then we could see if any of the Seine River boats are running."

"My leg is fine. Exercise is the best thing for it."

43

"Have you given any thought to leaving the Army?" Lee asked, still holding his arm. She felt at ease and secure in his presence.

"Strange that you should mention it. I've had twenty-eight years of service in the Army, which I've enjoyed. Having said that, I have a feeling that I would like to work at my forestry profession before I get too old."

"You're a forester then."

"Yes, the Maine woods where I was born and raised is becoming more and more attractive to me. My Dad passed away when Sam and I were young boys. Mother had been a very active woman over the years keeping the old homestead in Wilson River in one piece. She passed away while I was on Okinawa. I'm anxious to go back home, Lee. I don't know if it's a lack of ambition or what, but I have a feeling that there has to be more to life than what I've been doing for years. Maybe, if I'm lucky, I'll find the answers in the forests of Maine. The forest has been a sanctuary for my soul ever since my dad died when I was ten years old." Simon found it easy to share his thoughts with Lee.

"I always suspected there was a poet beneath those muscles and broad shoulders," Lee exclaimed. He was a quiet, serious man. She admired that about him. Strong gentle men were hard to find.

They were taken to a dimly lit section of the restaurant Lee selected and spent a pleasant hour and a half eating and talking small talk. Simon told her that the steak was the best he had eaten in ages. She could not finish all of her shrimp and seafood plate. During the course of the evening she had a feeling that Simon was a little more distant with her than he had been earlier in the day at the Medical center.

"Is anything bothering you, Simon? I have the distinct impression that sometimes you're with me, and then you seem to be far away again. Is it me, or am I being too bold to ask?"

"It's not you, Lee. I'm sorry if I've been distracted." He told her about his encounter with Miriam and General Carter, and that she was back at his hotel suite resting.

"Are you crazy, Simon?" cried Lee, aghast at the potential for trouble. "If Carter was to find out he would have you in irons in a heartbeat."

44

"I know, Lee, but what could I do? She was on the verge of a nervous breakdown."

Lee was angry with him for endangering his career in the Army and for being with her when he probably wanted to be somewhere else. His heart was not in their date. She had correctly sensed it all evening. "What do you suggest, Simon?"

"I apologize, Lee. I haven't been fair with you. Miriam knew about our date tonight and insisted that we keep it. She left me for another man, which you already know. It happened right out of the blue and hurt for a long time. You can appreciate how that feels. I hated her, and I hated the way she did it with impunity. Then the war consumed everybody's energy, including mine, for the duration. When I met her to visit Keith's grave all that anger and hatred simply disappeared, and I'm a little uncomfortable with that."

"Don't be angry with yourself, Simon," she said in a soft conciliatory tone. "I believe in plain talk, and the time has come for me to be honest with you. I probably would have the same mixed feelings you're faced with if I was to encounter my ex-husband under similar circumstances. We should not be sorry or feel guilty for having them. I've already admitted that to you. The first time you and I met at the Presidio I was attracted to you. It went beyond casual friendship. Our encounter at Guadalcanal confirmed my original sentiment. Today, when you walked into my life again, my whole world suddenly became alive with possibilities that were warm to contemplate."

"Lee, I..."

"No, Simon," she interrupted him, placing a finger across his lips. "Let me finish so that you and I will know where we stand with each other. I've dated a lot of men since my divorce. You're the only one I ever considered worth waiting for. You could have made me forget my ex. Now that I've bared my soul, the time has come to be honest with each other. I'm aware that we do not really know each other very well, but most people can tell within a short period of time if a relationship is worth cultivating or not. Is there a chance for you and I in the future?"

"Oh, Lee, how can I tell you with any assurance what my thoughts are? Right now I don't know. A few days ago I could have told you easily. I never forgot you either, Lee. After these past two days I'm all screwed up inside. I apologize for that. As for you and I, let me say that you have always had my respect and admiration. I'm awed at the dedication you display toward our wounded soldiers, and I have seen how you agonize with those unfortunate ones that don't make it. Anyone who could win a heart such as yours has found a rare gift. You deserve the very best, dear lady, and I am humbled to be the object of your thoughts. All of those things make a solid foundation to build upon. Right now I feel unworthy. Would I be interested in pursuing a longtime relationship with you? The answer is yes, but there are some obstructions in the road right now. Where do we go from here? I don't know. I would do anything to not hurt you, Lee."

A single large tear formed in Lee's left eye and ran down the bridge of her nose. She deftly wiped it away with a napkin. "Your answer is a maybe. I can accept that because I know you to be an honest man without deception. That always made you look attractive to me, Simon. Why don't we call it a night? Tomorrow may look differently to us."

"You're probably correct," Simon admitted hesitantly.

"I even had fantasies of going back to your suite for the night," Lee confessed boldly. "It would have been awkward with Miriam there, too."

"I'm sorry, Lee," said Simon, holding her hands in his across the table. "Be patient with me. I apologize for not being more definitive."

They left the restaurant and took a cab back to her apartment. She mentioned that he should keep the cab waiting for him because they are difficult to locate at night. He escorted her to the entrance of the apartment house.

"Goodnight, Lee." He held her in his arms and kissed her.

"Goodnight, Simon. I'll see you tomorrow." She opened the apartment door and closed it quickly. He waited long enough to hear her crying on the other side of the door.

With a heavy heart and a sensation that he had betrayed someone who did not deserve to be hurt, Simon retreated to the cab which took him to his hotel. A light was on when he opened the door to his suite. Miriam was gone. She left a note on the coffee table in front of the couch. He read the message with apprehension:

Dear Simon,

A note to say thank you for being concerned about my welfare. I did rest well. I think it is best for everyone that I leave before your return tonight. The bitter taste of tears of regret may be too late.

Many things have happened in my life that I am ashamed of. As of now, I'm taking steps to correct some of those mistakes. I'm leaving for the United States. A plan has been incubating in my heart for a long time. The day you came to Paris encouraged me to implement that plan while I have the strength to do so. Thank you for helping me find the courage to act. I've known since the first day of our arrival that Leroy has a woman in Paris. He had met her in the states and pulled strings to be posted in France to be with her.

He doesn't have the guts to divorce me outright and marry the woman because it would reflect badly on his record. If I leave him, it will make him look like an aggrieved person, a martyr. Then he can indignantly sue for divorce which is what we both want. What a shallow pathetic man he really is.

To be free of that monster will be the answer to years of praying to a benevolent God for some form of deliverance. I want you to know that I'm doing this for my physical and emotional welfare. Just being with you for a day was enough inspiration to take the drastic move. Thank you for the memories we shared. I am sorry that I proved unworthy.

Leroy robbed me of my self-respect. I must find it again. In order for it to have meaning, I need to earn it on my terms as you rightfully suggested. Thank you, dear heart, for being the strong decent man that you are.

I'll always love you.

Mim

Chapter Six

Simon was relieved to board the train destined for Metz and Montfaucon. He sat at the window seat of a crowded compartment, blocking out the idle chatter of passengers around him. The past three days had been stressful. His main reason for making the trip to France was to say good-bye to his son. He had accomplished that goal, but his relationship with Miriam was more unsettled than ever. He could not help worrying about her.

He was concerned that Miriam might do something rash, and blamed himself for leaving her alone. At the same time he was upset that he had spoiled Lee's night off. Thinking about her brought a smile to his lips. She was a remarkably strong lady. When he returned to the center the next day for a final check on his leg, the first person he saw was Lee. She was her usual good-natured self. He owed her an apology which he made with a promise to keep her informed of his progress in the days ahead. After his session with Dr. Connors, who approved his itinerary to visit the country in the vicinity of Montfaucon, Simon said good-bye again to Lee.

"Take care of yourself, Simon. I'll think often of you and wish you well. When you've had a chance to find yourself and are reasonably sure what is right for you, I hope you'll let me know. I'm not in the habit of making myself available or vulnerable to situations that could hurt me. I've made an exception with you. Don't let me regret that decision. Bon voyage, mon ami."

Simon lifted her chin and gently kissed her. "You're quite a lady, Captain Rogers. Thank you for the trust. I won't let you down again. Au revoir."

"Au revoir," Lee answered soberly.

Northeast of Paris the train passed through small towns that rekindled his memory of the time he and his brother, Sam, came to France in 1918 as young second lieutenant platoon leaders. Sam had served with the 27th Army Division, Simon was with the 2nd Army Division which fought ferocious battles in and around the area he was passing through. The towns of Belleau and Chateau-Thierry were places on the map that were forever enshrined with the valor and courage of the young American fighting men. Bouresches and Lucy-le-Bosages were also the scene of bitter combat and horrific losses on both sides. It was in this sector that American forces stopped the German onslaught aimed at Paris.

Since the war ended Simon had read every article, pamphlet and book he could obtain about the accomplishments of the Army he fought with and his brother Sam had died for. To his dismay and increasing anger, the main body of literature was overwhelmed by the exploits of the marine brigade which was a part of the 2nd Division. Casual readers would have assumed that the marines did all of the hard fighting. The sheer redundancy of the descriptive literature insulted every soldier that had served in the war.

When the two regiments of marines landed in France they were just as unprepared for combat as anyone else. The Army trained them, supplied them, and commanded them in every battle they fought. They had no artillery support and no logistical experience, so they were supplemented with Army support elements their table of organization lacked. Little or no credit was ever given to the soldiers who displayed the same valor, sustained the same rate of wounded and killed in action, and the same deprivation of food and medical needs at the front. The only thing different was recognition of Marine Corps units by the national press for courageous deeds and a tendency to ignore the contributions of the Army. This was the genesis of the bitter rivalry that still existed between the two services. The powerful and insensitive Marine lobby in Washington infuriated him, because truth and fairness were victims of their lust for self-glorification. Unfairness always aroused Simon.

The train pulled into the station at Montfaucon at six o'clock in the evening just as the sun was setting behind the rolling hills in the distance. An ancient Citreon taxicab took him to the hotel where he had made reservations. The cab driver would not accept any money for the lift to the hotel.

"Thank you for your help," said Simon.

"No, it is I who say thank you, Colonel." He drove off with an energetic wave of his hand.

The hotel was a relatively modern structure compared to the drab unkempt buildings he had seen in metropolitan Paris. When the United States Army captured Montfaucon on September 27, 1918, little remained of the original village. Four years of bombardment had destroyed every structure. A new Montfaucon rose like the legendary Phoenix next to the ashes of the original site where a large monument was built on top of the hill and old ruins.

The town was filled with village people and tourists. The impressive World War I cemetery and memorial attracted a large number of tourists from the United States. Consequently, many of the shop keepers and clerks in the hospitality industry spoke fluent English.

It was too late in the evening for Simon to go to the cemetery, so he enjoyed a leisurely meal at the hotel dining room and retired to his room to write a letter to Lee:

Dear Lee,

I arrived in Montfaucon after nightfall so I haven't visited the cemetery yet. My hotel window looks out on a towering Doric shaft with a figure of Liberty at the top. It is lit up with floodlights and is an impressive sight to behold.

I'm anxious to travel around the area. Even though it was twenty-seven years ago, I can still remember what it was like when Sam and I were young men fighting a war in a strange land far away from home. This region of France has been the scene of much conflict for centuries.

I've thought a lot about you today, and I want you to know that regardless of what transpires in the future, I will always remember you as a dear friend. I apologize again for hurting you, it was not intentional.

50

What a fool your husband must have been to give you up...

Love,

Simon

The next morning, sunshine flooded Simon's room, waking him up. An omen of good things to come! Sam's grave had been beckoning to him for a long time, and he rose with a renewed feeling of expectation and discovery. Twenty-seven years ago, he had visited the site of the original destroyed village of Montfaucon to say good-bye to his brother in the newly established cemetery.

It was not difficult for Simon to recall the devastation of the land. He had witnessed unspeakable desecration by the lethality of modern warfare. It had sickened him to see the gaunt black stubs of broken trees standing as silent witnesses, giving their mute salute to the savage struggle that had reduced them to shattered shreds of decaying wood fiber, devoid of life. As far as the eye could see, the landscape had been ravaged and plowed into pulverized lumps of soil mixed with human body parts and broken weapons of war. Scavengers had found the battlefields to be a bountiful food source.

Simon took a cab to the monument and rode around the perimeter of the cemetery so that he could view it from every angle. It brought out the same feelings of peace and solitude he and Miriam had experienced at Normandy. The granite tower at the end of the cemetery overlooked the fields of crosses and Stars of David. Near the top of the tower was an observation platform with a view in every direction. The figure of liberty holding a torch at the top of the structure was similar to the Statue of Liberty that France had presented to the United States at the turn of the century.

The cab driver told Simon that the tower had an elevator in the center of its shaft so he would have no problem getting to the observation platform. The view at the top was breathtaking. The Ardennes Mountain range in Belgium could be seen in the distance. The rolling farmland was similar to his native state of Maine.

The precise geometrical layout of the graves could be appreciated from the windblown platform. They stood in perfectly straight lines row upon row. Even when viewed from an oblique, they were evenly spaced and in alignment. The grounds were beautiful and immaculately maintained. He took one more visual sweep around the platform before leaving. Off to the east he noticed portions of what was once a building. Vines covered the rubble, and trees of four or five inches in diameter grew out of the debris. It was a ruin left untouched since the ceasefire was called.

On the way down the tower it struck him that he had not seen any evidence of recent fighting around the memorial and silently thanked the Germans for not desecrating the sanctity of the cemetery.

After all the years that had passed since the First World War, most of the days blended together with few exceptions. Days, weeks, and months had been filled with anxiety, fear, and the ubiquitous sound of gunfire somewhere along the line. Each day was the same. Fear of gas attacks were the most frightening. The yellow-colored mustard gas could quickly overcome a man before he placed his gas mask on correctly.

***

There was one day that Simon remembered with a clarity reserved only for the special occasions of his life. The morning of November 11, 1918, brought word that a ceasefire was ordered for 11:00 AM all across the front. The men huddled in their trenches listening for every noise. His platoon had held their fire ever since the warning order came down the line. The opposing German lines had done the same. Occasionally an artillery shell could be heard in the distance. Everyone wondered if it would be a false alarm. Uncertainty filled the hearts of each man holding his rifle at the ready just in case. How many times had each of them prayed for deliverance from the daily horror. They had lived with fear for so long it was difficult to relax. Laughter was scarce on the front line. Killing the enemy was serious business.

Suddenly whistles were blown on both sides along the front. The message that passed through was like a gift from Heaven: "Cease fire and hold in place." The guns became silent. For a brief period the men were numbed by the news. They leaned against the soggy trench walls and thanked God.

52

Survival was the most precious gift of all. Everything else was secondary and it took a while for that reality to sink into their consciousness. Shouts and cries of joy rose from the muddy, desolate battlefield. Their days of Purgatory were over.

Some adventuresome souls carefully poked their heads out of the protected trench line to take an unobstructed view of the contested land. Laughter and celebration hesitantly began to fill the air. Fires started at random all along the line so that coffee could be prepared. Simon was one of the first men in his section to stand on the edge of the trench. He breathed deeply several times. The air was void of the acrid, choking smell of gunpowder. It was cool and refreshing. He noticed that some of the German troops had climbed out of their holes holding rifles with fixed bayonets. Without hesitation they drove the bayonets into the earth and hung their unique heavy helmets on the butts of the rifles.

Simon ordered more fires to be started and motioned the men out of the putrid smelling trenches with any bit of foodstuffs they had. In a short time they were celebrating with coffee and hardtack. The much maligned hardtack never tasted as good as it did that morning. One of his platoon sergeants was a German immigrant from South Dakota. The tall, lanky, blond-headed, blue-eyed young man was asked to tell the Germans across no-mans-land that coffee was plentiful, and they were willing to share what they had with their former enemy. They should bring their own cups with them.

The German soldiers listened to the invitation. They had not built fires like the intrepid Americans. A few answered the call and started to walk towards the American side. They brought loaves of black bread to share with the coffee.

For months Simon and his ravaged platoon had fought the tenacious enemy, hating and fearing him at the same time. Now, watching them plod through the blackened mud, he and the rest of his men were shocked to discover that the enemy was just like them, battered, exhausted, hungry, and afraid. They shared the same deeply set eyes that stared off into space, seeing nothing and everything. Hours before, they were deadly enemies; now there was mutual respect that transcended nationalities or language. Above everything else, they shared the liberating joy of life itself. As for Simon, the joy he experienced on that day was equal to the rapture that he felt when he married Miriam and the day their son was born.

***

Simon walked along the promenade at the far end of the cemetery and was greeted by the caretaker.

"Hello, Colonel."

"Hello," answered Simon, acknowledging a man dressed in civilian clothes about his own age.

"I'm Carl Hathaway, the caretaker and curator for the monument. I watched you climb the tower after circling the cemetery. Is there anything I can do to help you?"

"I'm glad to meet you, Mr. Hathaway. I'm Colonel Hanley and am surprised to find someone who speaks English so well. Are you an American?"

"Yes, I was wounded at Verdun and stayed on after the first war. My brother was killed by the same shell that wounded me. He's buried here at Montfaucon. I work for the United States Battlefield Monuments Commission."

"What a coincidence. I came to this place to visit the grave of my twin brother, Second Lieutenant Samuel Hanley. We served in different divisions."

"I'm amazed at the large number of veterans of this recent war that have come to visit graves of relatives and friends. Would you like to come to the reception center? I can show you where your brother's grave is located."

"I'd appreciate that. I'm impressed with the immaculate appearance of the Memorial especially since the war ended such a short time ago."

"The Germans were a bitter enemy, but I'll say one thing for them. They scrupulously honored this hallowed place and most of the other cemeteries and monuments in France and Belgium. I was not bothered by the occupation troops. As a matter of a fact, the major that patrolled this area frequently stopped to see if I needed anything. My family was not threatened, so we remained close to the monument for the duration. I'm thankful for that. I married a French girl right after the Armistice in 1918. We had a son and daughter who lived with my parents during the war years in my home town near Boston."

"After all these years, you still have that clipped New England dialect. I'm afraid I never lost mine either. I'm from northern Maine."

"We're practically neighbors, Colonel," smiled the thin Carl Hathaway.

They went into the reception center near a small chapel. Hathaway directed Simon to a large map and relief model of the cemetery and pointed out the location of Samuel Hanley's grave near the geographical center of the burial ground.

"Would you like for me to arrange for a ride out there, Colonel Hanley?" asked Hathaway, uncertain if the walk was within Simon's ability.

"No, Sir. Thanks just the same. I'll take my time, I have plenty of that. My wound is healing, and exercise is the best thing for it. Being here in this section of France brings back a lot of memories."

"That's what this sacred place is all about. The world should never be allowed to forget. When our generation is gone, there won't be any direct connection to what took place here. That's why I'm so gratified to see second and third generations of family members showing up in such large numbers," said Carl Hathaway.

"The peace and serenity that fills the air here is a contradiction to the way these men died. I recently visited the grave of my son at Normandy and had the same feelings. I never expected it to be like this," declared Simon, looking over the endless lines of graves. He could feel Samuel's presence. Chills ran up and down his spine and goose bumps formed on his arms.

"Death is the ultimate state of grace, Colonel."

"Yes, I suppose you're right. Thank you for your help, Carl Hathaway. It's been a pleasure."

"You're welcome. Please call on me if you need any assistance. I'm usually around the reception center."

Simon slowly walked down the center paved walkway. Silence filled the air. The only sounds to be heard were the soft whir of the wind blowing through the grave markers and birds singing from every corner of the field of stones. He stopped to listen and closed his eyes.

In the depth of his consciousness he could still hear the sound of gunfire echo erratically across the land. Mixed with the disjointed cacophony of artillery were the human sounds of wounded men calling for help and screaming for their loved ones as they lay alone in the cold mud. After twenty-seven years, the cries of the wounded still tormented him.

Simon turned to his left, knowing that he would confront his brother's burial place. A cool breeze swept across his face. He recalled that Sam had that gift of smiling most of the time, even when things were not going well for him. Simon touched the lettering on the white cross: "Second Lieutenant Samuel D. Hanley, USA."

"Well, Sam, it's been a long time since we were together in France. I think often of you and all the good times we had together. I've felt guilty surviving the war, getting married and having a son. You were denied that pleasure. God, I've missed you, Sam...," Simon let the tears come. More than ever he needed the stabilizing influence of his brother, his best friend, his classmate..., yet, the emptiness continued. Time had not diminished the love he held for Samuel. The hollow void Simon experienced when he first learned of Samuel's death was just as painful.

While Simon was consumed with memories and overwrought with grief and loneliness at the grave of his brother, a woman with a young girl of six or seven years old were walking down the same pathway Simon had used and turned into the row where he was kneeling before Sam's grave. The woman was mesmerized by his presence. She watched him wipe his eyes and blow his nose with disbelief and wonder, holding ever so tightly to the little girl's hand. Simon turned to see who was behind him. Suddenly, her look held him speechless.

She cried out in a loud incredulous voice: "Mon, Dieu, Sam..." and fainted.

Chapter Seven

The little girl was pulled off balance when the woman passed out and fell forward. Nothing in his life so unnerved Simon as the words coming out of the woman's mouth and her subsequent collapse, partially on top of him. He quickly extricated himself holding the woman, carefully placing her on the freshly mowed grass. He held out his hand to the little girl as she began to cry.

"Please, don't cry. I won't hurt you. Please..." he tried to comfort her, but was unable to quell her fears. She was petrified of him, believing him responsible for making the middle-aged woman fall. His knowledge of French consisted of a few words. He felt paralyzed and helpless. "Please don't cry..." Simon pleaded.

Simon checked the woman to see that nothing was choking or restricting her breathing. She rolled her eyes once so that he saw only the white portion and was alarmed that she might have been injured. A few seconds later, the woman heard the child crying and sat up.

"I'm all right, sweetheart," the distraught lady said in perfect English. "Don't be afraid." The child embraced the woman as she sat on the ground and looked again at Simon. An air of disbelief, and fear consumed her. "No, no, it can't be..." she cried out with trembling lips. "After all these years, you can't be Sam. Who are you?"

Simon heard her voice and saw the shock on her face. "Lady, I apologize if my presence has disturbed you. Did you know Lieutenant Sam Hanley?"

"Yes, I knew him," she quickly replied, anxious to hear more from the stranger.

"I'm Simon Hanley. Sam was my twin brother."

"No..." cried the lady in disbelief.

"Yes, it's true," he demanded in a calm voice. "I've recently come from the United States to visit my brother's grave. Both of us were in combat near here during the First World War. How well did you know Sam?"

She straightened the beret on her head and modestly pulled her dress further down over her legs and began to stand. Simon offered her a hand which she accepted, quickly releasing it as soon as she regained her footing. She was embarrassed and avoided his questioning look. The little girl wore a blue dress with yellow flowers and a maroon beret similar to the one the lady had on. She was still upset and clung to the woman.

"I'm sorry that I've frightened the child," Simon said, kneeling down to her level, balancing himself on his cane. "Please don't be upset, young lady. I would never hurt you."

"Is everything all right?" asked Carl Hathaway, out of breath from running up the walkway. "I saw you fall, Lili, and heard you and the girl cry out."

"I saw Mr. Hanley and was surprised, that's all," declared Lili, taking a deep breath. "I'm all right now. I'm sorry that I intruded on your visit to your brother's grave. Good day, Sir. Thank you for your concern, Mr. Hathaway." Lili took the child's hand and started to walk away.

"Please Ma'am... is it Lili?"

"Yes?"

"You can't just walk away from here. You said you knew Sam. He never mentioned a Lili to me before he died," Simon exclaimed.

"Then you never knew, Colonel. I must leave now. My granddaughter has been upset enough for one day. Good-bye."

Carl Hathaway and Simon watched her walk down the pathway toward the reception center. Simon's head was filled with questions screaming for answers.

"Do you know this Lili, Mr. Hathaway?"

"Yes, she's Lili Becker. She's our Town Librarian and lives on the outskirts of the village in a modest country home she rents from a local farmer."

"I can't believe that she knew Sam."

"All I can tell you is that she visits the grave several times each year, always with the little girl. As I understand the situation, she came to town after the Germans occupied Paris. I never knew for sure. No one asked questions during the war. Knowledge of certain people could have been dangerous. I believe she left Paris for the country where it was easier to find food, and the Germans bothered the populace less than in the cities. I know that the people at the library think the world of her. She's intelligent and helpful in the library, but she has a reputation of being a recluse."

"Where does she live?"

"Her place is on the main road heading north several blocks from your hotel at the outskirts of the village proper. It's a small granite house with red shutters on the left hand side of the road right after you cross the bridge over the small stream that runs through the village. She raises a large garden and diligently works in the fields around the house. She doesn't bother much with people, and they honor her desire to be left alone."

"Thanks for the help and information, Mr. Hathaway. This has been quite a day!" observed Simon, shaking his head. He walked towards the town thinking about the incredulous incident that had just taken place.

He wracked his brain if there was anything he had forgotten or overlooked that could shed some light on the sudden appearance of the mysterious Lili Becker. When he and Sam entered France in 1917, they both participated in training exercises at a small town south of Paris. After completing the basic infantry training agenda, they were assigned to different divisions. They saw each other twice before the war ended. The first time was about February of 1918 before their respective units entered combat. Sam had mentioned how great the French people were to his men billeted in private homes nearby. He was positive Sam never mentioned a Lili.

***

The last time he saw Sam was at an officer's conference near Verdun after both of their divisions had been severely mauled by the Germans. At that gathering, Sam was his usual optimistic self. Nothing ever bothered him. It had been a ten minute reunion. They had embraced each other soberly before returning to their respective platoons. Simon could still see Sam picking his way through a mud-filled cart track behind a farmhouse. A hundred feet down the lane Sam turned to wave good-bye. That scene was permanently etched on his soul. In that moment, Simon had a premonition that he was seeing Sam for the last time.

***

The walk to the hotel made Simon's leg sore. It was the longest distance he had walked since he was wounded. The hike had weakened him, but it had also generated an appetite, so he went directly to the hotel dining room where he ordered pea soup and a ham sandwich. Partway through lunch a young man entered the dining room, removed his hat and approached Simon's table.

"M'sieur, Hanley?" the boy announced, holding a letter out to him.

"Yes," responded Simon, taking the envelope. "Thank you."

"You are welcome," answered the boy in broken English as if he had been instructed to memorize the words. He quickly left the room as Simon opened the envelope and read the letter.

Dear Colonel Hanley,

I expect that you must be filled with questions about our accidental meeting at Sam's grave. I understand the shock that placed both of us there at the same time.

Mr. Hathaway probably told you that I work at the village library. I will be free all afternoon if you would care to visit us at our home. I'll try to answer your questions at that time.

Sincerely
Lili Becker,
1497 rue Marne, Montfaucon

He fingered the message, admiring the flowing penmanship. It was now one- thirty in the afternoon. Simon completed lunch and anxiously went to his room to change and freshen up. The situation still baffled him. Surely, he admitted to himself, there had to have been some type of

60

intervention, Divine or otherwise, about the trip he had planned to make to Montfaucon. The fact that the mystery woman had offered to answer questions of her own free will interested him, and he was eager to hear what she had to offer.

He called for a cab which turned out to be the same battered Citreon that took him from the train station to the hotel. The friendly driver knew right where Lili Becker's house was located.

The cab driver turned into the driveway and refused to accept any money. The house was a small stone structure with vines growing on the south and west walls. It was neat and orderly. A large dairy farm could be seen half a mile down the road. A wooden fence separated the house from the adjacent sugar beet fields. A small spiral of wood smoke curled from the chimney, filling the air with its unique pungent aroma that Simon had not smelled since he left Maine. It made him feel a little homesick.

The half-acre of land within the protective fence was filled with vegetables and flowers neatly laid out in straight rows. Near the entrance to the house he noticed several tomato plants hanging heavily with large red tomatoes. He was tempted to snatch one and eat it. The door opened before he knocked. It was the little girl curiously watching him.

"Hello, young lady," he smiled. She returned his smile with some reservation. She was a pretty child with dimples on her two cheeks, but there was a sadness in her eyes that touched Simon and drew him to her. "Is your grandmother at home?"

"Yes, she wants you to come in the house," she answered, looking up at the tall soldier passing through the door.

Simon removed his cap and was met by a more relaxed Lili Becker. "Welcome to our home, Colonel Hanley. I'm glad you've come. Please, make yourself comfortable. We can sit in the living room. I started a fire in the fireplace. May I get you something to drink-wine, coffee, tea, cider?"

"This soldier never says no to coffee," answered Simon. She motioned him into the living room and left to start coffee.

The low-hanging ceilings made the room look smaller than it actually was. A small fire crackled in the field stone fireplace with a granite mantel. Large hand-hewn beams spanned the ceiling from wall to wall spaced every four feet.

The wall opposite the fireplace was covered top to bottom with books of every description. The top portion contained historical writings and a large number of classic novels all in English. There was a functional warmth and informality about the house that made him feel at ease the minute he entered it.

Lili returned to the room, taking a seat across from Simon in front of the fireplace. She was small and petite with fine facial features. She carried herself with an air of confidence and dignity, which bordered on aloofness and indifference that did not encourage familiarity. The dark blue dress with white lace trim she wore emphasized her trim lithe body. Her sandy hair was rolled into a bun at the back of her head. The pair of black rim glasses suspended around her neck completed an appearance that many people have associated with old-maid school teachers. Her dark brown eyes glowed in the reflection from the fireplace. She was more reserved than shy. Her penetrating glances evaluated Simon thoroughly. She felt comfortable with the decision to invite him into her home. She was a model of graciousness as a hostess.

"The coffee will be ready in a few minutes," she announced, noticing his approving looks at the bookcase. "Do you like books?"

"I'm a professional soldier. When I have not been fighting a war, I've been studying and attending Army schools all over the country to increase my skills as a leader of men in combat. I take that responsibility seriously, and study a lot. I like this room. It's warm and relaxing." Simon watched her without being too obvious. She seemed to be at peace with herself, even under the unusual circumstances of their meeting.

"This visit must seem strange to you. It does to me," replied Lili, staring at the fireplace.

"You've certainly been a surprise to me," observed Simon. "May I ask why you speak such flawless English living in France?"

"My parents were Scotch and English and I've continued the tradition with my granddaughter."

"Where did you meet Sam?" he asked, unable to hold his anxiety any longer.

"He was billeted in a house south of Paris next to the University where my father taught chemistry. We lived in an

62

apartment building that also housed several American soldiers while they were undergoing training. Sam was one of them. I met him one day when he was wandering around the University, and he asked me for directions to the Agricultural building. When I gave him directions he, too, was amazed that I spoke English. We talked a long time that first day. Afterwards, we saw each other as often as his rigid schedule allowed and became good friends. I am not ashamed to admit that I fell in love with him the first few times we saw each other. I've always believed that it was mutual," she claimed defensively, checking Simon for his response.

"I believe that the human heart is capable of doing anything," replied Simon.

"Sam came to our apartment and shared several meals with my parents and me. They liked him very much."

Simon was thinking back to that period when Sam had mentioned going to the homes of local people where they lavished foodstuff on him and others. Samuel never mentioned Lili. He was, in reality, a very serious person using his smiles and easy-going-attitude to hide and protect his private feelings. It was plausible that he wanted to tell Simon, but held it back for a more opportune time, which never came.

"I'm not disbelieving you, Mrs. Becker. My brother and I were identical twins. Our personalities were similar but different. The fact that he did not mention you by name to me or to our mother in any letter does not invalidate what you're telling me now. I have no reason to not believe you."

"You are exactly what I imagined he would look like if he had lived. He was a very caring and gentle man. My father especially liked him for his fine manners."

"I can believe that. You describe Sam correctly."

"The coffee must be ready now. Would you excuse me while I put my granddaughter to bed?" she asked.

"Of course, I understand."

"She has been sick lately and needs rest. She was the main reason I left the cemetery in such a hurry. Stress is not good for her," she said without explanation.

While she was out of the room Simon looked at the pictures on the mantel. He recognized Sam in uniform, smiling as usual, standing beside a tree in front of a set of buildings, probably the University Lili mentioned. There was another photo, a more recent one with better lighting and definition. It included Lili with a young man and a woman about the same age. There was something familiar about the eyes on the man. No matter where you looked at the picture his eyes seemed to follow you.

"I made some apple turnovers this morning. Please help yourself to them with the coffee," she announced, setting a tray on a stand beside Simon's chair. She saw him studying the pictures. "I have something confidential to tell you that will shock you, Colonel, and I do it because I believe you are entitled to the truth."

"The truth?" asked Simon, wondering what else he was going to discover about his twin brother.

"Yes," confessed Lili, nervously avoiding his searching stare. Simon felt the tenseness in her. She looked at the flames in the fireplace for several seconds and continued: "There's more... When Sam left for the front in the summer of 1918 I was pregnant with what became his son, Samuel, Jr. I never told him. I didn't want him to find out in letters while he was in combat at the front. It was my fervent prayer that he would return to me of his own free will because of his love for me. I believe he would have done that if death had not intervened."

"You and Sam had a son? My God, this is incredible! Where's the son?"

Lili jumped out of her chair to grasp the picture on the mantel Simon had looked at earlier. "This is a picture of Samuel, Jr. The Germans killed him and his wife, the young woman standing beside me. They had joined a group of Partisan fighters in Paris that had been penetrated by the Gestapo. They and others were shot in the streets of Paris." Tears formed in her dark eyes. She wiped them dry, trying to quell the outrage that still consumed her.

"I felt something when I saw the photo," exclaimed Simon, numbed by the discovery. He stood up to better look at the picture Lili was holding. "He favored Sam, but he had your nose and mouth."

"That's what people used to say," Lili admitted nervously.

"I'm sorry that I could not share your loss. Why didn't you ever try to reach me or my mother once you knew you were pregnant?"

64

"I've asked myself that same question a thousand times. You had a right to know, but I was afraid you would not believe me and look upon me as an immoral woman who took advantage of a lonely soldier away from home. My parents sent me away to a convent to have the baby. When I returned, they helped us, but I wanted to do things for myself, so I started work as a librarian at the University. Sam grew into a fine young man just like his father. You would have been proud of him, too."

"The child you just put to bed is your granddaughter. Where is your husband?" asked Simon with interest.

"My husband? I never married. My granddaughter is Samuel's daughter. You are Samantha's great uncle!"

Chapter Eight

Simon's face turned milk white. Lili was afraid that the knowledge was too much of a shock for him. At first he thought that he had heard her wrong, but the logic of the sequence of events seemed to be beyond dispute. Why should Lili intentionally lie to him? He got up from the chair and nervously walked about the room without saying a word. She put another piece of wood on the fire. Simon backed against the warming fireplace, clasped his hands behind his back, and rigidly arched his shoulders. His visit to Montfaucon was one he would remember for a long time!

"Are you unhappy that I told you, Colonel?" she asked with hesitation, unable to interpret what he thought about the information.

"No," Simon responded, turning to her. "How did you happen to come here from Paris with the child? Where were your parents?"

"They were in England visiting friends when the war started. A year later, both were killed in one of the German bombing raids against London. As for my coming here, it was the only place I could think of. You can't imagine how it was, and you don't know what real terror is until you've experienced what the German pigs are capable of doing to human beings. Samuel and Robyne were two of the most beautiful people this ugly world has ever known, and the Nazi's shot them down on the street like mad dogs! I almost lost my mind. I would have gladly joined any resistance group for revenge, but I had to think of Samantha. She needed care, and I was the only person available to give it to her. She's such a dear girl..." Lili started to cry, softly at first. Then, tears flowed down her cheeks faster than she could wipe them away with her small handkerchief

66

Simon looked on helplessly. The release of tears continued unabated for several minutes. She had never had a chance to mourn the loss of Sam, their son, his wife, or her two parents. The catharsis taking place in his presence was a release of years of pain and fear. He placed both hands on her shoulders to try and console her. Her body wracked with convulsive cries.

"Let it all out, Lili Becker. You've been carrying a heavy load for too many years. Take all the time you need to acknowledge your sorrow and hurt, and make no apologies to anyone, especially me."

Lili heard his soothing words. There was wisdom in what he was saying. Samantha had become her reason for living after the gruesome death of her mother and father. Simon handed her a clean handkerchief. She took it and blew her nose several times.

"You asked me why I came here?" she continued between gasps for breath, hiding her swollen eyes from him. "Samantha was only one year old then, barely walking by herself, when Samuel and Robyne were killed. I was babysitting Samantha the day they were shot. My parents had left a Ford sedan at the University. That evening I loaded Samantha into the automobile and left the city, certain that they would arrest me if I remained. I took every back road I could find on my way to Montfaucon. I knew that Sam was buried here. I had researched every cemetery in France and Belgium after the first war. Fortunately, I was never stopped by a German patrol.

"I also knew that a librarian job was available at the town library. The town had contacted the University placement service for possible applicants. I got the job the first day of my arrival in town. I'm a graduate librarian. One of the clerks directed me to the people who own the farm next door. They rented the house to me without asking any questions and have been most helpful over the years. I could not have managed without their kindness and support. Now you know more about me than any person in the world, Colonel."

"If you'll call me, Simon, I'll call you Lili. What do you say?"

"Yes, Simon sounds less formal than Colonel."

"I must say that you've shown a tremendous amount of courage and determination in dealing with the tragedies in your life, Lili. I admire the strong spirit of independence that has allowed you to find your way. I salute you, and I'm sure Sam is watching your performance with pride."

"I'm not strong, believe me," she confessed. "I need Samantha more than she needs me."

"Tell me about her illness," Simon requested in a calm voice.

"Samantha has a heart condition that will probably require surgery. Without getting into technical detail, she has a leaking valve in her heart. The family doctor here in town thinks she needs surgery to correct it. She's been a very sick girl for the past year and a half. All of this started when she became sick with rheumatic fever. We almost lost her once when the fever raced out of control. She has developed bronchial and throat infections on a weekly basis."

"How many different doctors have you taken her to?"

"Only the one here in Montfaucon. He's very good but limited as far as surgical operations are concerned. I've been saving money so that we can go to Paris to have her checked by experts in the field. That way, if an operation is needed, I'll be able to pay some in advance."

"May I see her?"

"She's probably sleeping. She frightens me sometimes because she sleeps so soundly that I can hardly hear her breathe. Walk softly; she's in the room off the kitchen," Lili requested.

She led him through the kitchen to her room, opening the door a crack to check on Samantha. The sun was starting to sink into the west, filling the room with subdued sunlight. Simon tiptoed around her bed and kneeled down to look at her. Small beads of sweat had formed on her forehead. Such a pretty child he thought. One of her pigtail braids had started to unravel. He pulled the loose strands of hair away from her eyes and looked at her for a long time. Lili stood by, watching. Simon was touched by her devotion to the child, Sam's granddaughter. Now he understood why some higher power had brought him to Montfaucon at this time.

He leaned down to kiss Samantha lightly on the forehead and thanked God for guiding him to her. Samantha opened her eyes halfway and fell back to sleep again. Her soft hand touched him on the cheek, moving him to tears. He quietly left the room and stared at the fire in the fireplace, hanging onto the mantel with both hands. His vision was still blurred. Lili followed him and took a seat. The room was filled with emotional silence. She had seen Simon's reaction to Samantha's hand touching his face.

"I've been running things through my mind, asking myself what would Sam do if he were in my shoes, and what would he want me to do in his absence?" Simon asked.

Lili cried and held her hands to her face: "No, I have not asked you for anything. I..."

"No, you haven't, and I admire your independence, Lili," Simon turned to her. "Right now, after what you've revealed to me, I cannot see that little girl, knowing that she needs medical care from the best there is without wanting to do something about it."

"It's not fair that my problems become your problems," Lili protested vehemently.

"Don't you think it would be more appropriate to say that your problems should be shared by a family that cares? When you confided in me that Sam had a son, I was shocked and didn't want to believe it, but I was proud of the prospect that a part of my beloved brother had survived him. Now I find that his granddaughter is in need of medical attention. If you knew Sam well, you'd know that he would not stand by and simply be a spectator."

"Yes, he would want to do something. Do you hate me for confiding in you?"

"Dear lady," scolded Simon. "Don't you ever get weary of fighting the world alone? Do I hate you for telling me that my brother found love and peace of mind in your arms before he died? Do I hate you for telling me, the last survivor of the Hanley family name, that my brother's granddaughter is in the next room? You might as well ask 'is there a God in Heaven?'

"I'm still in a state of shock, but I'm alert enough to know that you've given me some of the most beautiful news these tired old ears have heard in a long time. Samantha rightfully loves and respects you. No person could ever replace you in her heart, and I would be the last person to condone such a thing. Our chance meeting and the enlightening conversation we've just had, have, in a flash, changed many things in my life. You could have given this old soldier a heart attack; instead, you've made my heart sing for joy. Little Samantha is a living, breathing product of you and Sam. What a wonderful revelation! I thank you for that, Lili Becker. I think you're a courageous soldier fighting life's battles all by yourself. I'm positive that some power has guided me to this village for a reason. May I assist you in fighting it? Please don't shut me out."

Simon looked at her reaction to his words. She heard the spoken words and knew what was in his heart. She smiled at him. "Thank you, Simon. Sam loved you the same way you still love him and his memory. It's starting to get late. May I fix something for you to eat?"

"If I answer your question you'll probably laugh at me," teased Simon.

"I promise to not laugh."

"Okay then. When I walked into the kitchen I noticed some of the most luscious looking red tomatoes I've seen in a long time out there beside the door. I almost grabbed one and ate it before I knocked. If you have some bread I'd love a tomato sandwich."

Lili suppressed an urge to giggle. He was like a little boy, something unusual for a strong man.

"You just requested my favorite at this time of year."

"I don't know how long it has been since I could pick fresh vegetables from a home garden. We raised large ones when Sam and I were kids in Maine."

"Before it gets too dark, why don't you step outside and pick as many as you want? I'll set the table for us."

Simon selected a half dozen of the ripest tomatoes and placed them on the table in the center of the kitchen. Lili was slicing a fresh loaf of oatmeal bread.

"Do you want wine with your sandwich?" she asked.

"Only if you are. I had a problem with alcohol before the war. I still enjoy an occasional beer and glass of wine, but I don't want it to become a habit again."

"I can do more coffee or tea. I prefer coffee," suggested Lili.

"I'd like that better," replied Simon.

She placed a cutting board in front of him to slice the tomatoes. He cut them into half inch slices using up four of the tomatoes, and they sat down to make the sandwiches.

"I've told you all of the secrets in my life which is most amazing considering the reputation I have of being an old maid recluse. I know very little about you. Do you have a large family?" Lili noticed the wedding band he continued to wear after Miriam had left him.

"I combined this trip to Montfaucon with one to the Normandy cemetery. My only son was killed there. He was a West Point graduate and his mother and I were very proud of him. Do you know what I mean by West Point?"

"Yes, the United States Military Academy at West Point, New York. Why didn't your wife accompany you here?"

"She divorced me in 1933 for another officer. We met a few days ago to attend the commissioning ceremonies for the Normandy burial sites. It was the first time I'd seen her in five years."

"I'm sorry. That sounds terrible. Your son must have been unhappy about that."

"Even though his mother left me for another man, her love for Keith was genuine and unwavering. When I left Paris yesterday, she decided to leave her husband because he was unfaithful. She left me a long letter explaining her actions. Everyone is entitled to happiness, and I wish her no harm," Simon told her.

"The loss of a son leaves an emptiness that can consume you. Even now I still have a hard time accepting the finality of Samuel, Jr.'s death. I've been selfish in thinking that I was the only one to be burdened by such pain," Lili acknowledged. "We have that in common. My prayers are with you and your wife, Miriam, that you may find peace. It's elusive, but, with time, it can be found."

"Thank You, Lili."

"Sam told me about you and Miriam. He predicted that you two would be married the first week after you got home. He jokingly called you 'Sim and Mim'."

"That sounds like Sam," Simon chuckled, taking another bite of his sandwich. "This tastes great. I could eat another one."

71

"Oh, please help yourself. The coffee is ready to pour. I notice that you wear some impressive ribbons. I know what they stand for. How serious is your injury?" Lili asked.

"I should make a complete recovery without any lasting physical limitations. You're perceptive about military things. I've been a regimental commander' and sometimes it places me in demanding situations that nobody else can fulfill. I wear the ribbons in honor of those who served just as bravely and did not receive any recognition of their deeds," Simon explained modestly.

"You're correct. Many acts of courage go unheralded by the rest of the world, but that doesn't denigrate the value of your contribution. Keith must have been proud of his father," stated Lili soberly.

"I've been thinking about Samantha," said Simon. "Would you object if I arranged for an examination of her by an Army doctor I trust in Paris?"

"When would you do this?" she asked hesitantly.

"I'll call first thing in the morning to set it up. When would it be best for you? Is Samantha in school now?"

"I've been homeschooling her lately because she has been so fragile. I can take time from the library for something like that. Are you sure you want to do this, Simon?"

"Does the sun come up in the morning? Does night follow day?" he asked impatiently. "Of course I want to do something. If Colonel Connors, the Army doctor in Paris, suggests that she needs further care, we'll take her to the United States where we have the best medicine in the world."

"I don't know," cried Lili nervously. She was unprepared for such precipitant decisions. "I want what is best for her, and I'm willing to work hard to make it possible. I simply don't have that kind of money to do what you're talking about."

"First things first, Lili. Do you want me to help with Samantha?"

"Yes."

"Do you trust me to want only the best for her?"

"Yes, and so do I."

"Okay, then, we'll take it one step at a time," Simon suggested. "Personally, I trust the evaluation of Colonel Connors over most French doctors. Please don't take offense to that remark."

72

"No, I agree that Samantha could get better diagnoses and care in the United States than in France, which is still recovering from a bitter occupation and a devastating war. It's the money that frightens me."

Simon sympathized with her reluctance to relinquish decisions about Samantha. He understood that and did not want to be the stranger that suddenly appears in their lives and starts telling them what they must do. He would resent it if he were Lili.

"Would you accept financial assistance from me if it would make her well?"

"Yes, I'd accept it from anybody, but I would eventually pay them back."

"Then we don't need to debate something we don't have the facts on yet. When I phone from the Hotel..."

"I have a phone here at the cottage."

"May I make a few calls then?"

"Of course you may. The phone is on my desk next to the bookcase," Lili pointed across the room.

Simon removed his tunic and loosened his necktie, pulling a small notepad from his jacket pocket.

"I'm going to check on Doctor Connors first. Would you mind talking to the operators for me? I don't understand and can't talk a word of French."

"I'll be glad to." Lili took the receiver and placed the call to the number Simon gave her. A voice answered at the Army facility.

"Medical Center, Captain Lee Rogers speaking."

"Just a moment please," Lili requested, passing the phone to Simon.

"Hello, this is Colonel Simon Hanley. Is Colonel Connors available or still at his desk?"

"Well, hello, Simon. This is Lee. Have you been hurt or something?"

"Hi, Lee, I'm glad you're there."

"Incidentally, Connors is at the center if you want me to connect you to him?"

"That'll be great, Lee. A couple of questions first. Without going into a lot of detail, I have a six-year-old-girl that had rheumatic fever and has been diagnosed by a local French doctor as having a faulty heart valve. What are my chances of getting her into the center for a thorough examination by Doctor Connors without getting court-martialed?"

"All you need is a friend at the center who's willing to help you," added Lee flippantly. "I can handle it if Connors agrees. I caution you though, we cannot take any responsibility for treatment of her problems."

"Thanks, Lee, I feel better already. Put me through to Connors and thanks for being my friend at court."

"You're welcome, Simon. Who is the voice I heard on the phone? Is it Miriam?"

"No, it was not Miriam. I'll tell you about it sometime, Lee."

Simon spoke at length with Colonel Connors, telling him everything he knew about Samantha's condition and the background of her relationship to him. He agreed to see her the next day or the day afterward if it was more appropriate.

"I can't thank you enough, Doctor Connors. I know that it's an irregular request, but I wanted the advice of someone I could trust. We'll try to make it for tomorrow. If not, I'll call to let you know. Thank you, Sir, and thank Lee again for me."

"The United States Army seems to take care of its own," commented Lili, excited about having Samantha examined by a doctor more familiar with modern medicine than her country doctor at Montfaucon.

"Can you two make it for tomorrow? We should try to get as early a train in the morning as possible."

"We can meet any schedule you suggest." Lili called the station for a departure time in the morning and reserved tickets for the eight o'clock train to Paris.

"I should be getting back to the hotel; it's getting late. Would you call for a cab to pick me up? The driver has already given me two free rides. We're almost old friends," smiled Simon.

"If you want to wait until Samantha wakes up, I can take you back to the Hotel. I still have my parent's Ford."

"Thanks, but Samantha needs her rest uninterrupted. The cab will be fine. Do you think Samantha will like the trip to Paris?"

Lili finished making a call to the cab driver's home. "She has never been outside of the village. I didn't circulate socially within the village because I thought it would be better to maintain a low profile for several reasons. I know that they talk about me, but at least they're still uncertain about who I am."

"Mr. Hathaway has high regards for you."

"He's a regular at the library. He's working on a military book and has been doing a lot of research. I've helped to locate material and references. A single mother with a small child is enough to start tongues wagging. France is no different than England or the United States in that respect. People love to gossip. I simply chose to say nothing to anybody and I've followed that policy until tonight. Very few people have visited us and I did not encourage it."

"Grandmother," called a small voice from the door of the kitchen. Samantha was standing in the doorway, her hair disheveled, holding on to the arm of a rag doll.

"Come here, Honey," Lili called, holding her arms out. Samantha ran into them climbing onto her lap. Her color had improved from when Simon first met her.

Samantha looked at the food on the table and said, "I'm hungry."

"How about a poached egg on toast?" asked Lili, setting her beside Simon on a highchair. She shook her head and continued to look at Simon, uncertain if she approved of him or not. Simon was amused at her appraisal.

"I already know that your name is Samantha. Do you know what my name is?

"You are a soldier," she said, fascinated at the gold eagle insignias on his shirt collar.

"Yes, I'm a soldier, and I want to be your friend. You ask Grandmother what my name is." He did not want to be the one to tell her who he actually was.

"You listen carefully, Samantha. This soldier is your father's uncle, and I don't believe he will object to being called Uncle by you. Little children should use names that show respect instead of familiarity."

"Uncle Simon sounds fine to me. Let me hear you say it," Simon proposed.

"Uncle Simon," she repeated, proud of herself.

"That's very good, Samantha. You know Americans like myself have lazy tongues and we like short names. Would you object if I call you Sam instead of Samantha?"

"No," she shook her head, thinking about what he said.

"To be fair, I should let you have the same privilege. You may call me Uncle Si instead of Simon. What do you think of that?"

She smiled at him and said, "Okay, Uncle Si."

"There can't be too many Uncle Si's in the world, and every time I hear you say Uncle Si I'll know that you're either talking to me or about me," laughed Simon.

Lili caught the teasing nuance and laughed with him. "I think you might have lost her on that one."

"Did you like the tomatoes?" asked Samantha, looking at what was left on the table.

"Oh yes. They were the best tasting tomatoes I've had since I was a little boy about your age, and that's a long time ago. Your grandmother ate one sandwich. They tasted so good that I ate two sandwiches. Now my belly is full, and it feels good."

"I planted the tomatoes beside the door," Samantha smiled at him.

"Those are the ones I picked because I thought they were the best looking ones."

"I think you're making a conquest, Uncle Si," observed Lili, breaking an egg over a pan of boiling water on the gas stove.

Simon was beginning to detect an impish side of Lili's disposition. She smiled and laughed easily, in contrast to the air she projected when he first met her. Samantha had picked up her grandmother's trait of slightly hunching her shoulders in a rapid movement at things that were obvious and slowly moving her head up and down when she was pleased at something.

"You can pour yourself a glass of milk now. The eggs will be ready in a minute," said Lili.

Samantha took a glass from the cupboard and went to the refrigerator where she poured herself a glass of milk. She turned to him and asked; "Do you want some milk, Uncle Si?"

"No, thank you, Sam. I'm still enjoying the cup of coffee your grandmother fixed for me. Milk is especially good for little girls."

"I know," admitted Sam with a little giggle.

Lili served Sam the toast with two eggs on top and tied a bib around her neck. Sam took a fork and knife to cut the toast into bite-sized pieces and started to eat. Simon was finding her an alert and intelligent child.

"You've done a wonderful job with her. She speaks better English than a lot of adults."

"I never talked 'baby-talk' with her," Lili answered. "I'm biased, I know, but she's a very special little girl."

Simon noticed Sam taking in every word. "Oh, oh grandmother, you've got to be careful about all of that praise it could go to her head. Do you know what happens then, Sam?"

"No," she answered, anxious to hear the answer.

"Your head will swell up so big you'll have to go sideways through a door." Sam paused a second to visualize what Simon had said and started to laugh with Lili joining in. Samantha finished eating her supper and, at Lili's request, went to her room to change into pajamas.

"Maybe your Uncle Si would like to read you a bedtime story before his taxicab arrives."

"I'd love to, even if we have to make the driver wait for us."

Sam came out of the bathroom wearing bright red pajamas with white polka dots and rushed to a bookcase in her room to select a book. She pulled the blankets down and climbed into bed pulling them up to her chin. Simon read two short stories. Part way through the second one Sam fell asleep. He placed the book on the table beside the bed. He bent down to kiss her on the cheek and whispered: "Sweet dreams, little princess."

Lili turned off the lights and closed the door behind them. "She responded to you better than I expected. I hear the taxi outside."

"I'll get my jacket, and I'll see you in the morning at the station."

"It was nice to hear laughter around the kitchen table tonight. I would not have blamed you if you had ignored my note and left town, but I'm glad you didn't. Thank you for everything, Simon. Goodnight."

"Goodnight, Lili."

Chapter Nine

The train ride from Montfaucon to Paris took them through small farming communities and busy metropolitan centers. Sam sat at the window of their coach compartment mesmerized by the roads, bridges, and large buildings within her view. The large sugar beet farms with row upon row of beets being harvested especially interested her. Lili told her that table sugar is made from the white rooted beet. Sam believed her grandmother but wrinkled her forehead, unable to comprehend how that could be possible.

Simon watched Lili from his vantage point of the opposite seat of the compartment. She was dressed in a light blue dress with a dark blue blazer. Her dark hair hung about her shoulders. She was an attractive woman with a confident air and a serious demeanor. The small amount of lipstick she was wearing emphasized her expressive lips.

Lili looked out the window at the passing scenery but did not see it; her mind and heart were elsewhere. She was thinking about what the future held for Samantha. If the examination by the Army doctor confirmed what she already knew, not much would be resolved except the assurance of a second professional opinion. In her mind she had already concluded that Samantha would need surgery. That fact made her uncomfortable, yet, she could acknowledge and accept it because it would increase Samantha's quality of life. Her fragile granddaughter was too young and innocent to be burdened with such a debilitating illness.

After an hour of watching out the window, Samantha was tired. She laid her head in Lili's lap and stretched out on the seat. Simon watched her, amazed at how quickly she fell into a sound sleep oblivious to the world around her. The love on Lili's face was a manifestation of what was in her heart. Her eyes met his, and she smiled. Two days ago they were total strangers. Today, they were joined in a common cause. Behind Lili's smile and confident air there was a nagging feeling that something unforeseen was waiting to burst the aura of optimism that filled her heart since she and Samantha stepped on the train. She had learned to pay attention to her premonitions, for they had accurately foretold the future in several instances of her past.

She was aware that Simon had been studying her ever since they left Montfaucon and was somewhat uncomfortable that he knew more about her than she knew about him. Consequently, she observed and evaluated him closely at different times on the trip. He could be austere and severe, yet she had seen how easy it had been for him to be playful with Samantha. He was physically strong, and she had no doubts that he was a brave and courageous soldier. He resembled Samuel so much it was often difficult for her to differentiate if she was talking to Simon or his dead brother.

They arrived in Paris by noontime and took a cab to Simon's hotel where he requested a single room for himself. Lili and Samantha could take his two-room-suite, which was more appropriate for them. They freshened up, ate lunch in the dining room and left for the Medical Center where they were met at the reception desk by a smiling Captain Lee Rogers.

"Colonel Hanley," she addressed casually. "You're right on schedule."

"Lee, this is Lili Becker and her granddaughter, Samantha. Lili, this is Captain Lee Rogers of the Army Nurse Corps."

"I'm happy to meet you, Captain. I'm so grateful for this opportunity to have Samantha checked by an American doctor."

"It's nice to meet you, Lili, and you, too, Samantha," replied Lee, coming around the corner to confront Samantha. The little girl's eyes touched the maternal part of Lee's big heart. "Do you speak English?"

"Yes and French, too," answered Samantha proudly.

"Well, we're going to try to help you, Samantha. It will take a while, and the doctor and I will be asking you a lot of questions. Your ability to speak in English will help a lot. Colonel, why don't you make yourself comfortable? You can get a cup of coffee at the small canteen right around the corner. I'm going to take Lili and Samantha to see the doctor."

"Thanks, Lee." Simon watched the three walk down the hallway toward the doctor's office. Lili looked back at him with a hesitant smile even though she was frightened.

Two hours later, Lee and Lili returned with Samantha. Lili looked exhausted, but Simon noted a hint of relief in her eyes as they approached the reception center. Lee excused herself to go to the pharmacy at the rear of the reception desk.

"What did the doctor say?" asked Simon anxiously.

"He confirmed our local doctor's diagnosis. The blood and urine samples indicated that her white and red blood counts are normal, and her blood sugar is normal, eliminating any prospects of diabetes. The doctor said that he wanted to talk with us. He'll be right out," Lili replied, holding Sam's hand.

Simon picked up Samantha. She grasped him around the neck and placed her head on his shoulder. She was tired and weak. He continued to hold her when Doctor Connors approached them.

"Colonel, this little girl is in good health except for one of her heart valves. It's not uncommon for children to develop an irregular heartbeat and/or deformation of some of the heart valves when they have been stricken with rheumatic fever. I believe that Samantha needs surgery. The valve affected is not closing properly and can be readily corrected. I have an old friend who is a heart specialist at the Boston Children's Hospital. I would be willing to call him and set up an appointment. It all depends on Miss Becker and you."

"What do you want to do, Lili?" asked Simon.

She had committed every word the doctor spoke to memory. "I just want Samantha to be well again." Her eyes filled with tears, reflecting the fear and hope that was in conflict within her heart.

"There's an element of urgency involved," added Doctor Connors. "This beautiful child should not have to suffer one day more than is absolutely essential."

"Then the answer is obvious, doctor," admitted Simon, decisively interpreting Lili's desire. "We'd appreciate it if you could make the call and set things up as soon as possible. Our next step is to get Lili and Samantha a passport or whatever papers are needed to enter the country."

"I can expedite that by declaring it a medical emergency and have our Headquarters obtain the necessary papers. Stop by the office of Civil Affairs before the day is ended. I'll have specific times and dates ready for you. Incidentally, speak to them about the use of a regular Military Air Transport flight to New York. I'll do the same on my end."

"How can I thank you, Doctor Connors?" Lili was bravely fighting tears.

"I went into medicine to help people like you and Samantha. Your loyalty and commitment to your granddaughter has gladdened my heart. Today, dear lady, it is I who have been rewarded. Check into Headquarters today. Good luck. Colonel Hanley, give my regards to Doctor Goodwin at Walter Reed Hospital."

"It will be my pleasure, Sir," said Simon, watching the doctor walk back to his office.

Lee returned with a vial of pills in her hand. "These should be given to Samantha twice a day. They'll thin her blood and increase the oxygen in the blood cells. Samantha won't feel as fatigued if she takes these until the Boston physician tells you what to do. The prescription is basically aspirin and iron."

"Thank you, Captain." Lili accepted the bottle of pills. "You've been most kind, and I appreciate that."

"You're welcome. I wish you good luck with Samantha." Lee placed her arms around Lili and hugged her firmly. "I admire your devotion to Samantha. Your silent battle for her over the years is an inspiring example of what the human spirit is capable of." Lee released Lili and kissed Samantha on the cheek. "You keep in touch, Colonel."

"I will, Lee. Thanks again."

They returned to the hotel so that Samantha could rest before they visited the Civil Affairs office. An hour later, Samantha was still tired from the visit to the doctor. Simon elected to carry her to the headquarters because it was getting late, and he was not sure how much time they would need to get things done. Red tape was as widespread in the military as it was in the civilian government, and he knew from experience that it could take longer than expected.

They met a group of officers as they were entering the building. One of them was General Leroy Carter. Simon was holding Samantha in his left arm and the cane in his right hand. Military protocol did not require him to salute General Carter. "Colonel Hanley," announced Carter in a sarcastic manner. "I assumed that you had returned to the states with Miriam."

"I had nothing to do with her departure, Sir."

"Then I was wrong and apologize," saluted Carter, walking away with a sneer on his lips. Simon would have taken great delight in wiping it all over his face if they were not in uniform and he was not holding Samantha.

"Who was that?" asked Lili, amazed at the intensity of the short exchange. "I thought you two were ready to fight."

"That was Miriam's husband. He's a disgrace to the uniform he wears. I apologize for the incident. Come, let's see what we're up against here."

They were directed to the Judge Advocate General office. Doctor Connors had already called, as he promised, strongly recommending that Samantha and Lili be given emergency passports for entry into the United States. Simon encountered an old friend, Major Jack Burton, a military policeman. He facilitated the issuance of the two passports. Samantha and Lili had their pictures taken after filling out a number of forms. They could sense the air of expediency that existed in the major's office.

While they were waiting, Major Burton mentioned that a military plane was scheduled to leave Paris for New York in the morning. He was authorized to book passage on the plane. Lili met Simon's eyes and shook her head in agreement to the reservation.

Major Burton checked his desk for a large manila envelope and handed it to Lili. "This came in an hour ago by personal courier from the Medical Center."

"Thank you, Major," said Lili.

"I owe you one for all of this, Jack," promised Simon.

"I'm glad to help, Simon. I hope everything works out for the best, Miss Becker. We wish you well, Samantha," said Major Burton. "I have a daughter about your age back home in Oklahoma. Your passports are ready. They're good for the duration of Samantha's treatment and recovery. Bon Voyage."

"Thanks, Major. Everyone has been so kind and helpful," said Lili, taking the passports.

"The next time we meet, Jack, steaks and drinks are on me."

"I'll take you up on it, Colonel." Once again, Simon was proud to be a part of the United States Army and the brotherhood that functioned within it.

They returned to the hotel suite where they planned to order dinner from room service. That way Samantha could rest and they could review what Doctor Connors had included in the envelope. Simon excused himself for an hour or so, telling Lili that he would return to take dinner with them at the suite.

An hour later, Simon let himself into his single room placing a shopping bag on the luggage counter. He removed his tunic and hung it up in the closet. Checking his watch, he quickly grabbed the bag and rushed to Lili's suite on the same floor.

"It's me, Simon," he announced, knocking on the door.

"You're right on time. They'll be sending up dinner in a few minutes," Lili greeted him in a more relaxed and expansive mood. "Samantha has been resting well. I've given her one of the pills Captain Rogers gave us. We can have a quiet dinner together."

"That's good. I have a gift for her for being such a brave little trooper," declared Simon, placing a large package on the sofa. He held two separate small packages in his other hand. "I also have something for her grandmother. I hope you enjoy them."

Surprised and excited, she sat on the sofa to unwrap a bottle of fine perfume. She opened the bottle and gently sniffed it, savoring the scent.

"It's exquisite, Simon, thank you. I haven't had good Paris perfume for ages."

"The other gift is a practical one," smiled Simon, pleased with her enthusiasm.

Lili stripped the paper from the second gift and lifted a ladies wrist watch from the box.

"I've noticed that you don't wear a watch. In Boston you'll find one handy and practical while you're waiting for Samantha's operation and recovery."

"Oh, Simon," she cried, fastening it to her left wrist. A tear started to form in her left eye. "Thank you. You are too generous." She threw her arms around him in a spontaneous embrace, quickly releasing him to wipe away the tear.

"Lili Becker, you've elevated the memory of my brother to an enviable height. I'm glad you like the gifts. Surely, the good Lord that watches over all of us looks upon your loyalty with appreciation. I salute you, lady."

"You're going to make me cry, and I don't want to. I've been counting my blessings while you've been gone, and I'm speechless at the good fortune that has been visited upon Samantha and me since you walked into our lives."

"I didn't walk into your lives. You literally fell into mine," grinned Simon, offering her a clean handkerchief.

"Technically, you're correct," she smiled, blowing her nose. "Please, Simon, we have to talk. Let's sit down to discuss what we're going to do before Samantha wakes up."

A determined air of seriousness came over her. He took a seat at the table in the center of the room.

"I'm ready anytime you are, Lili, but before we get into the subject I think you're going to broach, please allow me to make a few comments. Whatever it costs for Samantha to have the operation, for you to live in Boston while she is recovering, and the other miscellaneous costs of travel, etc., are well within my ability to pay, and I'll consider it a privilege to do so. It's only money. Samuel would do the exact same thing for me and you know that. Now, I'll listen to what you think."

"Simon, what is there left to say? I'm a proud woman who has always stood on my own two feet and paid my way, no matter how difficult it was. I want to pay what I can. My savings are not enough to cover everything, but I insist on doing something. In the future, I will make timely payments to you for the balance. Do you understand that?"

"Yes, I understand your position. For the past five years I have been collecting combat pay for a major rating and then for my full colonel status. It has all been deposited in a Maine bank and has grown to a respectable sum of money. I'm frugal by nature and don't spend money unless I need something. My needs are modest and simple. So the few expenses accompanying Samantha's medical care are not an extravagance for me. Please don't be offended by my offer of

84

charity. I'm sounding like a broken record, but I do this simply because I want to, and it's the right thing to do."

"You're a good person, Simon Hanley. I accept your generosity for Samantha's sake. There's not another person in the world that I would take such charity from. I hope you don't think of me as a beggar, because I'm not!"

"To the contrary, Lili. I do this because Samuel cannot do it for his granddaughter, and Samantha can't do it for herself. I'll receive payment enough by an occasional hug around the neck and the privilege of seeing her jump, run, and laugh like any other kid her age. Please, end of conversation, okay?"

"Okay."

A knock on the door announced the arrival of room service with their dinner. Simon opened the door and was greeted by aromas of fresh baked bread, chicken, and fresh vegetables. Decanters of milk, coffee, and wine were accompanied by pieces of apple pie and cinnamon rolls. Simon tipped the young bellhop and closed the door behind him.

"I didn't think I was hungry until that cart was rolled into the room. Now, I'm starved," admitted Simon.

"Why don't we eat? I just checked Samantha. She seems to be sleeping soundly. We can keep her portion warm."

"Sounds great to me," exclaimed Simon, pulling the wheeled cart beside the table so that they could reach it.

"I ordered some wine. I thought we might toast our good fortune," Lili suggested.

"I think that's appropriate," Simon replied, placing two goblets for her to fill.

"A toast to give thanks for what we have been blessed with and to a kindly benefactor who has been the instrument of change and made possible that which I feared was impossible. Also a toast that the future will fulfill our dreams and hopes for Samantha to be well again. If that is not meant to be, give us the strength and discipline to accept God's will."

Just as they drank their toast Samantha walked into the room, rubbing her shining eyes.

"You're just in time, young lady. There's a package on the couch behind your grandmother. It's for you, and I hope you like it," Simon pointed to the bag. Samantha unwrapped the box in the bag but could not break the string around it. She held it up for Simon to break. He it did with ease. She removed the top of the box. Inside was a brown Teddy Bear about two feet tall with a large red ribbon around his neck. Her eyes opened wide, grabbing the bear and holding it to her cheek rubbing the soft fur against the side of her face. Simon watched the bear transform Samantha into a happy little girl. He felt a tightness in his throat. She turned to look at him and suddenly ran into his arms. He lifted her to his lap. "Thank you, Uncle Si. I love it."

"I can see that, Sam. You're most welcome."

Lili was beaming at Samantha's excitement over the stuffed toy.

"Can I sit at the table with the bear Grandmother?"

"I don't see why not. I'll pull a chair up for you and Teddy. We'll eat while it's still hot," said Lili.

Everyone ate as if they were hungry. Lili and Simon finished eating before Samantha, and they sat sipping their coffee while she emptied her plate. Simon asked her which she preferred for dessert, apple pie or a cinnamon roll. Samantha looked at each desert and selected apple pie.

"Now, Lili which do you prefer? I like them both, so the choice is yours."

"I'll take the sweet roll."

Afterwards, over coffee, they reviewed the material Doctor Connors included in the envelope. They had an appointment with a Doctor Alan Mitchell at the Boston Children Hospital any morning at eight thirty within the next week. Results of previous X-rays, blood, and urine reports were all included in the packet which combined with all of the reports Lili had from her local doctor. The file constituted a reasonably complete medical history for Samantha.

"We'll go to New York on a military plane which will be free of charge. Once in New York we can get a train to Boston and locate a decent hotel near the hospital so that you can come and go with ease. You can pick any morning you want to report to Doctor Mitchell."

"Things are happening so fast I can't believe it's true. I haven't been away from Montfaucon since 1940. Tomorrow we'll be in the United States of America. It's a little overwhelming. I have the last letter that Samuel wrote me. You may find it comforting, Simon. I've almost worn it out over the years. It was typical of Samuel. I'd like to share it with his brother."

"Thank you, Lili." Simon unfolded the letter with unsteady hands and read:

My Dearest Lili,

A few words tonight before I check sentry posts again. I've known you for just a few months, yet, I have a feeling that you've always been a part of me. Does that mean I started living only after I met you?

If something happens to me, and we can't deny that it's a real possibility, I want to tell you how much you have filled my heart with love and happiness. Your letters are a Godsend. This is no time to think of long-term relationships, but I can't help myself.

You'll like Simon and my dear Mother. I know they'll love you in return. I pray for that possibility. If it is not to be and I am called to our Maker, I want you to know that I will always be with you in the brightest of days and the darkest of nights.

I've found love for the first time in my life, and it sustains me these long nights in the trenches. Until next time.

Love you very much,
Sam

Chapter Ten

The Army Air Corps passenger plane was the same aircraft as a civilian DC-3 with an olive drab paint job. The flight from Paris to New York was filled with soldiers and airmen. The only civilians were Lili and Samantha. Simon sat with them in a double seat without an armrest in the center, making it possible for Samantha to sit between them. The cramped space was tolerated in order to maximize the seating capacity of the plane so that more soldiers could be returned back to the United States. During takeoff Samantha sat against the window, eyes bulging at the ability of a heavy metal plane full of people to stay in the air and fly like the birds.

Military flights were vastly different from civilian flights. Comfort was at a minimum. Snacks and drinks had to be provided by each passenger. Simon had anticipated the situation and brought along a supply of Coca-Cola and sandwiches made up in the hotel dining room. They carried a small bag with the food and drinks which they stored under their seats. Samantha slept during portions of the long flight across the Atlantic Ocean by laying her head in Lili's lap and her legs extended over Simon's. Later, Simon turned Samantha around so that Lili was holding her legs, and he held her in his lap for the rest of the trip.

Lili reclined her seat and watched clouds in the blue sky beyond her window. She closed her eyes and fell asleep. Simon watched her relax. There was a timeless wholesomeness about her. She was attractive without being showy. Her unpretentious ways reflected her pragmatic approach to life. Simon was impressed with the strength of character that had sustained her through the war years. Samantha was a lucky little girl to have a grandmother with the kind of grit Lili possessed. He watched her for a long time, understanding why the quiet unassuming librarian had captured Samuel's heart. She would be easy to love!

The flight was routine. Most of the soldiers were coming home for the first time since the war started. There was a jovial mood on board the aircraft. The closer the plane got to the continental United States the more restless and boisterous the passengers became. Samantha woke up and pulled the bag of food and drink from under the seat. She was hungry and shared sandwiches with Lili and Simon. After eating all they wanted, there was left-over food and several bottles of Coke. Simon suggested that Samantha offer whatever was left to the other passengers. At first she was hesitant, but Lili encouraged her to walk up and down the aisle for exercise, and then she would feel more comfortable distributing the food.

Everyone was kind to her. She represented what they had left behind and was the main reason they had gone to war. She passed out the sandwiches and drinks to a solid round of applause and handshakes from the young men. Simon knew the kind of exuberance the men felt. They were coming home alive. They had fought hard and won and, most important of all, they had survived the crucible. Life was the greatest gift of all.

A young navigator stepped into the passenger compartment to let them know that they were going to land at an alternate airport in Boston. New York was socked in with a heavy fog bank. There were a few cheers and a lot of groans from the passengers. Simon was pleased at the turn of events. Everyone on board strained their eyes for the first glimpse of the continental land mass. When it came into sight there was pandemonium on board. Clapping, whistling, and cheering drowned out every other sound. Even Samantha was swept up in the emotional euphoria and started clapping her hands with the men. The plane entered Boston Harbor and landed straight in from the sea at Logan Airport. They had come home! Simon shared the men's joy. The thrill of being a part of the war in Europe and Asia was a monument to the collective spirit of the American soldier. Most of the soldiers waved and said good-bye to Samantha as they rushed for the exit door.

"I've told you that you're a special little lady," said Simon, holding her on his lap while the soldiers evacuated the aircraft. Once off the plane, Simon and Lili were quickly processed through customs. He asked one of the cab drivers at the terminal door to take them to the hotel closest to the Boston Children's Hospital. They were taken to the Lennox Hotel on Boylston Street.

A two-room suite was assigned to Lili and Samantha. Simon took a small single on the same floor. His leg felt cramped from the long ride, and he started to walk through the hotel corridors to exercise it. Lili and Samantha joined him.

"Is your leg improving, Simon? I've been selfish these past few days thinking only of myself and Samantha."

"It just needs to be exercised, Lili. Yes, it's improving every day. The puncture wounds were still draining when I went to Paris. That's why I looked up Doctor Connors. That has stopped, and some scabbing is beginning to take place, which is a good sign."

"I'm glad to hear that. When we registered at the hotel I saw fatigue in your eyes for the first time. I know that the flight was tiring for everybody. I hope that your generous concern for Samantha and me has not overextended you."

"Perish the thought, Lili. I'll be fine after a shave and shower. To be real honest I'm hungry. We can eat in the hotel dining room if you wish."

"Let me check on Samantha. Frequently when she falls asleep so quickly, she wakes up shortly afterward with a temporary burst of energy as if her body had restored itself."

"I'm going to make one more trip around the hallway loop, and I'll stop by your room. This will be your first meal in the United States."

Back in her room Lili combed out Samantha's hair and rebraided it while they waited for Simon.

The Crest Room dining facility looked out over a large concentration of trains, rail and freight cars, and repair facilities for the New York Central Railroad. At the opposite end of the dining room Boston University's College of General Education could be seen across the street next to the exquisite Boston Public Library.

"There's an energy and vitality in Boston that is lacking in Paris," sighed Lili, watching the busy rail yard. "I think this country is full of doers like you."

"The men in my regiment were a typical cross section of the population. I agree with you. We just defeated two of the most powerful nations the world has ever known. Leading the men in combat was an honor for me," Simon remembered, scanning the menu. "I believe I'm going to have a steak. I had a good one in Paris. The only time during the war that I had a decent one was on an attack transport just before Okinawa. I've got a lot of catching up to do."

Lili ordered fried clams for her and Samantha. "I've heard a lot about your New England clams."

Samantha was quieter and looked exhausted. The dark shadows under her eyes worried Simon, and his heart went out to her. "We're going to bring you to the Boston Children Hospital first thing in the morning, Sam. I'm sure they'll make you feel well again." She smiled back at him, but it was a feeble attempt. They ate in silence.

"Samantha and I are going to retire," Lili decided when they had finished eating. "Tomorrow will be a big day, and we should be well rested for it."

"You speak for all of us, Lili," answered Simon, lifting Samantha from her chair. He carried her out of the dining room into the elevator. She fell asleep hanging onto Simon's neck. Lili opened the hotel room and turned on a small table lamp so that Simon could see to place her on the bed. Her color was not good. He helped Lili remove Samantha's shoes hoping that the trip was not too much for her. They stood over Samantha's tiny body and faced each other.

"Rest well, Lili. I'll see you in the morning. With luck tomorrow will be the first day of Sam's recovery."

"We hope so," muttered Lili close to tears. The strain was beginning to get her down. She looked so fragile and vulnerable. Simon placed his arms around her. She laid her head against his chest and softly cried.

"Tears are allowed, Lili. Hold on a little longer. Both of you have been so very brave about this whole thing."

"I don't know what I would have done without you," Lili sighed feeling secure in his arms. She lifted her lips to him. He bent to kiss her. It was a surprising moment of discovery for both of them.

Later that night, Simon recalled the warmth of her lips, spending much of the night staring at the ceiling. The next morning was cold and rainy. He looked out the window hoping that the weather was not going to be a bad omen of things to come. He quickly discarded it, letting the positive feelings in his heart be his guide.

He met Lili and Samantha in the hotel dining room eating breakfast. Lili smiled, giving no hint of what had transpired the evening before. Sam looked much improved. The recuperative powers of a night's sleep had put a sparkle back into her dark eyes. There was an air of urgency and expectation at the breakfast table, and the meal was hurried so that they could get to the Children's Hospital as soon as possible.

The reception desk at the hospital directed them to Doctor Alan Mitchell's office where he graciously invited them in to sit down. He was a short, stocky man with a dark complexion and a bald head. There was an air of jovial naturalness about him with a tendency to dramatize his talking points with flourishes of his arms. He was a passionate man who took his calling seriously. Simon took a liking to him instantly. They had come to the right place.

Plenty of time was allotted to Lili and Simon so that they could discuss Samantha's situation thoroughly. Doctor Mitchell listened and took notes all the while evaluating Samantha sitting on a settee between Simon and Lili. He reviewed, in their presence, the documents Lili had included in the folder. When he had finished, he dropped the folder on his cluttered desk and turned to Lili, removing his reading glasses.

"My dear Lili Becker. My old classmate Doctor Connors had some nice things to say about you. We, here at the Hospital, will do everything that mortal man and the limitations of medical science allow for Samantha. Today, I want to have her go through the normal tests for blood, urine, sugar, etc., and we will want several X-rays of her chest and stomach. This is done so that we know everything possible about her body functions before we attempt invasive surgery. That way we have fewer surprises on the operating table. Are you prepared for her to start today?"

"Oh, yes, Doctor Mitchell. The sooner the better."

"I concur," agreed Simon.

"That being the case, you can stay with Samantha while we take her through the tests. I'm not going to speculate, but I have a feeling that the French doctor may have been on the

92

right track. If that is the case, we can correct any deficiency we find; however, there is always a risk in any surgical procedure no matter how simple. The element of the unknown is usually our greatest challenge. Samantha is a precious child, and I'm sure that God is on our side in trying to make her well again."

Simon hugged Samantha and kissed her on the forehead before leaving the Hospital. He then embraced Lili on the way out the door, pressing some American money in her hand in case she needed it. She resisted, but he silently insisted and left them with the doctor. Samantha waved to him bravely and said: "I'll be all right, Uncle Si, you'll see."

Back at the hotel, Simon placed a call to the Walter Reed Army Hospital in Washington, DC, to inform the staff where he was and what he was doing. Doctor Goodwin warned that it would be prudent for him to return soon. They were still responsible for his care until he was discharged. Miriam had contacted the hospital requesting that Simon get in touch with her at her family home in Wilson River. It was about the Medal Of Honor (MOH) for Keith. Simon wrote her number in his notepad and informed the doctor that he would be checking in shortly and hung up before anyone could register a complaint. He was not about to abandon Lili and Samantha just to comply with Army hospital rules.

The thought that his son, Keith, might be the recipient of the MOH filled him with pride. It was the most revered award throughout the western world. It placed every recipient on a pedestal, not for his character, his intellect, or even for his patriotism; it was awarded for raw, uncomplicated human courage committed under the threat of death. The mystique of the award has been cultivated through the years by its rarity and the exhaustive evaluation of the act by the military command. Many brave soldiers were denied it simply because they lacked two firsthand witnesses to their act.

Simon recognized the number at Wilson River, Maine. It was Miriam's family home.

"Hello," answered a familiar voice.

"Hello, Miriam?"

"Yes, I'm glad you called, Simon. The hotel in Paris said you had left for Montfaucon where Samuel is buried."

"How are things going for you?" he asked.

"When I left Paris, I went to our house in Alexandria, Virginia, to clear out my things. I've moved out everything that was mine and have come home to Wilson River. Leroy has already started divorce proceedings. While I was at the house in Alexandria, a call came in from Fort Bragg Headquarters announcing approval of the MOH for Keith. President Truman wants to present the medal to us at the White House around Thanksgiving time. The White House Staff will contact us about the details."

"Our son joins a distinguished group of Americans," thought Simon out loud.

"Are you back at the Walter Reed Hospital?"

"No, I'm in Boston."

"Boston?" exclaimed Miriam.

"It's a long story, Miriam, and I can't really go into it now. I'll report back to you soon. Are you going to stay in Wilson River?"

"I plan to stay here until the divorce is final. I'm sure that Leroy will try everything in the legal book to brand me as an immoral woman, but he'll be wrong. At this point I just don't care; I want out! I need some time to find the person I was before I met him. Lord, I was frightened on that flight from Paris. He was blind with rage at my departure and the reason for it."

"I met him on the steps of the Allied Headquarters building. He was his usual caustic self. He was angry at me, but the presence of others forced him to be civil. It was a courageous act, Miriam. I wish you well. I'll fill you in on events later. Incidentally, how are things there? Is my mother's house empty? My cousin Ken Holmes used it for a year or so."

"Ken left it in good condition. I've walked around your place several times, remembering how it was with us," acknowledged Miriam with a low voice. "It has been nice reminiscing about the past. I can't believe what I saw in Leroy that would make me do what I did to you. He had an infinite capacity to hurt people. I ended up being frightened most of the time. Here in Wilson River, where I belong, I'm no longer afraid to be myself. I'm beginning to write more and in the process, I'm rediscovering myself. I would never have found the courage to make this move if you had not met me at our son's graveside. I like to think that he had something to do with the trip, also."

"That may be so. I'm glad that you've found some refuge back home. I hope to get up there before snow flies."

"It has been nice talking with you, Simon. Do take care of yourself and keep in touch."

"I promise, Miriam. I have the most unbelievable story to tell you. Maybe it's worth retelling in your book."

"Now you've got me to wondering. Why is it that when I'm with you or talking with you like this everything seems to be right with the world? I've missed that intimacy and feeling of wholeness. Thank you for helping me find it again. Good-bye, Simon."

"Good-bye, Miriam."

Simon hung up the phone and sat back, remembering how it had been in the small town in northern Maine on the fringe of organized townships. Miriam's parents had died from the flu attacks at the turn of the century when she was a young girl of four years old. Her older brother, Timothy, had raised her with the help of their grandparents who lived on a small farm a mile or so outside of the village. Tim was ten years older than Miriam. It was a town where people looked after each other.

Tragedy for any of them could be just a heartbeat away. Simon's father had also died in the same flu epidemic, leaving his resourceful mother to provide for the two boys. She taught at the elementary school in the village and raised a large garden in the summertime, trading potatoes for cordwood in the fall. As the twins grew stronger, they worked hard at cutting wood and tending an ever-expanding truck garden. Hard work was a way of life with every family in town. His mother was determined that the twins would go to college. She had scrimped and saved for that eventuality from the first day they were born.

The twin boys entered the University of Maine at Orono in 1913, graduating four years later. Samuel earned a degree in civil engineering, Simon became a forester. Upon graduating each were granted a commission as second lieutenants in the Army Reserves.

The Army had been Simon's life for twenty-eight years; now, he was ready to do something different before he was too old to make the adjustment. The attraction of Wilson River was strong. He yearned to cast a fish line in the river again and smell the spruce and fir forests that blanketed the rolling hills. Miriam had, also, in her hour of greatest need, returned to her roots to find herself and her place in the world. Simon's thoughts were clouded with memories of Miriam and haunting visions of Lili and Samantha. He had known them less than a week; yet, he could not imagine a life without them being a part of it.

After lunch, Simon returned to his room to dress his leg wound with a fresh bandage when the phone rang.

"Hello," he answered.

"Simon, this is Lili," she cried hysterically.

"What's wrong, Lili?" he asked apprehensively.

"They're taking Samantha into surgery now. She had a bad coughing spell and passed out. Doctor Mitchell ordered surgery immediately..."

Chapter Eleven

"Where are you?" asked Simon

"I'm in the Hospital Visitor Lounge," answered Lili.

"I'll be right over just as soon as I dress my leg. Don't worry," he replied.

"What a foolish statement to make," Simon thought, rushing to finish bandaging his leg. He was out the door within a couple of minutes and grabbed a cab. He burst into the Visitor's Lounge, spotting Lili sitting alone with a frightened look on her face.

"What was the last thing doctor Mitchell said to you, Lili?" Simon asked, trying to be calm.

"Samantha became excited and started coughing. She seemed to be short of breath and fell against me losing consciousness. A nurse was drawing blood from her left arm at the time. I caught her and yelled for the doctor. He took her from me and walked quickly toward the operating room further down the hallway. He would not allow me in the room. His last words were: '…don't be alarmed. I believe Samantha's condition has just announced itself to us. Pray for us and be calm, please…' I'd like to know how anyone could stay calm in circumstances like that," she dismissed his admonition with a nervous restlessness. Her hands were still shaking. Simon saw fear in her eyes for the first time.

"Lili, the doctor may have given you a clue. You're in the best children's facility in the world. All the professional assistance that could ever be needed is under this roof. Could you use a cup of coffee?"

"I'm not hungry at all. I'll take a coffee," she answered, not caring one way or the other.

"Listen, I just came by a soda fountain in a drug store next door. Have you ever had what we Americans call an ice cream soda?"

"No, I've heard of them but never tasted one."

"May I treat you to a nutritional beverage that will tickle your taste buds and fill your nervous stomach?" he declared, trying to lift her spirits.

"Since you put it that way, how can I refuse?" she said with a half-smile.

"C'mon, my treat. You can tell Sam about it later and bring sodas to her while she's recuperating. I guarantee she'll love them."

"I pray that will be so..."

"Think positive, Lili. Did anyone ever tell you what a lovely grandmother you are?"

"No," she responded shyly. Simon locked his arm in hers and walked out the door.

"Do you like chocolate ice cream?"

"Yes," she said, beginning to share his enthusiasm.

"Two chocolate ice cream sodas with an extra scoop of ice cream," ordered Simon of the lady behind the soda fountain. They took a seat at a small circular table near the store front window looking out onto Copley Square. The waitress served two tall frosted glasses of chocolate sodas overflowing onto two napkins.

"Thank you, Ma'am," said Simon, paying her. "Its been five years since I had one of these. This lady is having her first one."

"Enjoy it, Ma'am," smiled the waitress.

"Thank you," replied Lili, sticking a straw into the frothy mixture, drinking hard and long. "It's delicious, isn't it?"

"You bet."

Lili was amused with Simon's playfulness. Simple things pleased him. They grinned at each other over the straws of their sodas. She drank it all, sipping every last drop from the bottom of the glass.

"I'm filled to the brim, Simon."

"It is filling. Whenever Samuel and I had an extra penny or nickel we used to save them for a soda at the small drug store in Wilson River. I used to dream about these drinks when I was in the South Pacific where even the water tasted like it was full of mud. I'd order another drink, except that I'm afraid you'd think I was a glutton." Lili laughed out-loud at his ability to make fun of himself.

"Thank you for a nice respite," she said, wiping her lips on a napkin. "I'm thankful that she's in the hands of skilled doctors. I've been doing a lot of evaluation lately. I have not had very many experiences of the heart. Over the years I've dated few men. I just never had the time for such things. Responsibilities always got in the way, so I'm having a difficult time interpreting my feelings right now. Am I beginning to have feelings like I do simply because you have befriended Samantha and me, or are they feelings of the heart unrelated to Samantha's need? I don't know, and it troubles me. I thought I should mention it to you because it has occupied much of my mind during this demanding period Samantha is going through. I'm not sure whether I'm making myself clear or not. I certainly don't want to add to the complexity of the situation. I've enjoyed your friendship and warm generosity, and I'm afraid that I might be misinterpreting my feelings. Am I being too bold in sharing them with you?" Lili asked.

Stunned at her candor, Simon was momentarily at a loss for words. "Your honesty with others and to yourself is one of the virtues that defines you, Lili Becker. If I have gained your trust enough for you to share such personal feelings with me, then I would say that our relationship, built on respect for each other, has grown to a new level. We share the same commitment and desire for Sam. When I came to Paris, my life was in a state of turmoil and uncertainty, more so than I have ever been in years.

"This afternoon, just before you called me, I spoke to Miriam about our son, Keith. We're going to receive the MOH in his name sometime this fall. She has gone to Maine to live until her divorce is final. I was angry at her for a lot of years. The anger is gone now. The years that we shared together were good ones, and I think often of them."

"Are you trying to say that you still love your ex-wife?" Lili questioned.

"I care enough to want her happiness, but don't prejudge me, Lili. I've been living in a totally different world since I met you and Sam. For the first time in years, I've felt wanted, and a warm glow has settled in my heart when I think of the difficult years you've had raising a son and a granddaughter, and still remained true to Samuel's memory.

99

"I don't think either of us has sorted out the real possibility that my attraction for you may be based on your relationship with Samuel. The feelings you so beautifully confess make me feel good; nevertheless, we cannot deny that you may be confusing me for Samuel and that could be disastrous because I'm not Samuel."

"I'm not a lovesick teenager; I never was," Lili replied defensively, but still pleased that they could discuss such issues with each other. "I'm sorry if I've added an element of intrigue to our friendship. I understand fully that we're still strangers and must be patient."

"Yes, patience is the greatest of virtues," added Simon soberly.

"I noticed, as a neutral observer, that Captain Rogers is in love with you, Simon," Lili added as an afterthought.

"Lee is a fine person worthy of the best any man can give. She has my respect, admiration, and my friendship. Beyond that, I don't care to comment. I believe she thinks more of me romantically than I do of her. You can evaluate that any way you wish," Simon told her.

"I was not questioning your feelings or hers; I was simply expressing an observation and wondered if she was part of what is confusing you," Lili replied quickly.

"We should get back to the Hospital," suggested Simon, uncomfortable with the tone of their conversation.

"Yes, I'm sorry I brought the subject up. Sometimes my compulsion to speak up gets me in trouble," she said with finality and walked out the door behind Simon. "Thank you for the soda. It was delicious, and I'm sure Samantha will like them too."

They sat in the lounge of the Hospital for four hours reflecting on what had transpired. Every hour that passed increased the anxiety that Lili was finding difficult to control. The nurse at the information desk told them that four hours was not uncommon for a major operation. Finally, Doctor Mitchell opened the swinging doors of the operating room and walked deliberately towards them.

"How did things go?" demanded Lili, her eyes filled with fear.

"Samantha is resting well now. She'll be in intensive care for the next few days. You should be optimistic about the future. She not only had a faulty valve opening, she also had a small hole in her heart."

"My God no..." cried Lili.

"There's no cause for alarm now," noted the doctor. "It was not a simple operation by any standard, but it is one that we've done here in the hospital several times on children Samantha's age. The leaking valve and the perforation have been repaired. Normally a child with her condition would have been extremely lethargic, yet she was moderately active. Your granddaughter is a fighter; I felt that all during the operation. It is my professional belief that we have corrected her problem. Unless something unforeseen develops during her convalescence, I don't see any reason why she can't lead a normal active life after her recovery."

"Thank you, Doctor Mitchell," Lili cried, embracing him. "You can't imagine what those words mean to me."

"I understand, dear lady. Now, I have some advice for you. When you and Samantha walked through that door our concern was primarily for Samantha, but you are part of the picture too. The caregiver is frequently in need of assistance. You're exhausted and worn out. Go and rest for the next couple of days without worrying about Samantha. We're going to take good care of her, I promise. We plan to keep her sedated to keep movement to a minimum and maintain as much isolation as possible to eliminate the threat of infection. After that we'll start her on moderate exercise therapy. At that point, you'll be an important part of treatment and you should rest in preparation for that phase of Samantha's recovery. Until then, keep in touch and rest so that you and Samantha can rejoice in her total recovery together."

"I see," said Lili, her heart pounding.

"If everything goes well, Doctor Mitchell, what is the approximate itinerary for Samantha?" asked Simon.

"I would say that by Thanksgiving time she could return to her home and start living a normal life. One of the reasons we want to monitor her until that time is that we inserted a fiberglass tube in one of her arteries. If her body rejects that we'll know almost immediately. If there are no signs of rejection by Thanksgiving, I believe we're safe to declare a victory."

"What if she rejects the material?" asked Simon, wanting to cover every contingent.

"Then we'll have to go into one of her legs or arms for a short piece of blood vessel to replace the fiberglass tube. However, we've had a good history with the fiberglass."

"Thank you for everything, Dr. Mitchell. It looks as if we came to the right place. Do you have any more questions, Lili?"

"No," she answered in a state of euphoria.

"Remember, Miss Becker. You've shown admirable responsibility to your granddaughter. If you are going to continue, you must take care of yourself, because she'll need you just as much in ten years as she does now. Rest your body and mind for a couple of days. Samantha is in good hands."

"Thank you, Doctor."

Simon and Lili left the hospital. Surprisingly the good news left Lili in a more weakened state than when she first entered the hospital. Her defensive mechanism was no longer needed and had started to shut down. Physical and emotional fatigue, greater than she had known before the operation was beginning to be felt. The wise doctor knew what he was talking about.

They walked slowly along Boylston Street toward the hotel. The street was packed with automobiles. The evening rush hour was at its peak.

"Have you thought of what you'd like to do in the next two days?" asked Simon, looking down at her. She had removed the beret she had worn that morning and let her hair hang over her shoulders. There was relief on her face, yet dark circles were still visible under her eyes.

"No," she answered. "I could not sleep for two days. I admit that I've been keyed up for a long time. It will not be easy to relax on such short notice. I apologize for talking out of turn in the soda shop. Are you angry at me?" She searched his eyes for an answer.

"No, I'm not angry at you. I understand your position. We're two adults and if there was ever a time for speaking our mind, it's when we're at or near the fifty-year-old mark. We've earned the right by then. I've been thinking of a plan. You and I could go to Wilson River for the next two days. You could see where Samuel and I grew up. The house has been empty since my cousin moved out a year ago. I've planned to go back just to be sure that things are in order and to feel what it's like to go home again. I haven't felt as if I belonged anywhere, except to the Army, for a long time."

"I don't know, Simon," Lili hesitated, thinking about his proposal.

"If you're wondering about your safety, I give you my word of honor as an officer in the United States Army that I would defend your honor and reputation with my life if necessary," promised Simon.

"I have no doubt about that. I was only thinking of you. If you show up for a few days with a strange unmarried woman, people will talk."

"Then let them talk," dismissed Simon. "Actually a change of pace and scenery would be good for you. I promise to see that you relax. What do you say? I'd like to show you around the town. It's pretty small, but I think it's special. When I was in combat I sometimes blanked out what was happening on the battlefield, and once again I could hear the gentle wash of the river against the rocks and the cheerful call of the whippoorwills at dusk and just before the dawn. It's a sound you never forget once you've heard it. I firmly believe that home and all that it represents in memories was what kept me from going crazy."

Lili listened to him talk of home. She could feel the love and passion he had for it. Places didn't change; only people changed.

"If you really want to go, I don't want to keep you from going. A part of me is curious to see where you and Samuel grew up," sighed Lili.

"Good, then it's settled. As soon as we get to the hotel, I'll see about a rental automobile or better yet, a train to Newport and rent a car there for the hour ride north."

They decided to reserve the hotel suite for Lili and cancel the single room for Simon. Within an hour they were speeding northward on a Boston and Maine train. Lili slept most of the three hour trip to Newport, Maine, where they got off and looked for an auto rental garage. A station attendant directed them to a Socony-Vacuum station a block from the terminal. He called the garage and reserved a vehicle for two or three days. They checked their luggage and walked to the garage to pick up the automobile. The owner was about thirty years old, short and muscular. He looked Simon up and down and walked to the gas pumps with crutches. He wore a set of Army fatigues with master sergeant stripes attached to them.

"Where did you get yours, Colonel?" the owner asked, impressed with Simon's rank.

"On Okinawa. Sugar Loaf Hill was the most valuable piece of real estate I've ever known. What happened to you, Sergeant?"

"I lost my leg on New Guinea. I never want to see another rotten jungle as long as I live."

"I don't blame you. I want to rent an automobile for a few days. We're headed for Wilson River. I was born and raised there."

"I've got a 1942 Chevrolet there," he pointed to the green four-door sedan parked beside the station. "You can keep it as long as you want, Colonel. When you drop it off, if there's nobody, around just leave the money in the ash tray in the back seat. The rental is a dollar a day; you supply gasoline and oil."

"That sounds great, Sergeant. Thanks for the trust. I'm sorry to hear about your leg, but you and I at least survived."

"I'm thankful for that too, Sir. Enjoy your trip back home."

"Thanks, Sergeant," said Simon, saluting him. "I feel as if I was home already."

They drove the Chevrolet north. The night was illuminated by what his mother used to call a harvest moon. He could still see the symmetrical cone-shaped spruce and fir trees against the fading horizon. The sweet penetrating aroma of the northern forest, spruce pitch interlaced with cedar, filled his lungs as the wind swept through the canopies of the forest. The forest was beckoning him home!

Chapter Twelve

Simon had a gratifying feeling of belonging as soon as he left Newport. For the last five years of his life, his thoughts and prayers were centered around what he was now doing with Lili - coming home! Many were the times when he questioned if he would survive the war. Familiar places filled him with a melancholic yearning to return to the days of his youth and to recall memories of a simpler time in his life.

He recalled that one of the games the two boys used to play with their mother and other people in town, was swapping of identities. Their mother always dressed them alike, and they had the same haircut up until the last year of high school. At a distance even their mother could not distinguish between them. A frequent part of her dialogue with them was prefaced with the question: "Which one are you?"

Their Aunt Maude and Uncle Ken lived next door. They were hardworking people who suffered personal tragedies and financial struggles that followed them to their graves. They had lost two children in the turn of the century flu epidemic and an older boy of fourteen years was killed in a sawmill accident. Aunt Maude was a sister to their father. She used to bake Finnish boulla rolls, a heavy, sweet bread with the subtle taste of cardamom seeds. Sometimes if they could afford it, Aunt Maude would brush an orange glaze on the rolls while they were baking. The twins were addicted to them and never got enough to satisfy their cravings.

One day when they were about five years old, Simon was playing at his cousin Ken's house when Aunt Maude took two large pans of boulla rolls from the oven. He and Ken were given two apiece with a glass of milk, which was always plentiful on the small farm. They finished the rolls in record time, and Simon started home on the well-worn path between the two places. Once he was out of sight he turned around and walked back, meeting Aunt Maude who was hanging laundry on the clothes line. He told her that he had met Simon on the pathway and was wondering if he, making believe he was Samuel, could have a boulla roll like Simon had just eaten. Aunt Maude was a kindly soul. She loved the twins as if they were her own. She gave him two rolls and watched him eat it as if he hadn't eaten all day, laughing at the endless appetite of young boys.

That night his mother confronted the boys. Aunt Maude had mentioned that both of the boys had a taste of her fresh boulla rolls. Samuel had stayed in the house all day with a bad cold, so she knew about the trick Simon had played. She scolded him severely and made him admit his deception to Aunt Maude and apologize for it. He also had to carry firewood to the kitchen stove woodbox alone for several days. It was a lesson in humility and honesty that Simon never forgot. The twins idolized their mother. She was strict and fair. Conduct unbecoming or not up to her standards was not tolerated, and the boys learned early in life that misconduct was not worth the consequences their mother meted out to them.

Throughout their teenage years, Simon and Samuel occasionally swapped names and identities, but it never got out of hand, and they always owned up to it once it had taken place. She never spanked either of them, but she could make them feel sorry and full of remorse with her agile tongue lashing. Discipline was a daily part of their life, tempered with love and fairness. Laughter often echoed within the walls of their home. Later in life, Simon thirsted for that same level of unity and contentment that had been a part of his youth.

"A penny for your thoughts," said Lili after a long period of silence.

"I was just thinking about childhood pranks Samuel and I used to play on friends and relatives. Wilson River was a great place to grow up in. My mother taught school for forty years, so we were on good behavior most of the time."

"What grade did she teach?"

"Fourth and fifth. The classroom was split between the two groups."

"Then you and Samuel were in her class. That must have been strange."

"It was a little, but she never cut us any slack. She disciplined us like everybody else. None of the other students ever accused her of being easier on us than the others. As a matter of fact she was slightly more demanding on us so there would never be grounds for favoritism. What was your son like, Lili? I haven't heard you talk much about him."

"Samuel, Jr., was a joy that filled my life. He was all that a parent could ask for, quiet and studious, probably much like your son, Keith. He was a demanding and accomplished violinist, capable of lifting your soul to new heights whenever he played. He was studying at the University where my father taught. I was so proud of him. He was a gentle person like his father.

"I still have nightmares of the way the Germans dragged him and his lovely young wife, Robyne, from his apartment. I was there when they broke down the door of the apartment. They accused him of being a member of a partisan group, which he was. He defiantly spit in their faces as they beat him with their rifle buts. I wished that I had a gun then; I would have killed every one of the beasts. I tried to intervene, but they hit me with their rifles and kicked me with heavy black boots as I laid on the floor beside Sam's unconscious body. I still carry their marks on my back. They dragged his body down the stairs feet first to the street propping him up against a lamp post. They shot him four times and did the same thing to Robyne. I'll hate the German butchers until I die."

"I'm sorry, Lili. I didn't mean to have you revisit those hurtful memories." He reached across the seat of the Chevrolet and squeezed her hand, thinking that soldiers were not the only ones branded by war. It was hard for him to imagine how anyone would have reacted to such a tragic death of loved ones. Yet, she had the presence of mind to grab Samantha and miraculously escape from Paris with her, a courageous act under the most grotesque of conditions. Life had not been kind to Lili Becker!

"We're coming to the town of Guilford," announced Simon, changing the subject. "I know that it has been a long day for you. What do you say if we stop to get a few groceries for breakfast and lunch?"

"I was wondering what we would do for provisions."

"From here it will only take another half hour to the house. A cousin of mine used it for a year. He was badly wounded in Africa and was discharged in 1944. We kept in touch with letters. He installed a gas range which will make cooking a little easier. We could eat here in Guilford at a restaurant, or we could wait and fix something at the house. It's your choice."

"I'm tired but not exhausted. I slept most of the train ride. We could get the provisions and decide about eating afterwards," she suggested.

"Sounds like a plan."

Simon pulled into a First National Store beside the main highway. Lili went along with him to see what was available in the country store and was amazed at the variety of foods offered. Simon picked up several cans of baked beans and loaves of bread. "Peanut butter and strawberry preserve are staples," he chuckled at her. She smiled at his enthusiasm over jelly and raised donuts, purchasing a dozen. Coffee, ham, cheese, eggs, milk and butter rounded out their selection. Three bags of groceries for two days! The same amount of food would have been adequate for her and Samantha for a week or more.

"Should we eat here or back at the house?"

"If you don't mind I'd just as soon wait until we get to your house. You have a lot of food," suggested Lili, with an impish giggle.

"That's fine with me." Simon placed the bags in the back seat of the car. He opened the door for Lili to get in and ran around to the driver's side. "Tonight will be the first time I've eaten at the house since I graduated from Command and Staff School at Fort Leavenworth in 1939. I came home for a few days and was immediately ordered to Pearl Harbor at Schofield Barracks."

There was very little traffic on the road leading to Wilson River. A month had gone by since gasoline rationing was lifted on civilian usage. Many of the family vehicles were in disrepair because spare parts and tires were impossible to get during the war years. Production for the war effort had highest priority. The civilian population made do with those parts already on the dealers' shelves.

"You can't see much of the countryside at nighttime. Most of the land is composed of forest except for small clearings around scattered homes and farms. Essentially it's a forest products economy. The largest paper company in the United States is the Great Northern Paper Company in Millinocket, Maine, about fifty miles from Wilson River. They own thousands of acres around here. I have a standing offer of employment with them as a managing forester if I ever leave the Army."

"The extensive areas of forest does have an appearance and a feeling of isolation," described Lili. "At nighttime the wilderness can be forbidding and uninviting no matter where it is."

"Your description fits the spruce-fir forest type. Its unfriendliness is part of its attraction. Peace and serenity can be found within its vastness. Some people can't handle being alone. I've always looked forward to it," Simon confessed to her.

"That's strange," thought Lili. "You seem to be comfortable and most engaging in the company of people. Seeking solitude is almost a contradiction."

"You're perceptive, Lili. I did not mean that I would prefer to hibernate or become a recluse. It's a matter of balance for me. While I like being around people and interacting with them, I also need that uninterrupted time when I can examine myself with uncluttered focus. Samuel was similar in that regard. Perhaps I needed more solitude than he did; I'm not sure. Mother used to encourage us to take time every day to discover ourselves and find the courage to follow our heart."

"I like that," said Lili, listening carefully to every word. "The courage to follow your heart. I would have loved your mother."

"Samuel said it correctly in your last letter. I'm sure Mother would have loved you in return. She admired courage and discipline. She chided Samuel and me when we became young men to hurry up and marry so that she could enjoy her grandchildren."

"It's ironic," reflected Lili. "She had a grandson and never knew it..."

"I didn't say that to make you feel bad."

"I know. I was just regretting that I didn't swallow my pride and contact her," Lili explained.

"There's not a human being in the universe that doesn't carry around some regrets. The saddest words in the English language are 'If only I had...' Don't be hard on yourself. Mother would admire what you've done with Sam, Jr., and Samantha."

Lily replied modestly, "You're a kind man, Simon." She had always imagined and feared that the family would have disowned her. Now Simon informed her that his mother would have admired and loved her. She sighed forlornly for what might have been...

"We're coming into the center of town after we go over the old iron bridge that spans Wilson River. Our house is on the first left-hand street along the river about a third of a mile from the center of the village." There was excitement in his voice.

"It's a small town," observed Lili. She had often wondered what it would be like.

"If you blink your eyes passing through the town, you'll miss it," Simon joked, turning into a driveway and coming to a stop in front of a garage.

On the left was a two story building traditionally called a New Englander with a very high roof peak to shed snow. A barn half the size of the house was on the right. He turned off the ignition and sat quietly. The joy of familiarity brought peace to the discord that had been raging in his soul for years. It was as if a beckoning hand from the roots of his past was reaching out to say "welcome." It loosened tears that slowly formed in his eyes and ran down his face. The darkness shielded his vulnerability from Lili. Homecoming was an important milestone in his life, and he needed to let the reality sink in to his consciousness.

"I thought I'd never see this place again," he revealed to Lili. Fear of death on the battlefield and inability to accept what had happened to his marriage had made life a living torment for him. He went through each day searching for direction. At times, he simply gave up and drifted aimlessly from day to day.

She sensed his emotion and reached for his hand. She understood what the concept of home meant to a combat-scarred soldier. She took a small handkerchief and gently wiped away his tears. He closed his eyes.

"I didn't think I would be so emotional," he admitted.

"I understand, Simon. Home is where the heart is."

"I'm having a hard time believing that I'm finally here," he said, opening the door of the car. "Come, Lili, I'll show you around." He unlocked the door of the shed in the Chevrolet's headlights. "I'm going through the shed to turn on the master switch for the lights."

The kitchen door required a different key. He tried several on his key ring before finding the correct one. Turning the overhead kitchen lights on revealed a note placed on the large oak table in the center of the kitchen. Simon picked it up and read:

Welcome home Simon,

I saw your cousin an hour after I spoke to you and got a key from him. I took the liberty of airing out the place and turned on lights and the refrigerator. The water pump is already primed all you have to do is turn on the main water valve and start the gas hot water heater.

I wish you a rewarding visit. I know how much it means to you.

Miriam

"Well, that was thoughtful of her." Simon handed the note to Lili. She read it carefully and felt uncomfortable. "I see a frown on your face, Lili. Please, I don't want anything to spoil your visit."

"I'm happy for you, Simon, and that makes me feel good. I was just thinking that you may be called upon to explain my presence, and I don't want anything to mar your homecoming."

"Don't worry about that, please. I must tell you that coming here with you has had more meaning for me than if I had come alone. I'll be proud to explain your presence as you put it. Now, let me show you the rest of the house." He took her hand and led her into the large living room off the kitchen.

The downstairs included the spacious country living room and kitchen with a half bathroom between them. A beautiful hardwood staircase was in front of the main front entrance. Everything was clean and neat and orderly. Lili was impressed with the relaxed, informal feeling she was experiencing, wondering if it was a reflection of the happiness that had filled the house for so many years. Homes had souls just like people. She felt its power and energy as soon as she entered it.

Three bedrooms and a full bathroom were upstairs. There was a connecting set of stairs in the far corner of the kitchen as well as the main front staircase. The master bedroom was above the kitchen. It had four large windows extending from the ceiling to the floor on the south wall looking out on the river. A door opened onto a screened private balcony with a commanding view of the river. The full moon shined through the low cumulus clouds casting beams of light on the slow moving water. It was a beautiful sight. The peace and serenity that emanated from the walls of the room touched her.

"Mother used to sit here even in cool weather, correcting school papers and planning her days. She loved this balcony. Samuel and I slept in one of the rooms close to the stairs. "I'll show it to you. It's not very different from the time we slept there for the last time before going off to war. Mother wanted to keep it like that. I slept a few times in the room, but I was married soon after the First War ended and wasn't around much." He turned on the light.

The roomy bedroom had two windows with twin beds on each side and a dresser separating them. The flower printed wallpaper had darkened with age. Lili noticed the photographs displayed on the top of the dresser. She looked at each one with interest. One was of Simon and Samuel in their uniforms and wide brimmed campaign hats. She could not distinguish the two.

"I can honestly tell you that I'm the one on the left," laughed Simon. "This is a picture of mother taken the same day near the river." He held a full portrait of a middle-aged woman about the same age Lili was now. She was an attractive woman with a soft whimsical smile as if she was saying something when the picture was taken. Happiness shown in her face and in her sensitive eyes.

"She's a lovely lady. I always visualized her as looking something like that. Who is this?" Lili asked, pointing to a photo of one of the twins with his arm around a tall, slender lady.

"That's me and Miriam. It was taken at the same time, too."

"She's beautiful."

"Yes..." he answered without further comment. "I'm going to sleep here tonight. You can use Mother's room. I'm sure she would approve. What do you say if we go down and fix something to eat? I'm ravenous."

"Me, too."

They retraced their steps and made a pot of coffee on the small gas range. Lili put together ham and cheese sandwiches piled high with fresh ham. Simon ate two of them, consumed two cups of coffee and impishly put a box of jelly donuts on the table.

"I can't resist them any longer. Here, help yourself. I'm going to splurge with two donuts for good measure."

Lili felt at ease in the modest country kitchen. It wreaked with warmth and harmony. Across the room was a beautiful ornate cast iron wood-burning cook stove with a full woodbox beside it.

Simon followed her eyes and read her mind. "When Mother was baking or in the winter time when it was cold, that woodbox was always empty. We took turns filling it every night. Processing firewood consumed a lot of our time every day."

"I can believe that. I used a cook stove very similar to yours in the cottage at Montfaucon. It was our only source of heat. I bought dry fuel wood from the farmer who owned the cottage," Lili told him.

"I've already turned on the water heater, so if you want to take a shower there will be plenty of hot water. I want you to feel welcome here. It has been nice sharing this day with you. I'm glad you came home with me."

"I've enjoyed seeing you reclaim an important part of your life. To my surprise, I don't feel like a stranger or an intruder, and that pleases me."

"It's been a busy day, and we've covered a lot of ground. You must be tired. I confess that the excitement of coming home and everything has made me weary. I'll take our suitcases upstairs."

"Are you an early riser?" asked Lili playfully.

"Normally yes, but I wouldn't be surprised if tomorrow morning I'm later than usual."

"It'll be good for you, Simon."

They went upstairs together. Simon placed her suitcase on a chair next to the bed and turned the lights on, holding the door to the balcony open for her. The moon was partly hidden behind a cloud.

"I feel a powerful energy in this room. It's so peaceful," Lili described what had filled her heart the moment they turned into the driveway.

The earth was embraced in the solitude of the night. They watched the moon slowly roll out from behind the clouds, casting shadows and splashing beams of light across the glimmering water. Simon reached out for her. She came into his arms and lifted her lips to him, confessing what was in her heart.

"Simon, you should know that I'm not thinking of Samuel when I'm in your arms. He's been dead for twenty-seven years, and nobody knows that better than I." Their lips met, and an alliance of love passed between them.

"It feels right, doesn't it, Lili?"

"Yes. I love you, Simon."

Chapter Thirteen

It was an honest declaration of what had been growing in her heart for days.

"I've fallen in love with you, too, Lili.

"If we listen to our hearts how can it be wrong?" she questioned.

He kissed her again and silently held her in his arms. Suddenly a familiar sound, an echo from the past, filled the room. A whippoorwill called from the distance, singing his unique song (whip-o-will, whip-o-will). An answer from another bird close to the barn filled the evening hush. They listened quietly and heard what must have been a young bird singing near the barn. Instead of calling the distinctive three-syllable-song the young bird got mixed up, sounding out the first portion of the call (whip-whip-whip). They laughed as the bird stopped and started again, repeating it over and over.

"You know I've listened to that call for many years when I was growing up, and I never saw what the bird looked like. I've seen pictures of them but I've never seen one in enough light to identify it."

"It's a melancholic sound. Maybe the whippoorwills are welcoming you home."

"And welcoming you into our world," said Simon.

She rested her head against his chest and savored the happiness of loving someone and being loved in return. It was almost too good to be true.

"Simon," she said releasing him. "This is the happiest day of my life and it would be complete except for one thing I haven't told you."

"Not told me what, Lili?" he questioned.

"You must promise to give me the truth."

"Of course I do," answered Simon impatiently.

"I'm Jewish, and that's one of the reason's my son was killed so viciously. Does that make any difference to you?"

"Absolutely not, Lili," he answered, embracing her again. "The lady I fell in love with is special in every way. If it's her Jewish ancestry that has supported and sustained her courageous efforts, then I embrace that, too. Now I understand why you left Paris for the country and maintained such a low profile. It must have been horrible." He continued to hold her. "You don't have to fight the world alone anymore, dear lady. Now that you've come into my life, let me share your burdens. You've fought alone long enough."

She stood on her toes to kiss him. "Goodnight, Simon. I'll always remember this day."

That night she dreamed of the future and prayed for Samantha lying in the hospital intensive care ward. It was the first time Lili had been away from Samantha since she snatched her from Sam's apartment and fled Paris in mortal fear that they would be killed, too. Those five long years spanned a lifetime of never knowing what calamity the future would bring. Simon had successfully broken the chains of the past, which had held her in emotional bondage. Dreams and hope for the future were now within her grasp.

The next morning Lili awoke to bright sunshine erupting into the bedroom. A new day was being born, filling her soul with a quiet peacefulness. She dreamed of happier days filled with love and sharing. She felt like shouting it to the world. On the small table beside the bed was a picture frame containing a yellowed piece of paper with a poem written in beautiful flowing penmanship. Tears filled her eyes as she read the words:

He Is Not Dead
I cannot say, and I will not say
That he is dead, he is just away.
With a cheery smile, and a wave of the hand,
He has wandered into an unknown land
And left us dreaming how very fair
Its needs must be, since he lingers there.
And you—oh, you, who the wildest yearn

116

For an old-time step, and the glad return,
Think of him faring on, as dear
In the love of There as the love of Here.
Think of him still as the same. I say,
He is not dead-he is just away.

James Whitcomb Riley

"I would have loved you, Mother Hanley. If I had only known, I could have eased your tortured soul, and I know how deep that pain can be. I could have shared your grandson with you, but I failed because of foolish pride and fear of rejection. Forgive me. I love you though we've never met."

She stepped out on the balcony and watched the river slowly glide toward its destination, the Atlantic Ocean on the rocky coast of Maine, where its clear fresh water was dispersed to the far flung corners of the world. Tall pine and spruce trees lined the shore. A small boathouse with a canoe and a row boat were visible near the bank of the water. The pleasant aroma of coffee wafted up the kitchen stairway filling the room. Lili put on her robe and went to the bathroom. The first thing she saw was a note attached to the mirror over the wash stand.

"Good morning Miss Lili-of-the-Valley."

It warmed her heart, but a pang of worry clouded the joy. She was happier than at any other time of her life, and the fear that the attainment of such a comforting level of bliss might decline just as rapidly lurked in the shadows of her mind. She was apprehensive that happiness and love found in such a short time could be lost just as quickly. She showered and combed her hair, dressing in a sweatshirt and a pair of blue slacks, then rushed down the kitchen stairs. Simon was waiting at the foot of the steps. He grabbed her and effortlessly twirled her around. She circled his neck with her arms and kissed him.

"Thanks for the note. My father used to call me Lili-of-the-Valley."

"It's an appropriate title. Coffee is ready. I've already had a cup of coffee and donut. You'd better grab some before they're all gone."

"That sounds good."

117

"The phone in the house had been disconnected for quite a while. This morning I hooked it up and called the operator to have us relisted. So, if you want to call the hospital for Samantha, it's ready."

"She's been on my mind much of the night. I'll call after coffee. She has already accepted you. I believe she would be happy to know that something beautiful is taking place between us. It's been so sudden that some doubts still linger. Is it really real, Simon?"

He placed a cup of coffee in front of her on the table and kissed her on the forehead. "It's real, Lili, and when everything is considered, we deserve each other."

"Thank you for being you."

Breakfast consisted of two cups of coffee and two donuts each. Lili, anxious to learn about Samantha, then placed a call to the hospital. Doctor Mitchell was not in, so she spoke to the nurse covering the intensive care desk.

"Samantha is resting well, Miss Becker. She's still sedated enough that she does not recognize who's around her. Today, the medication will be decreased so that she can take some liquids and solid food by the mouth. She seems to be doing very well. Her blood pressure is holding steady and normal, which is a very positive sign. If you'll give me the number where you can be reached, I'll make a note for you to be called if anything changes, which is certainly not expected. You must be proud of your granddaughter, Miss Becker. She has won everyone's heart on the floor. Do not worry. We'll take good care of her for you."

"Thank you, nurse. I am proud of her. The heart condition has worried me a lot. I have faith in Doctor Mitchell and all of you on the staff. Fear is being replaced with hope, and I can't tell you how happy that makes me. The number here is Wilson River, Maine, 92-W." Lili hung up the phone, filled with encouragement and relayed the good news to Simon.

"That's terrific. Would you like to take a walk down by the river? I'll show you the remnants of a tree house Samuel and I built out of slabs and old boards."

"Yes, I'll put on my walking shoes and a light jacket. The air is brisk up here in late September."

He watched her run up the stairs with ease, smiling at her energetic ways. She was good for him. He was fifty years old and about ready to retire from the Army, yet he was astonished at the intensity of his feelings for Lili. Most people believe that love is for the young, but they're wrong, he told himself. The petite dynamic Scottish girl from France had succeeded in turning his life around, giving it new meaning. They walked hand in hand where long ago Simon and Samuel had played with friends and cousins. A band of willow, birch and maple trees that lined both sides of the river were displaying their red, yellow, and gold foliage, announcing that another season was passing. As beautiful as they were, there was a melancholic feel in the air. Fall colors celebrate the death of summer and prepare the landscape for the dormant winter months.

Simon described how the river is filled with logs when the spring melt arrives. Logs are harvested during the winter season and piled high along the banks of the river at its headwaters further to the north. The current brings them to different sawmills along the river where they collect the logs in booms connected together with heavy chains. Then they drag a log at a time onto the sawmill carriage where it is broken down into lumber.

When the river was full of logs, it was possible to walk across to the opposite bank without getting your feet wet. The boys tried it a few times until the day Samuel almost drowned. They were walking and running on the logs which were quite close together. Larger logs were more stable than the smaller logs which would sink several inches when one of the boys stepped on them, especially close to the end of the log. Samuel lost his footing and slipped off into the water hitting his head hard enough to knock him out. If Simon and their cousin had not been present to pull him out of the water, Samuel would have drowned. Simon pointed across the river where Samuel had fallen.

They sat on a rocky ledge overlooking a narrow section of the river filled with rapids. Simon told Lili that his mother believed that the rocks provided the music of the river. The rush of the water over the rocky obstacles drowned out their voices. They removed their shoes and socks and let their feet soak in the frigid waters until they turned blue. They laughed at the playful gesture.

Simon and Lili returned to the house hungry and in need of a rest. They had hiked along the river until Simon declared that he had walked enough. His leg was getting stronger every day, but he had reached his limit. They quickly devoured the sandwiches and coffee. After, they planned to scout around town in the Chevrolet. Simon pointed out the grade school where he and Simon attended and their mother taught. The town was too small to afford a high school of its own so they sent students to Greenville on Moosehead Lake.

They pulled into the local station to fill the automobile with gas and check the oil. The person running the station was a stranger to Simon. Suddenly a green 1941 Studebaker coupe passed the station and stopped. Miriam was driving by and had recognized Simon.

"Here comes Miriam," Simon prepared Lili.

"I thought that was you, Simon," Miriam exclaimed, staring at Lili. "When did you arrive?"

"Last night. It was nice of you to open the house up for us. Miriam, I'd like to introduce Miss Lili Becker. Lili, meet Miriam Carter."

Lili got out of the Chevrolet and came around to shake Miriam's hand. "I'm glad to meet you. Simon told me that you were in France to visit your son's grave," said Lili, evaluating the statuesque woman.

"The last time Simon and I talked he said he had a story to tell me. Are you a part of that story?" Miriam asked somewhat puzzled by Lili's presence.

"I told you it was a long story, Miriam, and this is no place to discuss it," corrected Simon.

"You've ignited my curiosity so much I can't stand it," said Miriam with a pleasant smile. "Could I invite the two of you over to the house for coffee or tea? I have some Pentagon papers that you might want to take a look at."

"What do you say, Lili?" asked Simon, leaving it up to her.

"Anytime is fine with me. I want one thing to be understood. My story, as you call it, is not going to become the topic of conversation for everyone in town. I've shared it with Simon, and I don't mind sharing it with you, Miriam, but that's where it ends. If that can't be promised then we're wasting our time."

Simon was proud of the fair position she struck. The situation was awkward for him. Lili's simple request left no room for equivocation. He knew that Miriam was going to like her straight talk.

"I agree, Lili. You have my word. You two have that far away look about you..."

"We could stop by now if you don't mind," proposed Lili. "We're riding around seeing some of the sights."

"That will be good for me, too. I'll head home and expect you shortly."

Simon opened the door of the car for Lili and climbed behind the wheel. "Is this going to be uncomfortable for you, Lili? I wasn't thinking when I mentioned your unusual circumstances. I had no right to include Miriam."

"No, I really don't mind. She looks a little formidable, but I think that's just a front. Sharing my story with her isn't what's bothering me right now."

"What's bothering you?"

"I don't know how to say it without sounding like a nag or a jealous girl friend. Are you certain that your feelings for Miriam are such that you can let go? I admit that I've fallen in love with you, and I understand that we've got to give it some time, for it has been sudden. It would hurt to learn that you still love your former wife, and I would not blame you. She's an attractive and desirable woman. However, I would never settle for half of you, and I would expect the same for you if the situation was reversed."

"Dear lady," said Simon, grinning at her. "You're a wonder. You go right to the point of contention. I can honestly tell you that when Miriam left me for another man, a part of my love for her died. I hated her for a long time, but that has passed. I don't hate her now. I'll always be her friend, and you've got to accept that, Lili."

"I do, Simon, and I'm not trying to make you give up something that's important to you."

"The day Miriam and I went to Keith's grave, maybe there was a good chance we might have tried a reconciliation to pick up the pieces where we left them in 1933. I say maybe because a lot of hurt over the years had to be buried and it might not have worked. And then, you came into my life with fresh new hope and a new dream for the future and changed everything.

I cannot exempt Samantha from my feelings because you two are a package. I think I'm a very lucky man to love a beautiful woman and a precious little girl that won my heart. Don't ever doubt my sincerity, Lili."

"I won't," she answered with a kiss. "I'm glad that bridge has been crossed."

Miriam had coffee and tea prepared by the time they arrived at her family home directly across the river from Simon's house. It was a similar styled New Englander with a view towards the village center. Miriam and Lili had tea. Miriam served Simon coffee without asking; she knew his preference.

Lili immediately began to share her story of Samuel and their son, Samuel, Jr. She went into more detail than she did with Simon about the brutal death of Samuel, Jr., and his wife. The bodies were discarded like pieces of garbage. Tears filled her eyes as she explained that she never knew where they were buried after the Germans killed them. She lived in constant fear of discovery because she was a Jew, emphasizing that fact and watching for a reaction from Miriam at the same time. Her flight from Paris had filled Lili with terror. The Nazi occupation of Paris and its suburbs was at its peak, and only those who had experienced their cruelty and cunning ways could ever know what fear is really like.

She went into detail about seeking refuge in the town of Montfaucon and her subsequent work as a librarian. Samantha was an important part of the story, also, and Lili brought Miriam up to date on her operation in Boston.

Miriam listened without interruption or comment, stunned by the tragedies in Lili's life. She saw what was in Simon's eyes every time he looked at her. Lili completed her story in a deliberate tone: "Now that I've divulged the story of my life to you, Miriam, you must vow to never repeat it."

Miriam got up from her chair and embraced Lili. "My God, Lili, of course I promise to remain silent. I've never heard such a tragic story in my life. All of those years of dealing with the death of Samuel, your son, and his wife, and then caring for your granddaughter all alone... Your faithfulness and courage are an inspiration. How I envy you for that. The death of a son is one thing we have in common, but you watched your son being brutalized. Surely, dear lady, you deserve more than that out of life. I'm so glad you dropped by. I would be honored to call a person like you a friend. May I?"

"Please do," cried Lili, filled with emotion. She released Miriam and started to sit down when she noticed a violin case in a corner of the sitting room. "Do you play the violin?"

"No, it was a family instrument we thought my brother's daughter would be interested in. She lacked discipline to be serious about it. Do you play, Lili?"

"Yes, my family was very musical. My mother played with the Paris Philharmonic Orchestra before the war. My son, Samuel, was a magnificent performer. May I look at it?"

"Yes, it might be a little dusty, but it's all there."

Lili opened the case, picking up the violin with both hands, examining it skillfully. "It's an exquisite instrument in beautiful condition. It's an original Gottlieb, one of the fine early German violin makers."

"Could you play something on it?" requested Simon with admiring eyes. Every day he was discovering something new about her. Lili plucked the strings with her long slender fingers.

"The strings are a little old, but they'll hold a tune. The bow is like new."

"Please try it out, Lili," invited Miriam, anxious to hear how it sounded. She had never heard anyone play the instrument in all the years it had been in the family.

Lili focused on tuning the violin. She finally got it so that she was satisfied. She checked the bow again, placed the violin under her chin and went through the scale with her nimble fingers running up and down along the strings.

"My personal favorites were the Irish and Scotch folk melodies. My all-time favorite is this one. I'm sure you'll recognize it," she announced with a smile.

She closed her eyes and started to play the beautiful melody of *Londonderry Air,* a sad song of a soldier going away to war while his loved one waits for him through the seasons. Lili passionately filled the room with music, creating the mood and tone of the selection. The violin is especially fitting for the song, and Lili was able to fill their hearts with the sorrow and tragedy of unrequited love. She ended the piece holding the refrain as if it was fading away, rolling through the Scottish highland meadows. Then, suddenly, she picked it up to the highest bars in the song with a resounding crescendo and ended it. Simon watched her closely. Lili finished the song with moist shining eyes. It was a profound musical experience for the three adults in the room.

"The sad ending never fails to bring tears to my eyes," explained Lili, replacing the violin in the case. "Thank you for letting me try it."

Miriam was impressed, "That's the most beautiful rendition I've ever heard for that traditional favorite. You play extremely well, Lili."

"Bravo!" exclaimed Simon, filled with pride.

"I need a moment to savor that interpretation, Lili. Thank you for playing it," Miriam said, viewing the petite lady from a new perspective. There was a depth and sensitivity about her that touched Miriam with a deep sense of pathos. "You made a point of stating your Jewish heritage, probably to extract a reaction from me. As you get to know me, you'll find that I do not judge people on the basis of their race or religion. Now, I want to make a statement to clear the air. I wasn't born yesterday, and I probably know Simon better than I know myself. He looks more content and at peace with himself than I've seen him in years. He's a fine man worth any sacrifice. As for you, Lili Becker, I have a feeling that you are one of the few that is worthy of him. He and I had a wonderful marriage until I destroyed it in a moment of confusion and deception. I've regretted it many times. I am not your enemy, Lili, and I have no right to compete against you for his favors; I'm still a married woman. If you continue to make Simon happy the way he is now, I'll always be your friend and supporter. If, however, you lead him astray I promise to scratch your eyes out."

Chapter Fourteen

Simon lifted his eyebrows and swallowed hard when Miriam delivered her threat. He watched Lili for her reaction.

She met his look with a whimsical smile. "I appreciate your position, Miriam. When Simon asked me to come to Wilson River I was reluctant to leave Samantha's side, and I was uneasy about meeting you. Simon and I had just recently met and I did not want to be the object of awkward gossip that is possible in a small town. Now that I've met you and heard your view on things I realize that my fears were unfounded. For the past five years I've avoided people as much as possible; yet, I had to work in order to survive. It was a difficult balancing act because that meant meeting people that came into the library. Every day I was afraid someone would report me to the Germans, but the farming community of Montfaucon never betrayed me. I'll always be thankful for their support. Now that the war is over and the Nazi threat removed, I'm looking forward to meeting more people, making new friends, and being a friend in return. Simon has helped me in that regard. The adjustment of living under the oppression of the German occupation to complete freedom has not been an easy one for me. I would like to be your friend; life is too short to be alone in the world."

"Lili, your grace under appalling conditions is becoming to you. I have a feeling we can be good friends," concluded Miriam.

Simon was amazed at the way things worked out. He knew that the potential for hard feelings were possible and was prepared to whisk Lili out of the house on a moment's notice.

"Did you say that you had something from the Pentagon?" Simon asked, changing the subject.

125

"Oh, yes. An envelope from the Department of the Army includes a copy of the citation for Keith's Medal of Honor and information on benefits pertaining to MOH recipients. I have the envelope in a drawer in the living room. You should have it. May I have a copy of the citation when you have a chance?"

"I'll see that it's done," promised Simon, receiving the manila envelope. "Well, Lili, what do you say if we drive up to Moosehead Lake?"

"I'd like that," she said, offering a hand to Miriam. "This has been an interesting visit, Miriam. Thanks for your encouragement. We'll be returning to Boston tomorrow. Samantha will be wondering what has happened to us. Good-bye. Thank you for welcoming me into your home."

"It has been my pleasure. Take care of yourself and Simon. I'll pray for Samantha's recovery. Little children are our hope for the future. Good-bye, Simon. I'll be in touch when the time for our visit has been set by the White House staff."

"Goodbye, Miriam."

Miriam watched them leave. Once the Chevrolet passed from view, she gave in to the anguish that was making her physically sick. Tears clouded her vision as she closed the door and rushed for the bathroom.

Simon and Lili spent part of the afternoon visiting the well-maintained hillside cemetery where Simon's parents were buried. His father had been a veteran of the war with Spain and died shortly after returning home from the Philippines. His mother was buried next to him. Several generations of Hanleys were also buried in the Wilson River graveyard. Lili was impressed with Simon's sense of belonging. She envied the fact that his roots were well established in the small community, while her own roots were nowhere and everywhere.

The road they traveled to Moosehead Lake cut through miles of uninhabited spruce-fir forests. Simon explained the importance of forest management to Lili. Much of the land around the lake was owned by the Great Northern Paper Company, a producer of newsprint for several of the largest newspapers in the country. The vastness of the forest enterprise and the concept of sound forest management practices such as sustained-yield harvesting had created a stable economy and a vigorous healthy forest covering a large part of northern Maine.

The forest produced pulp for the huge paper machines at Millinocket. An important part of the multiple-use concept of forest management was the creation of lush forests filled with a diversity of game, wildlife, and plant species. The forest also produced high quality water and recreational opportunities limited only by the user's imagination. The forests of Maine had supplied the forest products industry with raw materials for two hundred years. After World War Two the forest was more productive, healthier, and capable of sustaining an even larger annual harvest. It was an undeniable tribute to the feasibility and soundness of the management practices of the past. Simon had a desire to be a part of the professional team that made that fact possible.

Simon told Lili that he thought Moosehead Lake was the most beautiful body of water he had ever seen in his travels about the world. Her first view of the lake was from Indian Hill on the road approaching the lake from the south. Simon pulled the Chevrolet off the road and stopped. The dark blue water stretched northward to the horizon. The sun was beginning to sink in the west, sending its rays laterally across the glimmering waters interrupted by small islands in the foreground. Sharply pointed mountain peaks surrounding the lake pierced scattered cumulous clouds hanging high over the water.

"It's beautiful, Simon," said Lili, wiping a tear from her left eye.

Simon reached for her hand. "Is anything wrong?"

"No," she admitted softly. "Beautiful things always make me cry. I haven't felt like this for a long time. A part of me is afraid I'll wake up and find that it's all a dream."

"It's not a dream, Lili," comforted Simon. "Your days of hiding from the world are over. All in all, the world is not a bad place now that the war has ended. It's available for you, Lili, limited only by your ability to dream. Your reaction to it makes me proud of you. Don't ever change." Her youthful innocence and appreciation of simple things supplemented the mental portrait Simon was painting of her inner being. He was falling more in love with her every day.

127

Simon stopped at the regional office of the Great Northern Paper Company in Greenville, anxious to inquire about employment opportunities before he made a commitment to retire his commission in the Army. Lili waited for him in the Chevrolet. Half an hour later he walked rapidly towards the car with a smile on his face.

"You look as if you had good luck."

"I did, Lili. They're planning for an increase in every department, especially the forest management section. The day I leave the Army I have the promise of a full time job as a professional forester. You bring me good luck."

"I'm glad. If that is what you want then you should follow your heart."

"Of course I'll have to bone up on a lot of new forestry material."

"I can help you do that," stated Lili. "I remember reading about the conservation movement in the United States at the turn of the century. A significant amount of material has been added to the literature since you were in school. Don't forget I'm a professional librarian."

"Don't scare me off," laughed Simon. "There's a good restaurant on the water down along the southern shore of the lake. What do you say if we celebrate the good news with a steak dinner?"

"I'll have a steak with you," she said, pleased to share his joy of a job. Being with Simon and doing things with him was easy and fun. Life was free of discord as if his strength had built a protective cocoon around them, where anything seemed possible.

They spent the rest of the evening eating dinner and lingering over coffee, watching the sun go down at the far end of the lake. They discussed the future and mutually agreed that Lili would stay in Boston with Samantha while Simon returned to the hospital in Washington. He told her that the Army might not grant him another leave until his wounds were completely healed and physical therapy had restored his leg muscles to normal.

Simon and Lili toasted the future and gave thanks for the good fortune of finding each other. Their parting view of moonlight reflecting off the water as the waves gently broke against the rocky shore, would remain with them as a cherished memory, uniquely theirs.

The next morning they returned to Boston, anxious to see Samantha. Doctor Mitchell was the first person they saw as they rushed toward the intensive care room.

"You look much better than a couple of days ago, Miss Becker," observed Doctor Mitchell.

"How is Samantha doing?" demanded Lili.

"You granddaughter has been an excellent patient. Right now she's taking solid foods like jello and toast. She just asked me if she could have some cereal."

"She always liked cereals."

"You may go right in the room. She's awake and alert."

"Thank you, Doctor," said Simon, opening the door for Lili to look in.

Samantha was lying in a hospital bed looking at the ceiling with the large bear in her left arm. A nurse was taking her blood pressure and pulse. Before the nurse had time to record the figures in her clipboard, Lili was at Samantha's side.

"I've missed you, Samantha. Are you being a good patient?" Lili asked with moist eyes.

"Grandmother," cried Samantha. "When I woke up the doctor told me that you were gone for a while. I was afraid you would not come back for me."

"Oh, sweetheart, I'll never leave you," answered Lili, kissing her and wiping a strand of hair from her eyes. "I love you, dear girl. I'm sorry that I was not with you when you woke up."

"Your grandmother and I left because the doctor assured us that you'd be in good hands like the nurse taking care of you," Simon explained.

"She's been asking for the two of you. She has overcome the residual effects of the sedatives," explained the nurse, placing a thermometer in her mouth. "Samantha is a brave little girl, and everyone in the hospital has been concerned for her. She's doing fine. All of her vitals are strong."

"Even though your grandmother has been away, you've been in her heart, Sam. I took her to the small village where I was born and grew up," explained Simon.

He and Lili stayed with her into early evening. Sam fell asleep several times while they were in the room. Each time she woke, the first person she reached for was Lili. The hospital made a bed available for Lili in the room Sam would be moved to that next morning.

Simon went to the ice cream parlor to purchase a chocolate ice cream soda for Sam. He returned with a large soda and two straws so that she could sip twice as much of the drink at the same time. Sam was sitting up in bed ready to try the sweet treat. Her first swallow brought a wide smile to her face and a gleam in her eyes.

"Mmmm, it tastes good, Uncle Si."

"You're welcome, Sam. I knew you'd like it. Your grandmother tried one the other day while you were being operated on," Simon told her, looking at his watch. "I should catch the evening train to Washington. I'm still a soldier and have to obey orders. You take care of grandmother, and she'll take care of you, okay?"

"Okay, Uncle Si. Are you coming back to see me?" Samantha asked, not completely understanding why he had to leave.

"I promise, Sam. Now that we've found each other nothing could keep me from seeing you again. You've filled an empty spot in my heart." Simon looked across the bed into Lili's dark eyes. She smiled at him. "I gave you a promise, and I want you to promise me to listen good to the doctor and your grandmother so that you'll get well soon."

"I do promise."

Simon leaned down to kiss her. She still clung to the bear sharing her pillow. "I'll miss you while I'm gone. The next time we meet, how about the three of us going fishing? I haven't been fishing for several years, and I'm looking forward to it. It would be fun to share it with you and your grandmother. Would you like that?"

"I would like to try to fish. I used to watch people fish in the river near the cottage," answered Samantha.

"Then all you have to do is get well and be patient until we're together again."

"I will."

"Good-bye, Sunshine. Uncle Si loves you very much."

"I love you, too," said Samantha, waving her small fingers at him.

"I'm going to say good-bye to your Uncle Si. I'll be right back," said Lili, following Simon out the door.

They stopped at the main entrance where Simon turned to Lili. "My head is spinning at what has happened to us. A few days with you and my life has radically changed. Perhaps parting for a while will be a good test if it's real or simply an infatuation of two lonely people. Promise me that you'll let me know if you feel differently when we're apart. I'll do the same with you."

"I promise to tell you if anything changes," Lili replied in a low voice.

"I never liked good-byes, they've had a habit of being permanent. The French say it very well, au-revoir. It implies that there's a tomorrow and a future instead of an ending. Until next time, Lili." He held her by the shoulders and kissed her.

"Au-revoir, Simon. I'll miss you. Take care of yourself. What a difference you've made. I've started to live again these past few days. Thank you for the memories. My love goes with you, until next time." She watched him disappear in a taxicab. For a fleeting moment she felt panic and wanted to run after him, but the thought of Samantha in the hospital needing her brought a smile to her lips. She slowly walked down the long hallway.

Chapter Fifteen

The first thing Simon did after checking back into the Walter Reed Army Hospital was to write a letter to his friend in Paris, Major Jack Burton. If any information could be obtained about the whereabouts of Samuel and Robyne Becker's graves and the circumstances of their death, Jack was the man. Simon knew that Jack's title as Commanding officer of a Military Police Battalion attached to the Judge Advocate General section was partially a front for his intelligence work.

Simon first met Jack at an Army War College course on intelligence gathering and interpretation. Jack was the instructor. They became close friends and had kept in touch over the years. Jack was known as somewhat of a maverick who didn't hesitate to state his views to superiors or subordinates when he thought the situation warranted it. That may have accounted for his still being a major.

Sitting at his small desk in the hospital room, Simon typed the letter:

September 28, 1945

Dear Jack,

This is an unusual letter to write to an old friend, but, in my desperate situation, I can't think of anyone else known to me that is on the ground.

I'm asking you for another favor. You may recall the lady, Lili Becker, that was with me when you facilitated passports to the U.S. for her and her granddaughter, Samantha. I'm happy to report that the little girl is doing well after an operation at the Boston Children's Hospital. Her grandmother and I thank you for helping to make it possible.

132

Without going into elaborate detail, Lili Becker and my twin brother Samuel Hanley, Sr. (KIA-World War I) had a son, Samuel Becker, Jr.. My nephew, Samuel, Jr., and Robyne Becker were married in 1938 and had a daughter, Samantha. She was born in 1939 (the same Samantha you issued a passport to). Samuel, Jr., and Robyne were executed by the Germans on or about July 20, 1940 at an apartment building on rue de Mariniot, Paris.

Obviously it was a traumatic experience that she still carries in her heart. I promised Lili that I would try to locate their burial place, hoping that she may find some comfort in that reality. Lili was in the apartment when the Gestapo executed her son and his wife. They also beat her about the neck and back with rifle butts. She was able to escape from the apartment with little Samantha and successfully made her way to Montfaucon to the north where she was able to live in relative obscurity for the duration of the occupation. Any information you come up with will help this courageous lady put that tragic time in her life to rest.

If you can't help me, Jack, I will understand, for I know you to be a true champion of justice. I anxiously await your answer.

Best Regards,
Simon Hanley,
Colonel, USA

Four days after sending the letter, Simon was working on a treadmill in the physical therapy room when he received a phone call from Major Burton.

"Hello, Jack, this is Simon."

"I have your letter in hand, Simon. It certainly sounds intriguing. My answer is yes, I'll be glad to check into it. This Lili Becker sounds like a special lady. Very few Paris Jews survived the war. If they were not rounded up and shot by the Germans, they were exposed and delivered to them by French citizens. I can tell you that the deeper one investigates what took place during the German occupation the more rot you find within the French citizenry. I probably better leave it at that."

"I hear you, Jack. Thanks for offering to help. It will mean a lot to her."

"Is this lady special to you, Simon?"

"Yes, very much so, Jack."

"I make no promises and give no guarantee on results or time table," said Major Burton with conviction. "However, I'll pursue the information you've sent to me. When I have something I'll contact you. How long will you be at the Walter Reed Hospital?"

"Maybe a month. If I've been released, I'll leave a forwarding address for you. I'm thinking of resigning my commission and return to the Maine woods. I'll miss the Army life, but after twenty-eight years the time is right for me. How about you, Jack?"

"I'm going to stay on a little longer. Now that the war is over, things are beginning to get complicated in Europe. It looks interesting from my perspective. I wish you luck, Simon. The Army has been blessed with dedicated soldiers like yourself. You tell Lili that I'll do my best. Good luck with your retirement. I'll be thinking of you."

"Thanks, Jack."

The news from Jack was encouraging. If any information was available, Jack Burton was the person capable of sniffing it out. Simon decided to not say anything to Lili until he had something specific. Otherwise, it could only dredge up false hopes and end in another disappointment for her.

He had talked to Lili the night before. She sounded happy and content with Sam's progress. Sam was moving about, and they were taking slow walks along the Charles River. Lili had taken Sam to the ice cream shop. It soon became a tradition and every day they stopped by for a soda. Some days it was chocolate, and sometimes they varied it to strawberry. He could picture little Sam responding to treatment. There was a plaintive quality about her that had touched his heart the moment he met her. His brother would be proud of his granddaughter!

A month after Simon left Boston, he surprised Lili with an impromptu visit for a Sunday. He was nearing the end of his therapy and no longer needed a cane to walk. He called Lili's hotel room from the lobby.

"Hello," Lili answered.

"Hello," greeted Simon anxiously. "I just got in on the morning train from Washington. I can visit with you for a day."

"That's wonderful. Where are you?"

"Downstairs in the lobby."

"Well, why don't you come up? It'll be so nice to see you again. It seems like a long time."

"I'll be right up."

Lili was standing by the elevator doors waiting for him. She was dressed in a teal green dress with white lace trim. She was beautiful. His heart pounded the second he saw her. He lifted her off the floor and kissed her.

Lili wrapped her arms around his neck. "I was hoping to see you soon. I've missed you, Simon. The feelings have simply grown stronger."

"It has been a long month, Lily. You're lovelier than ever. My feelings continued to grow, too." They held each other, cherishing the moment.

"How's Sam doing?"

"She's doing better than expected. Doctor Mitchell told us she might be discharged in a week or so. That will be a happy day. I'm a little uncomfortable running up these large hotel bills, Simon. I understand what you told me about the money, but I can't change a lifetime habit of paying my own way and living modestly."

"If I were you I'd feel the same way, Lili. Please, don't worry about it. I can handle it," he told her.

"You don't use the cane now; that's wonderful. How is your leg?"

"It's doing fine. I can walk quite a bit longer now than when I left you. Have you had breakfast?"

"Yes, I was up early this morning," answered Lili.

"I wanted to see you and Sam today. I've missed you and received something you may be interested in reading. I contacted a major Jack Burton. You may remember him as the officer in Paris who approved your passports."

"Yes, I remember him at the headquarters building."

"Well, I asked him to try and locate the burial place of your son and his wife. Here's a letter I received from him." Simon handed the letter to Lili. She grasped it with shaking hands and sat down on the couch to read:

Dear Simon,

I'm writing this letter from my quarters on a plain sheet of paper. My reason for doing so has nothing to do with the validity of the information I'm passing on to you and everything to do with the methodology of its collection.

Samuel and Robyne Becker were buried in a common grave along with several other Jewish members of an underground partisan cell. There could be up to twelve people buried there. The cemetery is located at 20 rue Helene in the northern outskirts of Paris proper. This information has become available through several sources which I would classify as "Reliable". Evidently, Peter Gabineau, a French national who lived in the apartment directly above Lili's son and his wife was responsible for reporting them, and several others, to the German Gestapo. Peter Gabineau is an interesting fellow. He was a student with very meager financial resources at Paris University studying music when the German occupation began. All during the occupation he lived comfortably enjoying good food, clothing, etc. and was known to attend the races and opera on a regular basis in the company of well-dressed women and known French traitors. He became wealthy dealing with black-market goods, especially silk stockings, cigarettes, and good wine and liquor, which he sold to German officers anxious to buy and send such scarce items back to Germany for their families. He is currently residing at 214 rue Peuplier and appears to be financially successful...

I hope that this information will help Lili Becker bring that sordid past to a close. I personally visited the graves. They are unmarked in regards to the names of the people enclosed, but the date of July 20, 1940, corresponds with the rest of our information. The cemetery is maintained by a nearby Catholic Church. A priest told me that the bodies were delivered to them by a trucker contracting for the German authorities. He had told the priest that all of them were Jews. The day I was there I saw several fresh bouquets placed against the unmarked stone (the only one in the cemetery).

Fulfilling your request has been a revelation to me. Today I'm more aware and appreciative of the efforts of many brave French patriots who suffered greatly during the war.

Lili Becker is quite a lady. Her son is remembered by those who knew him as a beautiful violinist and a courageous patriot, loved by all.

I wish you the very best in your retirement years.

An old friend,

Jack Burton

Lili read it through once quickly. The second reading was much slower. A nervous twitch developed in her left temple as a seething rage continued to build seeking release. She erupted from the chair, startling Simon sitting beside her, and started walking aimlessly around the room. Her lips were compressed so tightly they were turning white. Simon was worried for her.

"I hope I did the right thing, Lili. I know Jack Burton well and would believe anything he said."

"And I know this Peter Gabineau. He was a close friend to Samuel and Robyne. Friends don't betray one another regardless of the reason..." she cried hysterically. The pain of her son's death was just as acute and fresh as the day it took place five years ago. Blood drained from her face as long excruciating howls passed her lips. Simon was concerned, but realized that the pressure of the sorrow and pain had to be

137

expelled in order for her to accept its reality. As painful as it was, it had to run its course, and he agonized for her, watching helplessly.

He directed her to the couch. Lili had never had a chance to grieve for her son. There were always too many things that had to be done and never enough time to do them. Now, five years later, she learned that an old acquaintance traded friendship for favors from the butchers and rapists occupying their country. She found it incomprehensible that another person could stoop so low. A part of her died with Samuel. A day never passed that she didn't think about him and yearn to hear his voice and feel his touch.

Simon witnessed the most heart-wrenching sounds ever coming from a human being. She sobbed uncontrollably, oblivious to his presence. Sweat beads ran down her face. Her catharsis was slowly draining her strength. Finally, when there were no more tears to shed, she sat quietly on the couch and stared into space as if she was remembering every minute of that horrible day in 1940. She was having trouble catching her breath. Her eyes rolled upward, exposing the white portions of her eyeballs, and she fell backwards against the couch in a dead faint.

Simon caught her and laid her flat on the couch, loosening the dress at her throat. He ran to the bathroom for a wet towel, wiped her arms and face, and placed it on her forehead.

She had witnessed the death of her son and had never confronted the reality behind it until she read the letter from Major Burton. Simon felt guilty; he should have saved the information and gone to Paris with her to visit the grave. The room was deathly quiet when the phone rang, making Simon jump. He answered it.

"Hello."

"Hello, is my grandmother there?" asked a little voice.

"Hi, Sam, this is Uncle Si. I just got off the train and am visiting your grandmother. She's busy in the bathroom right now. I'll have her call you when she comes out. You sound great. We'll be in to see you today. Are you being a good patient?"

"I just wanted to tell grandmother that I read all of my books to my friend Priscilla. She's in the bed beside mine."

"That's nice, Sam. I'm proud of the way you've recovered from your operation. You sound stronger than ever."

"Grandmother says that I've got too much energy now, and she can't keep up with me."

Simon chuckled with her. Lili heard them talking and sat up on the couch to clear her head. "Your grandmother is here now, Sam. I'll give the phone to her. I love you."

"I love you too, Uncle Si."

Lili breathed deeply several times and took the phone. Her swollen eyes avoided him. "Good morning, Samantha. That book I left with you last night was the last one. Did you and Priscilla like the story?"

"It was funny. The monkey always gets into trouble," she laughed, describing the antics of a little mischievous monkey in the *Curious George* children's book series. "Priscilla laughed with me, too, when I read it aloud. Can we get more books like that?"

"Yes, we can, Honey. If they don't have any in the hospital activity room we could try the Boston Public Library which is only a block or two away. Uncle Si has given us a surprise visit. We'll be over to see you soon. Love you, Sweetheart."

"I love you too, Grandmother."

"I'm sorry for my outburst, Simon." Lili's conversation with Samantha had helped settle her nerves. "I know that you meant well and wanted to help me put that part of my life to rest. It was bad enough to deal with the Germans and their brutal occupation, but the betrayal of a friend, a citizen of France, for monetary and personal gain is beyond my comprehension. Someday I'll confront Peter Gabineau. I want him to tell me face to face why he did it."

"If I were you I'd want the same thing, Lili, but you should not let that cloud the future," admonished Simon, holding her in his arms.

"I know that the past can't be changed; however, there's such a thing as justice and retribution. Consequences are an inseparable part of choices. My son had much to give to this world. The one responsible for his death should pay for something beautiful the world has lost. I don't know if that's revenge or not," Lili replied firmly.

139

"Neither do I," admitted Simon, wondering if he had done the right thing in opening up hurtful memories. "Why don't we go see Sam? Is it too early in the morning for sodas?"

"No," said Lili, relieved to change the subject. "Thank you for helping. Major Burton is a good friend. I'm sure it was not easy for him to gather the information. Please thank him for me."

"I already have."

They descended on the hospital in good spirits. Lili saw a remarkable improvement in the way Simon moved about without the cane. His long powerful legs made it so that she had to walk fast to keep up with him. She asked him to slow down as she was beginning to breathe hard.

They checked in with Doctor Mitchell. He told them that he had reevaluated Samantha's remarkable recovery from surgery. His original estimate of Thanksgiving as a possible date of release was based on a worst-case scenario. He thought that Samantha could be discharged in a few days.

"You know, Miss Becker," concluded Doctor Mitchell, "you may not thank us when you see how much energy Samantha has stored up and is screaming to be released."

"I've already had an indication of that, Doctor Mitchell. I'll manage somehow," Lili smiled with him. "It's wonderful to see my little girl able to run and jump like other children without being seriously fatigued in the process. Thank you. You and your staff have worked a miracle." She embraced him and kissed him on the cheek, an impromptu gesture that made him blush.

"You and Samantha deserve the new life that lies ahead for you. Good luck, Colonel, you're looking more fit also."

"I'm making progress, Sir. Your old friend Doctor Connors was correct in his recommendation of you. I thank you, too."

"Samantha has completed her tests for the day. She just told me that she was looking forward to her daily ice cream soda, chocolate I believe. Did you get her addicted to them?" he asked, with a twinkle in his eyes.

"I plead guilty," laughed Simon.

They rushed to Samantha's room. Simon saw a new Sam. Her color was normal and the deep-set eyes he recalled were replaced with sparkling brown eyes, alert and observant. As soon as she saw Simon enter the room, she jumped off her bed into his out-stretched arms.

"Grandmother and I have missed you, Uncle Si."

"I've missed you, too, Sam. What do you say if we go out for a walk and get a soda?" Simon suggested.

"Yes," said Sam.

"The weather is a little cooler today," stated Lili, selecting a warm jacket from Samantha's clothing locker.

They went directly to the ice cream shop where all three of them had a chocolate soda. Fortified with energy from the ice cream, they walked along the Charles River. It was a beautiful fall day. The wind from the northwest was cool and the sun shone across the river, glistening on the rippling waves. They walked around the Boston Shell where several musicians were practicing on the large stage. Lili watched and listened with an experienced ear.

"They must be members of the orchestra, they play very well. I have several recordings of the Boston Pops Orchestra. What a lovely setting this is for their concerts," Lili mused, holding onto Simon's arm.

They sat on one of the park benches listening to the musicians and watching the crew teams from several colleges as they rowed up and down the river. Samantha ran about the newly mowed lawn and tried a swing near the bench where Simon and Lili were sitting. Lili held Simon's arm, happy to be with him.

"The time is approaching when we must part, Simon. Samantha and I are planning to return to Montfaucon when she's released. I have unfinished work at the library. This has been a period of renewal and hope for Samantha and me. I shudder at what I would have done if you had not come into our lives," Lili told him.

"You would have found a way just like you always have, dear lady. Now that the doctor has given you a timetable," reflected Simon, reaching in his pocket for an envelope and passing it on to Lili, "I've purchased two tickets for you to return to Paris on a commercial flight. As soon as you learn the date of Sam's release, notify the airline to book your flight."

"I didn't expect you to do that, Simon, but thank you for your generosity," she responded, taking the envelope and

141

placing it in her purse. "This trip to Boston has probably saved Sam's life. How can I ever repay you for that?"

"By loving me as much as I love you, Lili. I had a feeling your departure might be early, that's why I came at this time. You and I are still strangers in many ways. It's sudden, we can't deny that. If I'm going to be true to the feelings I have for you, there's only one thing to do. Will you marry me, Lili?" Simon held out a small box to her. "This was my mother's engagement ring. I'm certain she would be pleased if you accept it. I love you, Lili Becker, and would be proud to call you my wife. The thought of you and Sam returning to France is unsettling to me. I won't deny that it's sudden for the kind of commitment that marriage requires, but I still had to listen to what my heart was telling me."

"How could anyone not love you, Simon?" she said between sobs. "It is sudden, and I believe we need a little more time. I accept your offer to be your wife and will cherish you as my husband." Lili took the ring from the case. "It's beautiful. I felt close to your mother when I slept in her room. You make me feel like standing up and shouting to the world how happy you've made me. Returning to France will be easier now. We have a future to plan and look forward to. It seems so right. I do love you, Simon, I'm not confusing you with Sam." Tears rolled down her cheeks.

Sam watched them from a distance, saw her grandmother crying and came running. "Why are you crying?"

Lili released Simon and held out her arms for Sam, pulling her onto both of their laps.

"What would you say if your Uncle Si and I get married?" asked Lili, wiping the tears of happiness from her face with a handkerchief Simon handed to her.

"It will be fun," answered Sam, hugging the two of them at the same time. "Does that mean you would come to live with us, Uncle Si?" she innocently asked.

"I'll always be with you and your grandmother. We haven't worked out the details yet," exclaimed Simon. "I thought we would go back to Wilson River where I grew up. Does that seem like a reasonable plan, Lili?"

"Yes, I would like that and so would Samantha. Are you certain about retiring from the Army? I would never ask you to do that, Simon."

"I had made up my mind before I met you, Lili. I'm really looking forward to work with the Great Northern Paper Company. However, you should be informed that one of the commitments an officer makes to his country is that he will serve again if a national emergency arises. I don't expect that, but it's always a possibility."

"I saw the enthusiasm in your eyes the day we were in Greenville. It will be a wonderful place for Samantha to grow up in. I'll be happy anywhere with you."

"I know that you have a number of things to settle in Montfaucon. Would you thank, for me, the good people in the village who have been a party to your successful evasion of the Gestapo? Also, what do you think about planning our wedding in the spring? I'll be settled in the house and new job by then."

"Spring sounds right to me, my dearest fiancé. Today you have made me the happiest woman in the world!"

Chapter Sixteen

A week after Simon's visit, Lili called his hospital room.

"Hello," answered Simon.

"It's me, Lili. I wanted to let you know that Sam has been discharged from the hospital."

"That's wonderful," he answered. "Miracles do happen, and dreams do come true. When are you leaving Boston?"

"I have a direct flight in the morning from Boston to Paris. When I opened the envelope with the tickets, I saw that you had enclosed some cash. You're too generous, Simon," she scolded.

"You may need it, and I don't want you or Sam to have any awkward moments for lack of pocket money. When you sign out from the hotel in the morning, you'll learn that I paid the bill in advance, so you'll be receiving more cash at that time. Put it in your pocket and enjoy spending it. I'll miss you two. We haven't seen each other much lately, but I've been with you in spirit every day. When you leave for Montfaucon, we'll be separated by a large ocean. That will make me miss you even more."

"I'll miss you, too, Simon. I'll write every day. Be sure to let me know when you leave the hospital for Wilson River."

"I will. The Medal of Honor ceremony will be coming up soon. The Army wants me to be in uniform for that event. I expect that my resignation will take effect shortly afterwards. I'm feeling physically fit. I've lost five pounds from all of the exercises they're making me do. Maybe I overate when I couldn't move around very well," he chuckled.

"Maybe you had too many donuts and sodas," Lili laughed playfully. "I hope you'll like my cooking after we're married."

"If it comes from you, I'll love it."

"There's another thing I wanted to mention to you before I left. I'm going to use the Ford automobile until we set the date to get married. At that time I thought I would give it to the farm family that owns the cottage. They've been wonderful to us. I've always felt safe and protected with them as neighbors."

"That sounds like a good idea, Lili. Thank them for me. May I speak to Sam for a minute?" Simon requested.

"She's right here waiting to say good-bye to you."

"Hello, Uncle Si."

"Hi, Sam. I'm going to miss you, but it will be for a short time. Promise to take good care of Grandmother for me and be sure to do what she asks you to do."

Sam giggled on the other end of the line. "I always listen to Grandmother. Are you going to come to the cottage for us?"

"Yes, I am, Honey. Your home is going to be with me after we get married. We'll have a lot of fun together."

"Grandmother has told me about the big house beside the river. Are there other little boys and girls nearby?"

"Of course, Sam. You'll have a lot of friends, I promise. I hope you two have a pleasant trip back to Montfaucon. Good-bye, Sam. Tell your grandmother I want to talk to her again. Uncle Si loves you very much."

"I love you, too. Grandmother wants to talk to you again," Sam replied happily.

"Hello, Lili?"

"Yes," she answered.

"I just wanted to see what you thought about something that's been on my mind lately. I'd like to legally adopt Sam after we marry. What do you think?" asked Simon.

"It's a beautiful gesture, Simon," she answered in a soft voice reflecting the warm emotions she felt. "It's the right thing to do. Thank you for being so kind and thoughtful."

"You've filled my days with happy thoughts, Lili Becker. 'Bon voyage'. I'll write often. I love you."

"And I love you, my brave soldier fiancée. Au revoir."

For the balance of the morning, Simon worked out vigorously in the physical therapy room. Later in the afternoon, he had a visit from General Alex Grady who found him fully dressed, sitting at the desk writing a letter to Lili.

"Hello, Simon," announced General Grady.

"It's nice to see you, Sir," greeted Simon.

"You look better than I expected to find you. There's a rumor making its rounds through the Army-Navy Club downtown that you're thinking of retiring."

"This time the rumor mill is correct," grinned Simon. "I've decided to try my luck at the forestry profession I've never had a chance to practice. I don't have that many more useful years left. I'll miss the Army and the companionship of fine men such as yourself, General." The General looked drawn and tired. Okinawa had taken its toll on him. "Okinawa was a hard one, wasn't it, Sir?"

"The toughest nut I've ever had to crack," replied General Grady soberly. "I'm going to join you in the ranks of the retired very soon. I've got eight more years on you, and I admit that I'm feeling my age. Before I left the Pacific Ocean area, the men in your regiment were asking about you. You left your mark on them, Simon. They wish you well."

"I think often about them. The three battalions I had on Okinawa were the best I ever served with. I have nightmares when I think of the things I asked them to do and was never disappointed. It was a privilege to serve with them, and that includes you, too, Sir. I sometimes wondered what was going to happen to the Army when all of us two-war-veterans leave, but I've been heartened by the performance of the younger men we've trained. After watching them perform against the Japanese and Germans, I don't worry anymore. The country will be well served by them."

"I just came from Fort Belvoir where arrangements have been made for awarding the Medal of Honor posthumously to Keith. Would you object if an old family friend accompanies you and Miriam to the ceremony at the White House?"

"We would be honored, Sir, and I'm sure I speak for Miriam," Simon replied without hesitation.

Simon confided to Grady about his involvement with Lili and brought him up to date on their plans for the future. General Grady knew about Samuel's death in World War One. As a matter of fact, he had met Simon and Samuel when they attended the same class he taught at Fort Bragg, North Carolina, on topography, map reading, and camouflage.

"This Lili sounds like a special kind of lady," added General Grady. "I hope things work out for both of you. I

146

always had the feeling that you and Miriam might have had a chance. I've known Leroy Carter for a number of years. He's a disgrace to the uniform. He's made passes at officer's wives on every post he's been assigned. I can tell you that now. It's been common knowledge among those who have served with Carter. I just hope Miriam will not be hurt by it."

"I believe that Miriam has accepted the consequences fairly well. Why don't I try to reach her while you're here, General?" Simon placed a call to Miriam at Wilson River. "Hello, Miriam?"

"I'm so glad you called, Simon," she answered. "I was going to call you later today. The ceremony at the White House is scheduled for the day after tomorrow at 10:00 AM."

"General Grady is here with me. I've invited him to accompany us to the White House. Do you have any objections?" Simon asked.

"I'd like that. He and his wife watched him grow up at Army posts all over the country. You tell him that I'll be pleased to see him again."

"I thought you'd feel that way. The Army is giving us chauffeur service from the hospital. Why don't you meet us here? Are you planning to stay at the Lookout Hotel?"

"Yes, I'll be coming to Washington tomorrow so that I can get a good night's sleep before the ceremony. How's little Samantha doing?"

"Sam and her grandmother just left for France. Sam's operation was a resounding success."

"That's wonderful. I received a nice note from Lili shortly after you two left Wilson River," continued Miriam. "I'll be in touch as soon as I arrive in Washington. Thanks for calling, Simon."

"You're welcome, Miriam."

"Well, that settles things nicely," said General Grady, picking up his hat and preparing to leave. "I'll meet you and Miriam here day after tomorrow. You continue to get well, Simon."

"Thanks for stopping by, Sir."

Two days later, Miriam arrived at the Walter Reed Hospital at 8:00 AM on the day of the presentation. She found Simon sitting at his desk drinking coffee dressed in his best

147

uniform. His brown jacket with several rows of ribbons was hanging over a chair next to his bed.

"Good morning, Simon," she greeted him from the doorway.

"Good morning, Miriam, come in. There's extra coffee and cups if you'd like some." He walked to the door to greet her, and she fell into his arms. He kissed her on the cheek.

"Thank you, I will have coffee. I've been a nervous wreck ever since I was notified of the time," replied Miriam. "When we lost Keith, we lost a large part of ourselves. I lost the only person left in the world that cared for me, and it was my own fault..."

"Please sit down, Miriam," motioned Simon, aware of her discomfort. She was wearing a black dress with a black blazer. Her small hat was covered with a veil she rolled up over her forehead to drink the coffee. Simon noted that she wore one of his old first lieutenant bars on her hat in remembrance. "You look lovely. How are things going with Leroy?"

"He and I don't talk person to person. His lawyer, a suave, slick-talking Irishman, has been threatening me with dire consequences since the divorce papers have been filed. I ignore him. I'm not laying claim to anything. All I want is to be free of him."

"I should tell you that Lili and I have become engaged. If everything goes as planned, we'll be married in the spring."

"I'm happy for you, Simon. You deserve to be happy. I'm not surprised, I saw it all over both of you at the house. I like Lili. I'm a little jealous of her, but I like her just the same."

"I've also made up my mind to retire from the Army. I've accepted a job from Great Northern Paper Company as a forester, and returning to Wilson River. All during the war years I dreamed of going back home."

"It'll be nice to have you home," claimed Miriam. "Simon, you're the first person to know. I have a publisher who has contracted to do my book. It should be out within a year."

"That's wonderful, Miriam, I'm proud of you. It's quite an achievement."

"It has been good therapy for me. Maybe I should thank Leroy for providing the nightmares I used the book to escape from. Those who know Leroy and me will find the book to be a bombshell to Leroy's reputation."

"I can honestly tell you that he's not universally loved within the Army, but you must know that by now."

"Yes, I've known that for years," she confessed with a sigh. They reminisced over coffee until General Grady arrived to join them for a quick cup.

"It's nice to have an old friend with us," exclaimed Miriam, nervously embracing him. "I hope you can forgive me for the outrageous choice I made. I'm in the process of correcting that mistake."

"I never stood in judgment of your marriage to Leroy. Now, I believe you have arrived at a wise decision, Miriam. I wish you well. It's nice to see you again." The tall thin General with the sad eyes wore his full compliment of ribbons for the occasion. He was the recipient of two Silver Stars and was known throughout the Army as one of their best division commanders. Troops under his command idolized him for his calm demeanor under pressure and his sincere concern for their welfare.

A young hospital orderly came into the room to announce that a sedan was waiting for them at the front entrance. Simon buttoned his jacket and buckled the Sam Brown belt he liked to wear.

"How do I look?" Simon asked nervously of Miriam.

"You look like the proud father you are, Colonel," she answered in a soft voice.

"This is the first time I've ever attended the presentation of a Medal of Honor at the White House," declared General Grady.

The three walked to the hospital main entrance to the waiting olive drab 1942 Plymouth sedan. Miriam and Simon sat in the back seat; General Grady climbed in the front seat beside the driver. Within a few minutes they entered the driveway security check point leading to the White House.

They were met by two immaculately attired Army aides to the President at the White House receiving area. One offered Miriam his arm and escorted her down a long carpeted corridor to the Oval Office. The second aide fell in beside Simon as they followed Miriam. General Grady took his position at the end of the column. They waited outside the door for several seconds. Miriam's heart was pumping so loud she was afraid everyone could hear it in the silent hallway.

The aides asked if anyone needed a drink of water or anything else. They all shook their heads negatively just as the door opened.

"The President will see you now," announced an orderly in a formal manner. He instructed them that they were the only ones to be receiving the Medal of Honor at this hour. President Truman watched them come through the door and walked around the desk to greet them.

"Welcoming the families and friends of our fallen American heroes is one of the saddest duties this old soldier has to carry out." The President greeted them with warmth and sincerity. "Your son, and countless others like him, have added to the legacy of valor which has made this the greatest nation on the face of the earth. It's an honor and a privilege to welcome you to the sanctity of this magnificent Oval Office. I confess to you that this office continues to awe this country boy."

"We're proud and saddened to represent our son, Lieutenant Keith Hanley," Simon replied in a strained voice. "We're accompanied by a dear friend of the family, Keith's Godfather, Major General Alex Grady."

"Welcome, General Grady," said the President, shaking his hand, noting the large number of ribbons on his uniform.

"It's an honor to be here, Mister President."

The president adjusted his glasses and made eye contact with Simon and Miriam. "This nation is blessed with families that produce such a fine soldier as we pay tribute to today: First Lieutenant Keith Hanley of the United States Army, a proud graduate of our Military Academy at West Point. The distinguished array of ribbons you wear, Colonel Hanley, humble this old artillery captain. Your son must have been as proud of you as you are of him."

"That is very true, Mister President," added Miriam, taking Simon's hand in hers.

"I especially honor the Combat Infantryman's Badge you've earned, Colonel. It represents distinguished service under fire." The President paused to step behind his desk where he selected a large notepad and repositioned himself directly in front of Simon and Miriam. The President wore the mantel of the Presidency with grace and dignity. He was respectful and humble.

The President threw his shoulders back, in a swift movement, and started to recite the citation accompanying First Lieutenant Hanley's award in clipped precise diction: "In the name of the Congress of the United States I present the Medal Of Honor Posthumously to First Lieutenant Keith Hanley of the Army of the United States of America, First Platoon, Company A, Fifth Battalion, Ninth Regiment, One Hundredth Division. He was Killed In Action in France near the Belgium border. On September 29, 1944, Lieutenant Hanley's Platoon was advancing across an open field near a wooded area when it came under heavy fire from several well hidden enemy machine guns. Lieutenant Hanley quickly organized an attack and personally led his men against the fortified positions coming under heavy fire from different directions. He carried several satchels of explosives, which he accurately threw like hand grenades at each of the enemy positions threatening his company's line of advance. Two of the enemy strong points were eliminated. Lieutenant Hanley's assault against the third machine gun nest was also made under withering direct fire. He was mortally wounded by long bursts from the machine guns, yet continued to its perimeter, where he threw his two remaining satchel charges, destroying its occupants. His indomitable spirit and exceptional courage saved his company, inspiring them to advance rapidly into the woods and relative safety.

"Lieutenant Hanley's conspicuous gallantry and intrepidity in action at the risk of his life above and beyond the call of duty reflect great credit upon himself and were in keeping with the finest traditions of the United States Army.

"The privilege of awarding this Medal of Honor is my most cherished duty as your President. The nation mourns your loss and you have my personal sympathy."

The President took the medal from a satin-covered box on his desk. The Medal is composed of heavy silver, plated with gold, and suspended on a ribbon with thirteen white stars on a light blue field. A bar below the ribbon has the word "valor" inscribed on a scroll. The ribbon is attached to a sash worn around the neck.

"It's an honor to award this Medal of Honor to Lieutenant Hanley's mother," the President said, placing the sash around Miriam's neck. He shook her hand and embraced her briefly.

The President offered his hand to Simon and General Grady. They both noticed a moist film covering the President's eyes.

"God bless both of you. May your sorrow be lessened by the collective mourning of a grateful nation. Thank you for coming. My prayers are with you."

"Thank you, Mister President," Simon and Miriam said in unison as the Army orderlies gently escorted them from the room, down the long corridor to the waiting sedan in the White House driveway.

Chapter Seventeen

The airplane ride across the Atlantic from the United States to Paris was much more thrilling to Samantha than her previous trip. She was no longer the sickly lethargic child that had left France literally in her mother's arms. On the return trip she spent all of her time at the window excitedly watching clouds roll by and ships sailing beneath them going to and from Europe and North America.

Lili read very few of the magazines she had purchased at the terminal; instead she relaxed in the seat and reflected on the changes that had taken place in her life in the short span of time since she had met Simon. The thought of him brought a smile to her lips. The future was all she could ever hope for and she prayed for God's blessing to make their dreams a reality. They had a five hour wait at the Paris train station for a train to Montfaucon, arriving at their cottage exhausted from the long journey.

The next day, Lili registered Samantha in the local school and reported for work at the library. Her superiors were pleased to have her back. During that first week of work she took two days leave from the library and left Samantha in the care of their farm family neighbors. A burning desire to pay tribute to her son Samuel and his wife Robyne had dominated her thoughts ever since she learned from Simon's friend where they were buried. She told no one where she was going.

The ride to Paris was filled with anticipation and sadness, uncertain about what she would find. Lili was hoping that her pilgrimage to Samuel's and Robyne's graves would calm the rage that she had lived with for the past five years; yet, her desire to confront Peter Gabineau was stronger and more immediate than ever. She intended to pay an impromptu visit to his residence before locating the graves. Her desire for answers could not be avoided any longer. The brutality and

153

suddenness of their deaths still haunted her daily. Sometimes she woke from a sound sleep screaming in protest of the torment that raged in her heart. Lili took a cab at the Paris train station and tried to relax, but every nerve in her body was alert. The moment of revelation was at hand. She was eager to learn the truth behind the despicable betrayal of her son and daughter-in-law.

Lili asked the cab driver to let her off at the beginning of rue Peuplier, the street where Peter Gabineau lived. It was a neighborhood of fine homes with large gardens enclosed by wrought iron fences to insure privacy and exclusivity. Her heart was pounding rapidly. A firm resolve propelled her down the street until she came to number 214, two blocks from the end, surprised at how calm she was. The house was a large granite structure with three floors. The lawn and garden were well groomed. An elderly gardener was kneeling, tending a flower bed beside the walkway. Lili spoke to the gentleman in French without a trace of fear or apprehension.

"Good morning. Is this the residence of Peter Gabineau?"

"Yes, Madam. I spoke to him a few minutes ago. He is in the kitchen eating breakfast. Follow the walkway to the left around to the rear of the house. The kitchen entrance is unlocked. You'll find him there."

"Thank you," replied Lili, walking slowly down the pathway.

Each step that took Lili closer to a confrontation with Peter Gabineau eroded some of her determination. Maybe she was making a mistake. Perhaps it would be prudent to let the past remain unknown... She hesitated near the door for a moment to collect her thoughts. Then, she recalled the vision of pain and terror on Samuel's face as he fell to the floor of his apartment. The image of rifle butts pounding against his bleeding skull was indelibly engraved in her memory, hastening her steps to the kitchen entrance where she knocked firmly.

"The door is unlocked, come in," called a deep voice from inside.

Lili opened the door and stepped inside, coming face to face with Peter Gabineau, standing behind a dining table covered with food in the middle of the kitchen. Her heart was racing so fast she was speechless. He had not changed that much. Peter Gabineau was still a young-looking man. Tall and slender with long arms and big hands, he still had the same sophisticated and haughty air about him that used to infuriate many of his old friends. His mouth was usually formed in a sneer as if he was looking down in disgust at everybody around him. It took a few seconds for him to recognize Lili.

"What are you doing here?" he snapped at her. His arrogant demeanor changed the instant he recognized her. He was unsteady on his feet and quickly sat down. His face turned white. Lili triumphantly saw fear in his eyes. That empowered her even more.

"I see that you recognize me, Peter. It has been a long time, hasn't it? I've come to ask you some questions. You were a guest in my home on several occasions and were a friend to Robyne and Samuel. How could a friend betray my son and daughter-in-law? What did you gain by informing the Gestapo about their presence? They never did anything to you. They were French patriots that loved their place of birth. I'm looking for some answers, Peter," she stated in clear precise diction, hoping that the fear she harbored did not show.

Peter saw the courage that motivated Lili and he scorned her with impunity. "Lili Becker, my old friend's mother has found the righteousness to confront me," he taunted her as if she was a worthless beggar from the streets. "You and your kind always made me sick. Samuel was always so sure of himself. Music came easy to him. His beautiful wife never knew I existed. I often tried to date her before they were married, but she turned me down as if I was nothing. They thought they were so superior."

"That's a lie, and you know it!" Lili cried in protest.

"The day they were arrested, they deserved what they got. I'll tell you exactly what happened," he continued to taunt her, enjoying the agony he saw in her contorted face. "The night before the Gestapo came to their apartment, Samuel had left for a meeting with that group of student patriots he was so fond of. I came down from my upstairs apartment to spend some time alone with Robyne. She refused my advances, but I still had my way with her. I showed her who was in charge even though she screamed and fought like an alley cat. She didn't have the guts to tell you what had taken place between us when you came to their apartment the next day to help them take care of the baby. For your information I think she liked it. I always wanted to try a Jew..."

"You pig," she cried, striking him a stinging blow in the face with her open hand. The sound echoed around the room. Peter's face turned red. The attack surprised him, momentarily wiping the smug expression from his face.

Enraged, he grabbed her by both breasts and violently threw her against the wall. Lili cried out with pain. He continued to hold her against the wall in an iron grip. "Jews were being rounded up all over France. At last the civilized world was recognizing the threat that your kind posed to mankind. The Germans were pleased to arrest them, and they eliminated a large Partisan cell at the same time. I showed the Zionists who was important! I was rewarded for my efforts and became an important businessman in the city..."

Lili listened as if it was a bad dream, fearing for her life. His taunting tirade fueled her inner rage. All she wanted was to shut him up and make him stop hurting her. Panic gripped her as she pounded on his face with her fists. She knew that she was in a dangerous situation, for he was much stronger. Then, she saw a bread knife on the table beside them and desperately lunged for it. Peter was holding her pinned against the wall, cruelly crushing her breasts. He contemplated her move, but was too late... She grasped the knife in her right hand and swung it in an arc with every bit of strength she possessed, driving it into his groin area. He immediately relaxed his hold on her and opened his mouth to scream, but only a muffled moan passed his lips.

"That was for Samuel," she cried in a low delirious state of mind. "And this is for Robyne and me, you miserable excuse for a human being." She pulled the knife from his groin and stabbed him two more times leaving the knife protruding from his body as he crumpled to the floor. She spit in his face. He looked at her with bulging eyes filled with horror and disbelief. The surly sneer was gone!

Lili straightened her clothing and casually walked past the gardener who was still working in the flower gardens. Her heart was pounding so hard she was afraid he might hear it. By the time she reached the street she was crying. Every muscle in her body was trembling uncontrollably from the unexpected turn of events. The more she walked the more composed she became. Conflicting and mixed emotions flowed through her mind. Luckily for her the streets were sparsely populated. She had administered justice where justice was desperately needed.

Lili walked the streets of Paris for hours in a trance, not caring or noting where she was headed. She had remembered Peter Gabineau as a sullen, undisciplined musician who envied others like Samuel who had more talent. It was difficult for her to imagine how simple petty jealousy could turn a person into the vile individual he ultimately became. Lili wasn't sure if she had killed him or severely wounded him. What frightened her the most was that she had no regrets or remorse. She did not view it as revenge. In her heart it was simply justice. Peter Gabineau had betrayed his friends for monetary gain. The consequences of that choice took five years, and she administered the verdict in a way he would always remember, if he lived...

She walked through a small public park in northern Paris with benches beneath large English sycamore trees, and sat for a long time, reflecting on what to do next. She gave in to her desire to visit Samuel's and Robyne's grave, and stopped a cab. Within a half-hour, she was dropped off in front of a magnificent Catholic Church with a large cemetery located behind the buildings.

She walked among the monuments, looking for a grave without markings. She found one near a fence at the rear of the cemetery. Several fresh bouquets of flowers were placed beneath a recently carved plaque with the following inscription: "This tomb holds the remains of twelve Jewish patriots who died for France. Their identity known only to God, but their courage and loyalty will always be remembered by their partisan compatriots. Rest in peace, brave souls. Erected September, 1945."

Lili dropped to her knees and wept. Five long years of days and nights filled with terror and anguish of not knowing were now coming to an end. Her pilgrimage and search for answers had come to an end. An elderly Priest noticed her sobbing beside the tomb and cautiously approached her.

"May I help you, Madame?" he asked in a consoling voice. She did not acknowledge his request, so he repeated the words: "I'm Father Latulipe. Are you all right?"

Lili felt his presence and saw his shadow on the ground. She heard his voice the second time he spoke. She looked up with swollen tear-stained eyes. All of the agony and torment that had filled her heart for years was visible on her face. The kindly Priest was frightened at the intensity of her grief.

"My dearest lady," he exclaimed, helping her to a nearby granite bench. "Please sit with me for a while." He glanced at the tomb and surmised the reason for her forlorn distress. "Some patriots erected the plaque at the tomb last month. I was the parish Priest when the bodies were buried here. I examined each one and administered the last rites that they may find peace. I gave them a Christian burial, even though they were Jewish. I can confide to you, my dear lady, that I hid a Jewish family in my quarters for the duration of the occupation. One of the members of the family was a Rabbi. He conducted committal services for the souls after dark when no one would notice."

Wiping her swollen eyes, Lili listened to the words the Priest spoke. She rummaged through her battered purse locating a portrait of Samuel and Robyne when they were married two years before their death.

"Father, could you tell me if these two people were among those buried in the grave?" Lili pleaded, handing the photo to the Priest.

"Yes, my child," answered the Priest. "They were on the first truck load of bodies… I remember how sad I felt. They were so young and innocent. Though they died violently, they entered God's Kingdom with a pure heart. It was a sad day for France when we buried them." He was relieved that the information he passed on to her was beginning to calm her wracking body.

"Thank you, Father," she cried, wiping her swollen eyes. "They were two beautiful people with much to offer this troubled world. I've been searching for some meaning in their deaths, but the answers have alluded me."

"I'm not able to give you the answers that would put your troubled heart to rest, dear child. It's only natural that you mourn their loss. If you live your life as a tribute to their memory, then they will share that life with you and live on in your heart. Did you notice the flowers at the base of the tomb?"

"Yes," sobbed Lili.

"Every other day two people, a young lady and an elderly gentleman, come to the cemetery bringing fresh flowers. I do not know who they are and have not wanted to intrude on their tribute to lost loved ones. Maybe you can find some comfort in knowing that others are sharing your loss and are paying tribute to their memories. You are not alone, dear child. Now that the war is over, the time for healing has arrived. It is not easy and will not be done quickly, but, we who have survived have an obligation to embrace life with a renewed passion to pay tribute to those courageous souls who have fallen and sacrificed so much for our freedom."

"You're a wise man of God, Father," replied Lili. She stood up and looked at the granite tomb. "I'll be back as often as I can. Thank you for helping me. I leave here secure in the knowledge that my beloved son and his dear wife have found peace and that God has welcomed them home. Thank you for your kindness."

"You are welcome, dear lady. Go with God's blessing. I will pray for you."

"Good-bye, Father. Would you please tell the people who come with flowers that I'm with them in spirit?"

"It will be my pleasure. It's always a comfort to know that we're not alone."

Lili left the church cemetery satisfied that she had accomplished her two missions in Paris. A picture of Samuel and Samantha filled her heart. She walked several blocks, reflecting on the events of the day. She had no regrets about what she did to Peter. In any court of law self defense would free her, but there were no witnesses... The more she thought about it, the more troubled she became. Doubts crept into her conscience, overshadowing everything else. Suddenly, she was frightened and feared that she might never be able to carry out the dreams she and Simon had for the future.

The only person Lili could think of to talk to in her chaotic condition was Major Jack Burton, Simon's friend at Allied Headquarters. Once she made the decision to seek him out and ask for his advice, she felt comfortable that it was the right thing to do. She hailed a cab. Sitting in the rear seat of the Citroen she noticed that her right jacket sleeve had blood stains. She tried to wipe them off but was unsuccessful, so she removed the jacket and carried it over her arm. Traffic snarls were numerous. It took them almost two hours to reach the headquarters building. When she arrived at the front entrance Lili was afraid that everyone had already gone home for the day, and she would be too late. She inquired for Major Burton at the reception desk and was told that he was at the Officers' Club just down the street.

Lili checked her watch. It was now six PM. Her train was scheduled to leave the Paris station for Montfaucon at eight PM. She reluctantly walked to the Club and inquired if he was present. The hostess directed her to a table in one of the small rooms. The smell of food made her hungry. She had not eaten all day. She approached the table with some misgivings, unsure whether it was the right thing to do. Major Burton looked up at her as she came abreast of his table. He was alone.

"Major Burton?" she inquired.

"Yes," he answered, standing to acknowledge her. "I know you from somewhere. Ah, yes, now I remember. You were with Colonel Hanley. Your name is Miss Lili Becker."

"Your memory serves you well, Major," replied Lili. Her palms were wet with sweat.

"Please sit down. What can I do for you?" he asked, studying her demeanor carefully. He knew that something very serious was troubling her. Lili's eyes betrayed the anxiety she felt. The horrifying prospect that she might be jailed for murder was a distinct consequence of her actions. She took a seat opposite him where they could observe each other. "May I order something for you?"

"I don't want to be a bother," answered Lili, starting to shake all over. "Maybe some tea or coffee." She was rapidly losing her ability to think rationally. Fear and regret was consuming her.

"I'm enjoying a tasty roast beef dinner. May I order one for you, Miss Becker? You look as if you could use a little bit of nourishment right now."

"That does sound tempting, Major. I've come to you..."

"Miss Becker," interrupted the Major in a firm, reassuring voice. He called a waiter and ordered dinner with rolls, salad, and some hot tea for Lili. When the waiter had left, he turned to Lili with a serious look and explained: "Before you tell me what's on your mind, I have some information that may be of interest to you. After you've heard my story you can decide if you want to tell me what you came here for."

"Whatever you say, Major," Lili answered, confused about what he was trying to say indirectly.

Major Burton took a long sip of coffee after Lili had been served hot tea. He then proceeded to tell her: "A half hour ago, just before leaving my office for the day, a message came over the teletype from Paris Police that one Peter Gabineau was in a hospital suffering from multiple stab wounds from a bread knife to the groin and lower abdomen."

Lili heard the words and melted in her chair. She was holding a tea cup and was so unnerved it spilled all over the table.

"Bear with me, lady," requested Major Burton in a calm voice. He reached across the table with a paper napkin, wiping the spilled tea. Then, he took her two hands in his. "Don't worry about the table cloth. The waiter will take care of it. Please, don't be alarmed at what I'm telling you. The report stated that Gabineau did not recognize the assailant and that he will survive. The wounds will leave him with permanent deformities in the private parts. My own personal thoughts on this event, after reading the full bulletin, are that the little weasel of a traitor got off too easy. I'm surprised that he has not been assassinated. It may come yet! Now, I'm going to assume that you wanted to tell me something about your granddaughter. What was her name? Samantha?"

"Yes, she's fine, Major," answered Lili in a low voice. She knew what the Major was doing. "The operation has transformed her into an active young girl. I'm so thankful for your participation in making it possible."

"Simon is a good friend, and I'd do anything for him. My advice to you, Miss Becker, is to return to Montfaucon as soon as possible."

"I have a train to catch at eight o'clock."

"That's good. Go home and erase any bad feelings you may have about making this trip to Paris. I thank you for letting me know how well Samantha is coming along. I see that your meal is on its way."

As soon as Lili finished the roast beef dinner, Major Burton accompanied her to the train station. "You're a brave lady, Miss Becker. Tell Simon that I'm going to collect on that steak dinner sometime in the future. You've made my day, lady. I hope that you can put those ugly thoughts you've lived with for years to rest. Simon told me about your engagement. He's a lucky man."

"Thank you, Major Burton, for being such a good friend," she replied, kissing him on the cheek. "True friends are a rare treasure. You've helped me more than you know…"

"Bon Voyage, Miss Becker," interrupted the Major, helping her board the train. Without another word, he smiled and waved as the train pulled out from the station.

The next day, Lili brought fresh flowers to Samuel's grave at Montfaucon. She was up early, refreshed by a good night's sleep. There was a soft dew on the ground and a quiet hush descended on the cemetery, bringing a calm comfort to her being. She kneeled on the mowed grass in front of the cross and gently placed a large bouquet of flowers in the vase she always left at the grave.

"My dear Samuel. I have good news to share with you today. For five long years I've lived with a consuming hatred in my heart. That hatred has been replaced with a feeling that justice has been done. I have avenged the death of our son!"

Chapter Eighteen

Simon examined himself in the mirror. For the past twenty-eight years he had proudly served his country as an officer in the United States Army. His commitment to the institution had required a great deal of personal sacrifice from himself and his family. Today he removed the uniform he had proudly worn, and a feeling of sadness and melancholy hung over him. It marked the end of an era in his life and the beginning of a new adventure that held much promise.

The regulated Army life had been compatible with his personal sense of order and had contributed to a feeling of security that had isolated him from the cares of the normal world of everyday working people. It had been a good life, and he could never forget the brave men that had served with him in two world wars.

Simon checked the white shirt and blue slacks he had just purchased with a twinge of guilt. By voluntarily hanging up his uniform was he abandoning a way of life? Was he making a mistake at this late period? Was this a decision that he really wanted to make? He was no longer a young man, and the older he became, the more difficult it was to implement drastic changes in his life. The mental image of Lili standing on her toes to kiss him brought a smile to his face and a quickening of his pulse. Thoughts of her and Sam erased any lingering doubts he may have had.

"Yes," he said to himself in a firm voice. "I'm ready for the change."

Before he vacated the hospital room he sat at the desk and wrote a letter to Lili.

November 30, 1945

Dear Lili and Sam,

This will be my last letter from the hospital. I'm leaving for Maine right after I post it.

I didn't realize how difficult it would be to leave a way of life I've known for twenty-eight years. Much has taken place since Samuel and I first signed up for the Army fresh out of college. I'm thankful that my wounds have not limited me. Right now, I'm in better physical condition than I've been in years. I don't mean to imply that I'm regretting resigning my commission, because I'm not. The future holds much promise for the three of us, and I'm anxious to prepare for that eventuality by getting a steady job close to home. I'm also anxious to get some painting and paper hanging done in the old house before we settle in, so I'll be busy for a while and am looking forward to the challenge.

I think of you and Sam often. I've started proceedings to obtain the necessary immigration papers for the two of you. They should be in hand sometime this winter. If we need any additional help, my old friend Jack Burton is in a position to speed up the process.

I have an announcement that will surprise you. My cousin, Ken Holmes, is an excellent mechanic. He has located a 1941 Studebaker Commander four door sedan owned by a retired school teacher in Wilson River. It has been idle for most of the war years. He's going to meet me in Newport with it. My job at Great Northern Paper Company comes with a small truck for my personal use. That way the car will remain at home for you to use as needed.

I was glad to learn that Sam likes the school in Montfaucon. It's an amazing accomplishment for such a young child to be so fluent in two languages. I'm a lucky guy to have two wonderful women in my life.

I'll write from Wilson River tomorrow.

All my love to both of you,
Simon,   (Uncle Si)

The city of Washington had grown several times in size over what it was when Simon had served as an aide to the Army Department during the mid-thirties. He was glad to be leaving. General Grady accompanied him to the train station to wish him well. It was typical of the General with the deep-set eyes.

"I'll miss you, General," said Simon as the train pulled into the station. "You and I have been in and out of some difficult situations, and I want you to know that serving under you was always a privilege. I hope that this parting is not a good-bye, but a so-long. Let's keep in touch, Sir."

"I'd like that, Simon. I'm following in your footsteps next month. The wife and I plan to spend the winter in upper New York State. As soon as the ice freezes on Lake Champlain, I'm going ice fishing. I haven't tasted fresh water salmon for years, and I'm going to get my fill this winter," General Grady smiled.

"I wish you well in your retirement, Sir. Nobody is more deserving than you and Mrs. Grady. The two of you will always be welcome anytime at Wilson River. I have a few favorite fish holes I'd like to share with you."

"That sounds like an invitation the wife and I can't resist. You take care of yourself, Simon. Good luck in your new profession."

Simon watched the tall elderly soldier wave from the platform and leaned back in the seat to dream of Lili. Simon's train arrived in Newport early the next morning. He spotted the light green Studebaker parked beside the station and was anxious to try it out. The last automobile he had owned was a 1929 Nash. He had given it up when Miriam divorced him in 1933.

His cousin Ken grabbed Simon and gave him a bear hug. Ken was shorter and heavier than Simon with a round face and red cheeks. He was a happy-go-lucky person with an engaging personality. German machine gun bullets had left

165

him blind in his left eye, over which he wore a patch. The same burst of bullets had also shattered a bone in his right leg. He walked with a limp but never complained about the limitations the war had imposed upon him or dampened his spirits. Simon found him to be the same cheerful cousin he had grown up with. They were about the same age.

"It's nice to see you again, Simon."

"Ken, you haven't changed," replied Simon, pleased to see a familiar face. "You had us all worried for a while. How are you doing really?"

"I'm adjusting, Si," Ken replied, hunching his shoulders. "The bullet that got me in the stomach bothers me the most, but medication seems to be handling that problem for now. You look real trim, Si. You know I'm so used to seeing you in uniform I hardly recognized you in civies."

"I'm feeling great, too. Let's take a look at the Stude," said Simon, staring at the automobile in the parking lot.

"The car is as clean as a new one. You remember how neat and orderly the Carlsons were. It even smells like a new one inside. It goes over the road nice and smooth, but I think my forty-one Ford would take it on the start," Ken laughed, handing the keys to Simon.

Simon drove his new car to Wilson River impressed with the fine engineering and spirited performance. He did concede to Ken that his Ford might take it at the start, but the Studebakers were renowned for their fuel economy and longevity. It was a treat driving his own vehicle after all those years without one. It contributed to his newly found sense of freedom and independence by giving him mobility at his fingertips. He was sure that Lili would like the car as much as he did.

The house that Simon and Samuel grew up in was next to Ken's place, separated by a small stand of white pine along the road. Simon told Ken about Lili and Sam and their plans to marry in the spring. Ken offered to help Simon with some of the house remodeling.

"The interior work, mostly painting and paper hanging, can be done before you get settled in. The shingles on the roof are still in good shape. I cleaned the chimney when I moved out a few months ago. You may want to give some thought to a new oil-fired furnace. You and your new bride will enjoy the

166

convenience of one. Now that the war is over, fuel oil will be plentiful. I like the heat of a wood fire but they need a lot of tending and care. They also use a lot of wood which could be difficult to get cut if you have a full time job away from home."

"That makes a lot of sense. I hadn't thought of that," replied Simon, listening to the practical advice Ken offered.

"If you did want to put in a hot air furnace, the pipes and registers should be done before any other remodeling is done," suggested Ken, wondering if he was putting a damper on Simon's homecoming. "Don't be overwhelmed by the repairs to the old house, Si. Sleep on things for a while, and we'll talk specifics later. Drop me off at my place. It's going to be nice having you back as a neighbor. I'm glad for you and Lili. We always hoped that you'd find someone after Miriam left you."

"Have you seen Miriam lately?"

"About every day," answered Ken as Simon turned into his driveway. "I understand that she has applied for a job teaching at the grade school in town. She's filling in as a substitute now. I've heard that she wants to teach the fourth grade full time next year. She seems happy with her decision to return home."

"We all gain in wisdom in our older years, Ken. I've dreamed about making this move for a long time."

"Welcome home, Simon."

The winter months came to the small northern Maine community of Wilson River with the same fury and intensity it always did. For months heavy snow blanketed the region, making travel in the forest impossible without snowshoes. Temperatures dipped below zero degrees frequently during the months of January and February. Simon and Ken worked diligently painting and wallpapering the interior of the house. By the end of February everything was completed including the oiled-fired heating system. Simon had contracted with a reputable firm for installation as Ken had suggested. He was anxious to have all of the interior work on the house completed before bringing his new bride home.

Throughout the winter Simon and Lili wrote daily to each other. Absence nurtured the love they shared. Late in March the phone rang just as Simon was sitting down to a supper of baked beans and hot dogs.

"Hello," he answered.

"Hello, Simon," exclaimed Lili in a strained voice.

"What's wrong, Lili?" demanded Simon.

"I'm calling because I just don't know what to do. I have to tell you something that I can't describe in a letter or talk about over the phone for fear that others might learn the truth."

"The truth," gasped Simon, dismayed and worried. She sounded frightened. "Have you or Sam been hurt or something?"

"Oh, no, we're both all right. Would it be possible for you to leave your work for a short period and come to Montfaucon? I need to talk to you in person, Simon. It'll determine whether we have a future or not…"

"Have you found someone else?" Simon asked in a state of near panic.

"No, my dear Simon," she answered softly. "My love for you is stronger than ever. Please believe that because it's true. I can't go into any more detail over the phone. Trust me."

Simon recognized the urgency and seriousness of her request and replied: "I'll be able to take the time off from the company. Maybe I can get a flight out of Portland. It'll take a day or two before I can get there, Lili. I'll call for reservations as soon as we hang up."

"I'm sorry to ask this of you, Simon," whispered Lili, desperately holding back tears. "I need you now more than ever."

"Are you sure you're okay, Lili? I'll be there as quickly as I can, I promise."

"Sam and I are well. I understand how this conversation must sound to you, my dear Simon. Everything will be made clear when I can tell you in person. Then you can decide what you want to do."

"That almost sounds like an ultimatum."

"Please trust me," she pleaded.

"You know I do," responded Simon, feeling helpless that she needed him, and he was thousands of miles away.

"As soon as you get your plane reservations, call me and I'll meet you in Paris."

"I will. Give Sam a big hug for me and tell her that I've missed her a lot this winter. Don't be discouraged. I love you very much, Lili."

"I love you, too, Simon." She hung up the receiver with trembling hands and released the tears of desperation and fear that had been bottled up inside her.

Two days later, Simon stepped off a commercial flight at the Paris International Airport. Lili was waiting for him at the exit of the Customs Department and ran into his waiting arms.

"I'm so glad you're here with me," she cried breathlessly, clinging to him. She lifted her lips and kissed him softly. They were warm and his heart beat a little faster.

"How could I stay away knowing that you needed me?" he said, releasing her.

"I know that you're full of questions, and I don't blame you for having them. Let's pick up your suitcase and get away from this public place. I'll tell you what has happened once we get to the privacy of the automobile."

Simon collected his luggage and followed Lili as she rapidly walked to the automobile in the parking lot. She climbed behind the wheel and skillfully threaded her way through the streets of Paris northward toward Montfaucon, avoiding major streets and boulevards wherever possible.

There was a desperate look on her face that did not encourage conversation, and that troubled him. He rode in silence trying to check his imagination, which was on the verge of running wild with speculation of all kinds of problems. The congested traffic eventually gave way to the more open and less-traveled roads of the rural countryside at the outer fringe of the metropolitan city. Large rambling estates of the rich and famous dotted the area with their high wrought iron fences and ornate main entrance gates.

"Are you angry at me for being so mysterious and secretive?" Lili finally asked, glancing sideways at him. She saw the bewilderment and nervous impatience that was almost overwhelming him.

"You must admit, Lili, that it's unusual behavior," he answered, trying to be understanding and supportive.

Lili pulled the Ford off the main road onto a secluded overview of the Marne River near the small city of Reims. Maple and willow trees lined the shores of the slow moving

169

river, shielding the overview from passing traffic. A cool damp breeze flowed through the valley. Lili rolled her driver's side window up to ward off the chills that ran through her body.

"Now my dear patient, Simon," said Lili, turning to kiss him. "I'm so sorry for bringing you into this thing."

"What are you talking about, Lili?"

She took his hands and pressed them to her face as she began to tell what had happened shortly after her return to France in the fall. She gave him a complete report of what she did to Peter Gabineau and her consequent visit with Major Burton. She tried to describe her feelings as accurately as possible without any rationalization. Simon listened intently to every word, trying to visualize the horror and fear that she must have felt, yet she kept it to herself.

"Why didn't you share that with me?" Simon asked, irritated that he was kept in the dark all that time.

"Believe me, Simon. I wanted to, but I was afraid, even paranoid, that in some strange way I might be the object of a police investigation. I never knew for sure, so I decided to keep it to myself so that you would not be implicated in any way."

Lili paused to catch her breath and continued: "I was able to get on with my work at the library and dream about our future until one day I noticed a small news item from a Paris newspaper. You can read it for yourself." She handed Simon the news clipping.

"I can't read a word of French," admitted Simon impatiently.

"Of course," said Lili, taking the slip of paper and reading it aloud: "Local business man dies under mysterious circumstances. Peter Gabineau, a local merchant in fine wines, was found dead in his apartment last night. The cause of death appeared to be a single bullet to the head. Several months ago, Mr. Gabineau was assaulted by an unknown intruder, requiring extensive medical surgery as a result of the attack. He was still recovering from his wounds when he was killed in his apartment. The police are investigating the whereabouts and identity of a middle-aged woman described by the gardener of the apartment complex where Gabineau resided."

"My God," he exclaimed incredulously. His first thoughts were to contact Jack Burton, hoping that he was still stationed at the Allied Headquarters in Paris. "I've got to call Jack Burton."

"That has already been done," Lili looked at him and smiled. "The same day this bulletin was in the paper, Major Burton called me. I told him that I had seen a certain notice in the paper. And he advised me to contact you and have you come as soon as possible." Lili nervously looked in the rearview mirror and checked the watch on her wrist. "I notified him of your flight number and estimated time of arrival."

A Citreon sedan pulled behind Lili's Ford. Two men climbed out of the vehicle and approached them. Simon recognized Major Burton and Sergeant Jones dressed in civilian clothes.

Chapter Nineteen

Simon was aghast at the sight of the two men he most wanted to talk to at this troublesome time.

"I can't believe my eyes," he exclaimed, getting out of the Ford to greet them.

Sergeant Jones and Major Burton had their overcoat collars turned up around their necks and their hats pulled down low over their eyes. Simon realized that they were intent on keeping their identity away from any possible prying eyes.

"Why don't we all take a ride," announced Jack, ignoring Simon's outstretched hand.

Simon and Jack got into the back seat with Lili between them. Jones slipped behind the wheel and drove the Citreon over the road several miles to another more obscure rest area beside the highway. Not a word was said until Jones shut off the ignition and quietly got out of the sedan to check the surrounding area.

"This must be driving you crazy, Simon," grinned Jack.

"That's an understatement, Jack. Is Lili in any danger?"

"I don't believe so. I don't think the police have any idea who Miss Becker is. Evidently Gabineau kept her identity a secret. However, assuming that he did divulge her identity at the time of the knifing incident, the police would first exhaust their search of the metropolitan Paris area. Miss Becker's secret flight to Montfaucon during the occupation will keep any investigator busy for a while, even if they are looking for her, which I doubt is the case."

"What do we do now, Jack?" asked Simon, searching for some plan of action that would remove Lili from any potential danger.

"Well," Jack drawled, looking out the window collecting his thoughts. "I haven't discussed a plan I've had in mind with either of you, and it's full of assumptions on my part. I can't

172

tell you why, but I strongly recommend that both of you get out of France as soon as possible, and leave no clues behind as to where you're going. I'm sure your phone line is clear, Miss Becker."

"Whenever I've called Simon these past few months I've used the public phones in the village square at Montfaucon."

"That's good..."

"What are you suggesting, Jack?" requested Simon.

"If I were in your shoes, I'd take Miss Becker and her daughter out of here tomorrow. On a hunch that you might take my advice, I've made reservations for the three of you to embark on an Army freighter departing at noontime tomorrow from Le Havre. You're booked as Colonel and Mrs. Hanley with granddaughter Samantha. The Army Quartmaster can marry the two of you just as soon as you step foot on that ship, which, as you know, is considered sovereign American soil. If you want something else done I'll try to help where I can, but I must tell you that Sergeant Jones and I are doing this at some risk. I won't say anything more."

Simon looked at Lili. She was as surprised as he at the sudden turn of events. "Is Lili in danger?" he asked again.

"As far as I can tell, she's not threatened at this moment," continued Major Burton. "However, prudence dictates that the sooner she's removed from potential discovery in France, the less chance there is of detection. I think the police are aware of Gabineau's traitorous past. And their investigation will most likely be superficial at best. France is doing a lot of national soul searching right now, and I'm sure that many patriots on the police force feel that justice was done when Gabineau was killed. If that is not the case, then France is in real trouble."

"Le Havre is almost two hundred miles from Montfaucon. How can we ever do that in time to be on the ship when it departs?" Lili asked wearily. The tension of the past few days were taking a toll on her; dark circles were showing around her eyes. She felt emotionally and physically drained. Lili looked up at Simon and asked: "Do you want to do this thing, Simon?"

It was a direct question filled with all of the uncertainty of having to make hasty decisions about important matters that would affect the three of them for the rest of their lives. She was afraid that the circumstances of her plight would be too demanding for Simon, and she would understand if he wanted to stop and methodically plan their special day in a more rational and formal manner. Simon was quiet as he kissed her on her forehead.

"I want to do it, Lili. It appears that time is of the essence. What do you suggest, Jack? I have a feeling that you've thought this thing through in detail. I trust your judgment and intuition." His decision gladdened her heart.

"You and Miss Becker should continue to Montfaucon and pack up your things, the fewer the better. Sergeant Jones has volunteered to pick you up and drive you to the coast in this car. You should leave Montfaucon no later than 4:00 A.M. tomorrow morning."

"What about the automobile and my job at the library?" asked Lili.

"You should disappear without leaving any trace of your destination. Call your superiors and tell them that emergency family matters dictate that you must leave, or something like that."

"I'll come up with something," she replied, satisfied that a workable plan was beginning to develop.

"Is this going to get you in trouble, Jack?" Simon asked. "I appreciate all that you've done on our behalf. The fact that you've already sheltered Lili from potential criminal charges, all in the name of justice, humbles me, my friend."

"Justice would not be served if Miss Becker became involved in the sordid, disgusting finger-pointing that is taking place in Germany and France at this time, Simon. I've been a servant to the principle of justice all my life, and if my actions can strike a blow in the name of real justice it's worth any risk that I may be taking."

"You've proven to be a true friend, Jack. I won't forget your support," Simon replied, holding out his hand.

"It's moments like this that make our military fraternity so special," answered Jack, shaking Simon's hand. "Now, you two have got lots to do, and I know how difficult it will be for you. Sergeant Jones will be picking you up in this car at 4:00 AM at the latest. Good luck and God speed."

Sergeant Jones got back in the Citreon and drove it beside Lili's Ford. Jack opened the door and stepped out from the back seat to help Lili.

"Thank you, Major Burton," said Lili, kissing him on the cheek. "Your daughter is lucky to have a father like you."

Without any further acknowledgment or words Jack got in the front seat of the Citreon and they drove off without a backward glance. Lili asked Simon to drive her car the rest of the way to Montfaucon. She needed to think about what she was going to do about this most important change in her life.

"As soon as we arrive at the cottage I'm going to take the automobile to my farm friends. I've got to pick up Samantha anyway. I'll tell them that I must leave in a hurry to tend to an emergency family situation. They'll understand without asking any questions. I'd like to bequeath my library to the town library custodian. She'll also accept my resignation and whatever reason I give for leaving, without bothersome questioning."

"That sounds reasonable, Lili," said Simon. "It's going to be a long night. What about some of Sam's friends?"

"They'll just have to wonder, that's all," declared Lili. "The more explaining I do the greater the chance of discovery. The town will talk some, but nobody will know for sure why I'm leaving with Samantha. Their speculation is inevitable and should not concern us."

"You're right," answered Simon. "Can you believe that we'll soon be married?"

"Oh, yes, Simon. I'm eager to be your wife. This is not the way I had dreamed or planned, but it will be a day of joy. I'm prepared to physically and emotionally leave France without looking backward."

A white frost had formed on the ground around the small farm cottage where Lili and Sam had felt safe from the outside world. Lili sorted out her wardrobe and packed a minimum of clothing. Her family records, personal papers and photos took up one large suitcase. She ultimately packed everything that she and Samantha needed in four pieces of luggage, leaving an assortment of household utensils and foodstuff for the farm family. Food was still scarce in France.

Sergeant Jones drove into the cottage driveway two minutes before 4:00 AM. He piled the luggage in the trunk and asked Lili to wear a large kerchief over her head, requesting that until they cleared Montfaucon she should refrain from looking out the window. He suggested that Sam stretch out

175

and recline on the seat for as much of the trip as possible. A half-hour later on the road toward the Channel coast, everyone breathed a sigh of relief. So far so good. Lili thought about what they had done and was certain that even if there had been some questioning among the townspeople of Montfaucon, no one could know of their plans to flee France.

Hours later, the smell of the sea filled their nostrils before it came into view. Jones asked Lili and Sam to crouch below the windows while he drove the vehicle down the dock beside the towering Army freighter. He stopped the car beside a deserted gangplank and asked all of them to remain out of view until he told them otherwise. Then he casually walked up the gangplank and disappeared.

"Can I sit up in the seat now, grandmother?" asked Sam, becoming restless.

"No, Honey. Be patient a little longer, and we'll be able to get out of the automobile."

"We've got a big surprise for you, Sam," promised Simon, lying on his side in the front seat.

Sam clung to the large bear Simon had purchased for her. She had slept on the floor most of the way to Le Havre and was now full of questions.

"I know it has been difficult, Samantha," said Lili, caressing her brown hair. "When we get out you'll be surprised. We're going aboard a large ship. When we do that, you take my hand and be a big girl for Grandmother and Uncle Si. That's important, Honey."

"I will, Grandmother," she promised, intuitively aware that their unusual flight from the cottage worried her grandmother.

Five minutes later, Sergeant Jones returned to announce, "They have a stateroom prepared for the three of you. The military police have cleared the dockside."

"I have a feeling that there's more about this situation than we've been told. Is there anything more you can tell me, Sergeant?" asked Simon, looking around at the vacant dock.

"I can't tell you about the specifics, Colonel Hanley. Major Burton wanted every precaution taken to get you three out of the country. I have a feeling that he's gone out on a limb to see that it's done correctly. There are a lot of power plays taking place in France right now, and he did not want you to get involved. That's about all I can tell you, Sir."

"You've done a wonderful job of removing us from a potential nasty entanglement, and we thank you for your loyalty and competence, Sergeant."

"I'm sorry if I've placed you in danger, Sergeant Jones," confessed Lili. "Thank you for everything."

"It has been my pleasure, Miss Becker. I'll help carry your luggage aboard. Major Collins, the ship's quartermaster, is expecting you." He led the way up the gangplank with two of the suitcases. Lili took one of the lightest bags in one hand and grasped Samantha's hand firmly with the other. Simon followed them up the boarding ramp with two more bags.

"They want to lift anchor as soon as possible, so I'll say good-bye to both of you. If you ever get to Warrensburg, New York, look me up. I wish you all the best," said Sergeant Jones setting the suitcases on the ship's deck.

"Thanks, Sergeant, I'll make a point of looking you up. It's a small world. I was assigned to Warrensburg, N.Y. to help construct the Civilian Conservation Corps (CCC) barracks at a demonstration forest run by the College of Forestry at Syracuse."

"It was called Pack Forest," added Sergeant Jones with a ready smile.

"You're right, Jones, Pack Forest was the place. I stayed there for several days. What a beautiful facility it is."

"I'm being mustered out of the Army on July 1st. I worked at Pack Forest before the war. Just thinking about it makes me homesick."

"I know what you mean. Enjoy your return to civilian life, Jones. The Army and the Nation are losing a faithful and dedicated servant. I wish you all the best."

"Thank you, Colonel."

Lili wrapped her arms around the young Sergeant and embraced him. "You've helped to give me a chance for a new life in your wonderful country. I thank you for being so kind. Your mother must be proud of you."

Sergeant Jones blushed at the compliment and smiled as he kneeled down to Samantha. "Good luck, Samantha. Take good care of your grandmother and your Uncle Si."

"I will," answered Sam, watching the proud soldier walk down the gangplank.

"Good-bye, Sergeant Jones," Simon and Lili spoke in unison.

"Bon voyage." The ramp was removed as soon as Sergeant Jones stepped off at the dockside.

"I've been instructed by the Quartermaster to escort you to your staterooms," announced a ship officer, taking two of the suitcases, directing them to a suite of three rooms on the first deck level. "Normally these rooms are reserved for the Quartermaster. Major Collins relinquished them for your use as soon as he learned that you would be making the trip to New York with us. He's busy on the bridge and will join you shortly."

"Thank you," said Simon, pleased at their accommodations.

"I see the Quartermaster coming down from the bridge," the first officer answered, leaving the room.

"Welcome aboard, Colonel Hanley," greeted a short heavy-set Army officer from the doorway. "I'm Major Collins, the ship's Quartermaster."

"Thank you, Major," answered Simon, shaking his hand. "May I present my fiancée, Miss Lili Becker, and her granddaughter, Samantha."

"It's a pleasure having you on board for the crossing. We've been expecting the three of you and are now getting underway." He had a dark complexion with a large nose and dark eyes. He was a gregarious man with a fine sense of humor who seldom took himself seriously, a powerful officer who wore his authority with grace. Simon instantly liked him. "We rarely carry troops because there aren't enough bunks for them. Our specialty is heavy equipment, and we're returning to the states with a full load of trucks, tractors, and tanks."

"I'm surprised to see an Army officer commanding a ship," confessed Lili.

"Actually, Miss Becker, the Army has more freighters and tankers than the Navy. I came into the Army through the Merchant Marine Academy. In the Army I'm called a Quartermaster. If I wore civilian clothes I'd be called the ship's Master. In the Navy and Coast Guard I'd be the ship's Captain. Different names but the same authority. This is our

VIP suite. I use a small room off the main bridge where I can run the ship easier."

"We thank you for your consideration, Major. My friend, Major Jack Burton has informed us that you will be able to marry Lili and me. Is that correct?" asked Simon. Lili squeezed his hand and smiled at him.

"Oh, yes, Colonel, I can marry you right now, but I would prefer to cross over the twelve mile International boundary before I do. It will eliminate any possible question about the validity of the marriage vows and my authority to execute them. Some countries of the world control absolute powers within their territorial waters. Be patient for a while, and my authority will be undeniable. Now that I've had a chance to meet both of you, it will be a pleasure to join you in holy matrimony. I've done quite a few in my twenty years as a Quartermaster."

"How long will that be?" asked Lili.

"It'll take a half hour to clear the harbor and an hour to cross into International waters. If you'll excuse me for a while, I want to assist my first officer in taking the ship through the harbor into open waters. I'll be back in an hour or so with papers for you to sign before we conduct the ceremony. Please make yourselves comfortable. The ship's bridge and upper decks are available for your use. The lower decks are off limits."

"Understood, Major," answered Simon.

The ship's loud steam whistle announced that it was leaving the dockside. It startled Sam and Lili as they checked the two bedrooms. Once the Quartermaster left the suite, Lili wrapped her arms around Simon's neck.

"Can you forgive me for being the cause of all this sneaking around business? This isn't the way I wanted to get married. Are you sure you don't have second thoughts? It's still not too late to change your mind."

"Now, why would I want to do that?" he asked, kissing the top of her head. "I love you more now than ever before. You had the courage to do what any caring mother would do for her son. Don't forget, it was also an act of self-defense. I'm going to be proud to be your husband. Believe me, if I had second thoughts I would not be here. We have a whole week ahead of us on this slow lumbering ship. What a great place for a honeymoon. It's perfect."

That afternoon, Major Collins, wearing his dress uniform, came to the suite to marry them. It was a simple and brief exchange of vows that fascinated Sam with its seriousness and solemnity. She held the two rings that Lili and Simon placed on each other's fingers. Major Collins obviously enjoyed the role he played in uniting the couple. He kissed the bride and shook Simon's hand with conviction.

"Congratulations, Simon and Lili Hanley. This may not have been a grandiose setting for such important vows, but the commitment you share in your hearts is a sacred pledge to face the future together as a team. You have graced this ship, and I thank you for letting me preside at your ceremony. It's the one authority I enjoy exercising the most. Refreshments are available in the officer's wardroom down the deck next door to your suite. Meals are served at six in the morning, noontime and six o'clock in the evening. Snacks and sandwiches are always available," announced the Quartermaster, leaving them alone in the suite.

"Do you feel any different, Mrs. Hanley?" asked Simon, taking her into his arms.

"Yes, I feel blessed, my husband," she answered, holding back tears of happiness.

"Don't cry, Grandmother," pleaded Sam, seeing the tears.

"Honey, I'm crying because I'm happy. So much has happened to us since I met your Uncle Si at your grandfather's grave. I'll work hard at being a good wife."

"Just be yourself and always love me," requested Simon.

At the evening meal in the officer's wardroom, they enjoyed a celebration hosted by the ship's officers. They had decorated the room with crepe paper streamers and had the cook bake a chocolate cake for the occasion. Major Collins mentioned that he was temporarily suspending the long-standing custom aboard American vessels regarding alcoholic beverages. He produced a bottle of vintage champagne and poured eight glasses for those present.

"As Quartermaster of this ship it has been my privilege to marry Colonel Hanley and his lovely new bride, Lili. May their days be filled with clear sailing and smooth waters. I also toast little Samantha, who brightens our table. May this ocean voyage be the beginning of a full and rewarding life as an American citizen."

Later that evening, after Sam had fallen asleep in her room, Lili and Simon took a walk on the deck. It was a beautiful night at sea. The English Channel was calm and the heavily laden freighter sliced its way through the water with a gentle slow-motioned rocking movement. A quarter moon partially hidden by thin wisps of cirrus fair-weather clouds reflected against the gentle waves. Vast dark voids between the clouds were filled with stars that brightened the heavens, highlighting the immensity of the universe and the relative insignificance of the small ship as it sailed across the dark waters of the Atlantic.

They stopped at the bow of the ship. Simon stood behind Lili, encompassing her with his strong arms. They watched a shooting star blaze its fiery arc from horizon to horizon.

"It looks as if the heavens are celebrating our marriage," said Simon, kissing the top of her head.

"The night is beautiful," replied Lili, cherishing the warmth of his embrace. "Ever since Sam and I left you and returned to France I've lived in a constant state of anxiety, mostly as a result of my actions. I was so afraid that I had lost you and Sam and that I would be put away in prison... I can't erase it from my mind. A part of me regrets what I did because I gambled with my future and came close to losing the things that mean the most to me. Samuel's death and the death of our son left me alone and afraid. Everyone that I loved in the world was gone, and I've been frightened and unsure about my place in this mixed up world until you came into my life, Simon."

"You're my wife now, and that makes you an American citizen," assured Simon. "The deck of this ship is the same as being on the mainland. You're safe now."

"I understand that," Lili sighed. "Your friend Major Burton has helped to make it all possible. I'm indebted to the friendship you two share and the honorable sense of justice that motivates him. I have no regrets in leaving France, except..."

"Except what, Lili?"

"There's a part of me that feels as if I had abandoned Samuel and our son. They're alone now, and there's no one left to remember them except you and me."

"My dearest wife, I was planning to visit your son's grave and pay tribute to his memory with you. A visit to his grave is out of the question right now, but in our hearts we can be with him and Robyne. I'm sure that they look upon your actions with approval and admiration for the courage that you showed in confronting Gabineau."

"A day never goes by that I don't think of them," Lili replied. "They are always in my prayers. I don't know what I would have done if you had not accepted Sam the way you have. This voyage is lifting me out of darkness to a new world of light and hope."

"I love her because she's a precious child who has touched my heart and given a new meaning to my life. The fact that she is a product of the twin brother I loved, and the one I now call my wife makes her even more of a blessing. I will always be there for her." Simon embraced her tightly and continued: "Twenty-seven years ago Samuel's bodily remains were buried at Montfaucon. Your loyalty to his memory has made him proud, and in that dimension where my brother dwells I believe that he looks upon our marriage with approval, for he is with us in our hearts. I feel his presence here with us now at the bow of this ship. I've always known when he was near me. Over the years it has happened often, especially when my life was falling apart or when I've been frightened in combat, which was often."

"Could we come back to Montfaucon sometime in the future, Simon?"

"Of course, Lili. I honestly believe that Samuel was the driving force behind my coming to France in the first place. He saw that you and Sam and I needed each other, and he guided me to you. I really believe that with all of my heart."

"Yes, I believe that, too," agreed Lili.

"We leave France without regrets, and look to the future," said Simon. "There's still one thing that I must do. I owe Lee Rogers, the nurse that helped you and Sam at the medical center, an explanation. I promised to let her know when I've made up my mind."

"The nurse in Paris," recalled Lili. "Yes, you owe her the truth. It was quite obvious that she loved you, Simon."

"Yes, I'll be proud to tell her about us. I think she saw it coming the last time we met."

That evening, Simon wrote a note to Lee so that he could post it in the ship's mail pouch which was picked up several times by escorting destroyers on the passage across the Atlantic.

Dear Lee,

A short note to let you know that Lili and I have just become married. I hope that you can wish us the best. Little Samantha was miraculously cured of her heart problem by the good doctors at Boston Children's Hospital. I look forward to being her guardian and watching her grow to adulthood.

I promised to let you know what my choice was. I'm a little late, but I wanted you to hear it from me. Your friendship has been special, and I hope that never changes. You deserve the very best, dear friend. I am sorry for any heartache I may have caused you and would erase it if I could.

Lili joins me in thanking you for your friendship and sincerity. Somewhere there's a special person for you that will appreciate the fine qualities that define you as a person. May God take your hand and lead you down the road to fulfillment.

All the best,
Simon and Lili Hanley

Chapter Twenty

On the second day of their voyage, Simon and Sam were walking around the deck from one end of the ship to the other. They had already developed their "sea legs" and were accustomed to the gentle rocking motion of the large vessel. They had just passed an open door leading to the crew's quarters below decks when a small dog darted out of the door in front of Sam, almost tripping her. A sailor followed, chasing the dog.

"Jeb, come here!" he hollered as the dog sped past Sam. "Excuse me, little girl, but I've got to catch the pup before he slips overboard."

Simon placed a steadying hand around Sam's shoulders as they watched the puppy try to climb a set of stairs to the bridge. He successfully climbed two of the steps and was having trouble negotiating the third step when the sailor picked him up. Sam laughed, watching the puppy.

"He's an independent little tyke," smiled the broad shouldered sailor, kneeling down in front of Sam. "His name is Jeb. We named him after the English sailor that found him in a bombed out building at the port of Cherbourg. He's very friendly and sure does like to eat."

Sam was excited. The energetic puppy licked at her hands and wagged his tail back and forth as she patted him. "May I pick him up?" asked Sam.

"Sure, just hold on to his collar. I let go of it for just a second, and he was out the door," said the burly sailor, standing up to address Simon. "It's not very often that we have passengers on the ship. The North Atlantic is not too bad in the spring, but the winter months can be a harsh experience. I hope you enjoy the passage."

"Thank you," answered Simon, pleased to see the way Sam took to the puppy. "Children and puppies seem to be a natural combination."

"That's the truth, Sir. I'm still on watch duty, so I've got to run, little girl..."

"My name is Samantha," she informed the sailor, handing over the small puppy.

"My name is Seaman Peterson. I'm glad to meet you, Samantha, and you too, Colonel Hanley."

"We're enjoying the ride, Peterson. The last time I took a boat trip was for Okinawa, and that was not a pleasure trip."

"I can appreciate that, Sir. Jeb could use more exercise. Would you like to take him around the deck with you I've got a leash in my pocket. Just be firm with him, and you'll have no trouble."

"Can we, Uncle Si?" she asked with pleading eyes.

"Of course, Sam," approved Simon. "It'll be fun. Maybe we can take him to your grandmother and show him off."

"That would be great," said Peterson. "When you're finished, you can find me in the machine shop just behind the bridge on the second deck. If you have any trouble finding me just ask for machinist mate Peterson."

"Thank you, Peterson. I believe your puppy has made a conquest."

"You're right, Sir. Well, I must be off. Thanks for exercising Jeb."

Simon showed Sam how to place her hand through the ring at the end of the leash and grasp the leash so that the puppy could not pull it out of her hand.

"He's a cute little pup. We'll take him around the deck one time. On our second trip around on the other side of the ship we'll let grandmother see him."

"Okay, Uncle Si."

"Have you ever had a puppy?"

"No, Grandmother could not afford to feed one."

"Well, when we get to Wilson River, we'll see what can be done."

"Could I have a puppy all my own then?" asked Sam with wide eyes.

"Sure, but you'll have to clear it with your grandmother first. I have a feeling that she'll like that too."

Sam pulled Jeb close to her. They ran up and down the deck together, happily laughing at the cute antics of the uncoordinated puppy. Simon was glad to see her play the way she did. He took a natural pride in being responsible for her welfare. Whatever made her happy made him happy also. Simon saw a lot of his brother Samuel in her facial expressions as he watched her run and play. When they approached their cabin door Simon placed Sam directly in front of the opening and knocked.

"Come in, the door is unlocked," said Lili from inside the suite.

Simon motioned for Sam to be quiet and knocked again. A second later Lili opened the door, and Jeb bolted through it, dragging Sam with him.

"What's this...?" exclaimed Lili unexpectedly. Jeb checked out a couple of corners of the room and started jumping up against Lili, a soft bundle of excited energy.

"This is Jeb, Grandmother," announced Sam. "One of the men let me walk him for exercise."

"He's a cute little mutt, isn't he?" Lili knelt down to pick up Jeb. She saw the contented look on Simon's face.

"Maybe when we get settled in Wilson River, we can locate a puppy for Sam," he suggested.

"That would be nice. I always had a dog growing up and I've missed not having one."

"Then it's settled. We'll find a puppy, and it'll be Sam's responsibility to care for it."

"Oh yes, I will, I promise."

The trip across the Atlantic was a wonderful time of discovery for Simon and Lili. They became more familiar with each other's likes and dislikes. Traditions and routines were established that became a regular part of their daily lives. Even Sam, at her young age, could tell that when Simon and Lili were together they became something that was greater than the sum of their individual selves. Anything was possible as long as they had each other. Their strengths flowed to each other creating a world where dreams can come true and worries of the past were soon forgotten. Their first boat trip had created a legacy of trust and happiness that became one of their most treasured memories in the years ahead.

The morning they landed in Boston Harbor was a partially cloudy day, but their enthusiasm of being back in the United States of America dispelled the gray, damp weather. The officers and crew of the Army transport went beyond the call of duty to make the trip across the North Atlantic a pleasant one. Sam had won everybody's heart. The crew had adopted her as completely as they had Jeb. She walked the lengths of the transport with confidence, recognizing many of the crew and calling them by their names. Seaman Peterson was especially saddened to see her leave. Their luggage was placed on deck near the gangplank, and a call was placed for a taxicab as soon as the ship was secured to the pier.

"There's something special about tying up at an American port," claimed Quartermaster Collins, joining them on the main deck. "No matter how many times I've done it, I still get a catch in my throat. I can imagine what this must mean to the three of you. This old ship has been graced by your presence, Mrs. Hanley. Little Sam has been a real trooper, and we'll miss her smiling face. I say good-bye and wish you well. It has been a pleasure."

He shook hands with Simon and Lili and kneeled down before Sam and hugged her. "Good-bye, young lady. We'll remember you for a long time. Seaman Peterson has something for you. He speaks for the ship's company."

Peterson and several crewmen gathered around the trio. "The crew and I have decided that if your uncle and grandmother approve, you can have Jeb and take him to Maine with you." Peterson paused, looking for approval from Simon and Lili.

"You have our approval and thanks for your kind offer," said Simon, winking at the Quartermaster. He and Lili had known about it for the past two days.

"With that being the case, we have Jeb all set to travel," exclaimed Peterson, directing the other seamen to bring Jeb on deck. The crew had made up a small case with a handle on top for carrying Jeb around.

"Jeb is comfortable in the case. We had him sleep in it for the past two days so that he'd be used to it." One of the young crewmen held out an Army gas mask bag filled with dog food and a small dish for water. "This bag contains enough food for a few days. It should last you until you get settled in your new home," he said shyly.

"Thank you," cried Sam, hugging Peterson and the other crewmen. "I'll take good care of Jeb."

"Good-bye, young lady. You've reminded us of loved ones we've left at home. Thanks for the memories."

The seamen carried their luggage to a waiting cab. Sam insisted on carrying Jeb down the gangplank with Simon's guiding hand. Each of them experienced some difficulty in walking on solid ground. They were excited as the cab sped them from dockside to the train station.

"Wait until we get on the train," laughed Simon. "It will be an altogether different motion to get used to."

Simon had left their Studebaker at the garage in Newport where he and Lili had rented a vehicle on their first trip to Maine. That had been in the fall when cool days and nights forecast the harsh winters that are normal for northern Maine. The air had been filled with a melancholic tinge of sadness that the death of summer was taking place and the land was preparing for the dormant season of winter.

Now, on their return trip to Maine as a family of three, the land was experiencing a rebirth of life, awakening as it always did each year, anxious to fulfill the promise of fall. The fields were already a lush green, and the trees were forming buds reaching for the sun prepared to explode in full leaf. Apple blossoms had bloomed and were fading away, littering the green earth with their pink and white petals. For everything there is a season. The rhythm of life never changed.

Lili's heart was full of happiness as she watched the passing countryside from the train window. For years she had been dormant, not daring to hope or dream for a better future. Life was filled with problems in need of solution, and she was becoming weary from the struggle. Then Simon appeared at Samuel's grave. She smiled, thinking how he accused her of literally falling into his life. She sat across from him and watched as he, too, looked out the window at the rural landscape. Sam was stretched out in the seat with her head on his lap, sound asleep. Jeb rode silently and contentedly in his box beside Lili.

Simon turned from the window and caught Lili watching him. He smiled at her. She liked that about him; he smiled easily even though he was by nature serious and studious. He was dressed in a pair of green gabardine pants and a light jacket. Even without his uniform he looked like a soldier with his erect posture and authoritative air. He had a presence about him that was difficult to define. He was not showy; as a matter of fact, he was quite self-effacing; yet, a stranger could see the strength of character that was a large part of his makeup. She catalogued those intangible characteristics under the heading of leadership abilities and prayed that he would never have to face the terror of combat again.

"A penny for your thoughts, Mrs. Hanley," he said in a low voice so as to not wake Sam.

"I was just thinking how much I love my husband and how wonderful it is to be traveling to our new home. I'm so excited I feel like shouting to the world and thanking God for the happiness I feel. Home is where the heart is. I never completely understood that old saying until now. What an amazing adventure the three of us are beginning."

"I feel like a kid again," admitted Simon, winking at her. "Some kid with gray hair, huh?"

"It gives you a stable look of maturity, my dear husband."

"I hope you're going to like the changes Ken and I have made to the house."

"I'm sure. It'll be the first time in my life that I can call a house a home. Even as a child growing up in France and Scotland, my parents lived in apartments."

"A new furnace has been installed. We can plan what we want to do with the exterior of the house now that spring is here. I'm really looking forward to planting a garden, even if it only has tomatoes and cucumbers."

"I remember how you like tomato sandwiches," she grinned.

"Wilson River will be a nice place for Sam to grow up in. The house and the small town are parts of her birthrights as a Hanley. I'm going to be proud to show the two of you off to old friends. I have a lawyer working on the paperwork necessary to legally adopt Sam. I'm proud that she's a Hanley, but I never forget that she's also a proud Becker. The bloodlines from you are filled with legacies of courage and the gift of creativity. I'll never let Sam forget that part of her legacy."

Lili tilted her head the way she often did. Her eyes relayed what was in her heart. Words were not necessary. Simon saw and understood.

When they arrived at Newport, Simon had Lili drive the Studebaker home to Wilson River. Sam rode in the back seat with Jeb who licked at her hand through the opening in the wooden slats of his cage.

"This car is a lot smoother and more powerful than the old Ford I had in France," said Lili. "The shift on the wheel is easier to use. I've always liked to drive. Fuel is so expensive in Europe that driving for pleasure was a rare occurrence and never thought of during the war."

"Now, you can take a ride and drive as much as you want, Lili. I'll be using the company truck every day, so this will stay at home for your use. I'm glad you like it. The Studebaker Company is a manufacturer of reliable vehicles. The car has only twenty thousand miles on it, so there are a lot of trouble-free miles left for us." Simon reached across the seat and squeezed her hand. She kept her eye on the road and smiled with him.

"I've been thinking about school for Sam. I'm wondering how we'll handle it with the school officials. We don't have and won't be able to request transcripts from Montfaucon," said Lili.

"I hadn't thought of that," reflected Simon. "I'm sure they can accept her and evaluate her progress in a reasonable period of time even if she has no records. It's not as if she had years of school. You're an American citizen now. Sam will be as soon as we receive the adoption papers. That'll document her citizenship status. Miriam is teaching at the school. We can ask her how to handle it."

"You know Miriam wrote me a couple of letters that made me feel good. She probably surmises by now that we're married. I have a feeling that we can become good friends."

"I don't see why not. She and I are still friends. The past is behind us. When Miriam congratulates people, she means it. She's not a hypocrite or a phony. You two have a lot in common, and I'd be surprised if you did not become close friends."

Lili drove the Studebaker into Wilson River across the bridge at the center of town and slowly turned onto the first left. Her heart was beating wildly. She was coming home!

Simon watched Sam as Lili pulled into the driveway and came to a stop in front of the garage. Sam looked at the white house and then at the barn with the garage between them.

"Is that the river you mentioned, Grandmother?" she asked, pointing towards the water.

"Yes, Honey, that's the river," replied Lili, flushed with excitement.

Simon opened the back door for Sam and Jeb. "You can take a look at the river with Jeb if you want, Sam. He probably will feel like stretching his legs after the long ride in the cage. This is going to be his new home, so you might not need his leash."

Sam ran rapidly to the edge of the river, glad to have a chance to run freely. Jeb kept close to her side without the constraints of the leash. They stepped out onto the small wharf beside the boat house, not daring to go too close to the edge.

"Now, Mrs. Hanley," announced Simon, taking Lili into his arms. He kissed her and held her close. They checked to see that Sam was careful on the wharf. "This is an old American tradition," he said, lifting her off her feet, holding her like a baby. He ran to the front door and carried her across the threshold.

"Welcome home, Mrs. Hanley!"

Chapter Twenty-One

Life in the small town of Wilson River was a rewarding experience for the Hanley family. They became a part of the community of hard working men and women turning their energies to living life to the fullest after the horrors of the war were put behind them. Simon spent five days a week on some portion of the vast acreage of the Great Northern Paper Company north of Wilson River and Moosehead Lake. On weekends he dedicated his time to working around the house; watching Sam grow into a healthy young lady; and savoring the sheer joy he experienced just being with Lili.

Lili was offered a part-time job as the town librarian at the small brick building that housed the town's moderate collection of volumes and historical records. She worked three afternoons a week. It did not take the people long to recognize that they had made a wise choice in selecting her for the position. She also held tutoring classes twice a week at the library for several students at the grade school in need of additional attention. She felt comfortable in the close-knit community.

Those who got to know Lili found her positive and energetic disposition contagious. It generated increased usage of the library. No question was too difficult, for Lili was able to come up with answers. She was responsible for obtaining hundreds of reference volumes from state and inter-library loan programs, believing strongly that the world's books of knowledge were the true basis of any worthwhile library, and that volumes capable of answering many questions should be a part of its basic inventory.

The first visitors to welcome them to the community were Ken and Edith Holmes, their next door neighbors. They showed up on the evening after they noticed the Studebaker parked in the driveway, carrying a staple dish in northern

Maine: baked beans, homemade bread and sliced ham. It was a warm gathering that dispelled any doubts Lili might have harbored about how the small town would receive her.

A few days after their arrival, Miriam also dropped by the house. It was a warm Sunday afternoon in late May. Simon and Lili were expecting her at any time. She pulled her Studebaker coupe in front of the garage, waving to Simon and Sam fishing on the wharf. Simon told Sam who the visitor was.

"I recognize her," said Sam. "She's the fourth grade teacher, Miss Olson."

"Miss Olson," mused Simon, not surprised that Miriam had changed back to her maiden name. "Do you want to go up to the house?"

"If you do," answered Sam, reeling in her line. Lately, every time she and Simon went fishing together off the wharf, she ended up catching the larger fish, and he kidded her about it.

"Are we going to keep quiet about the fish you caught today, or are you going to brag about it to Grandmother and Miss Olson? I have a feeling you have more experience at fishing than you've told me, because the big ones keep coming to you. I'm beginning to feel like an amateur," Simon smiled, collecting their can of worms on the dock. Sam looked up at him with her bright eyes. They had become pals.

Jeb was sitting on the bank waiting for them to step off the wharf. Earlier, on their first day of fishing, Simon had told Sam that the best way to drown-proof the puppy was to drop him in the water beside the wharf, promising her that Jeb's natural instincts would prevent him from drowning. As Simon predicted, Jeb frantically paddled to the shore none the worse for the lesson. However, from that day on, Jeb would not walk out on the wharf with Sam and avoided Simon whenever they were near the water. He preferred staying on firm ground as an observer rather than run the risk of having Simon throw him in the water again.

"I apologize, Jeb," said Simon, reaching down to pat him. Jeb was wary of Simon's gesture and was prepared to run away from him. "I guess I over-estimated you."

"If I carry him onto the wharf he starts shivering all over," added Sam, defending Jeb and scolding Simon.

"Well, at least we know that he can swim. In time he'll forget that I was the bad boy who threw him in the water," laughed Simon. He and Sam were inseparable whenever he was not working.

"Hi, Miriam," Simon greeted her, entering the house through the garage entrance. "I used to think that I was an expert fisherman on the river, but Sam has been making me look bad lately. She caught a nice brook trout today."

"Hello, Simon," said Miriam, sitting at the kitchen table with Lili. "I wanted you two to get settled before I barged in on you. Congratulations. You've turned this old house into a home again. I felt a wonderful energy the minute Lili met me at the door. It shows on all three of you. I think that's a marvelous achievement. So, this is our new third grade student I've been hearing such nice things about."

"Samantha, this is Miss Olson, one of the teachers at the school you attend," introduced Lili.

"I've seen her at school," answered Sam shyly, shaking the hand Miriam offered her. She held the fish in a wicker bag and excused herself to put the fish in the refrigerator and wash her hands.

"It's nice to see you again, Miriam," said Simon, accepting a cup of coffee that Lili placed in front of him. "Thanks, Lili."

"I'm glad to see this place filled with a happy family again," reflected Miriam. "I didn't plan to stop for long. I wanted to congratulate you and welcome you to Wilson River. I've been thinking a lot since that last time when you played the violin at my home, and I want to speak to you about a proposition. Would you be willing to give violin lessons to a few children in town? I have two students in my fourth grade that have expressed an interest in learning to play, and I'm sure there are others willing to pay you for lessons if you agree."

"My, I didn't expect this kind of offer, Miriam," exclaimed Lili, instantly enthused with the idea. She looked at Simon for his reaction.

"You can think it over. It was just a thought," added Miriam.

"I'd really like to do something like that," answered Lili. "I don't want to have too many outside activities that take my time away from..."

194

"Lili," interrupted Simon. "If giving violin lessons to children appeals to you, don't you dare to refuse because of us. Sam and I would be proud to have you do that."

"I can honestly say that lately, I've been thinking that Sam was ready to start with an instrument of her choice," admitted Lili. "Music enriches one's life so much."

"Precisely," Miriam agreed emphatically. "Samantha, would you please go out to my car and bring in the case that is on the passenger seat?"

"Yes, Miss Olson," answered Sam on her way out the door. Seconds later, she returned with a violin case and placed it on the table in front of Miriam. Lili recognized it as the violin she had played at Miriam's place.

"I'd like to give this to you and Samantha as a welcome home gift. I can't think of anyone more worthy of a fine instrument than you, Lili. It belongs in the hands of a master. There is no one in our family remotely interested in playing a violin. I want you to have it."

Sam listened closely to what Miriam was saying. When she saw what was inside, she thought it was the most beautiful thing she had ever seen. Lili accepted the instrument from Miriam with caressing hands.

"Thank you so much, Miriam. I've never played a finer instrument. I must confess, I've missed not having a violin these past few years. Thank you..." Lili left the table and embraced Miriam, touched by the sincerity of the gesture.

"A home like this is even better when filled with music," Miriam exclaimed.

"You're very kind and generous," added Simon.

Sam was excited about what had taken place. She was awed by the shiny instrument and gently plucked one of its strings. "Can you play it, Grandmother?"

"Yes," replied Lili, surprised that she should ask such a question. The violin she had owned was left in her Paris apartment when she fled with Samantha to Montfaucon, so Samantha had never seen her grandmother with an instrument in her hand.

Lili removed the bow from the case and plucked each of the strings, checking for proper tune. Then she placed the violin on her shoulder and played a medley of Scottish and

Irish folk songs ending up with *Clair de Lune* and *The White Cliffs of Dover,* a popular song during the war years.

"That's beautiful, Grandmother." Sam was enthralled by the music.

"That instrument is in the proper hands now," announced Miriam, getting up from the table to leave.

"How can I thank you enough for passing on a family heirloom to us? I'd be happy to start violin lessons. The students may be children or adults. That way I can express my appreciation for a wonderful gift. Thank you so much, Miriam."

"You're truly welcome, Lili," answered Miriam.

From that day on, the Hanley home was frequently filled with music. Sam was Lili's first student and became a promising violinist. She had discipline and passion for music, much like her father had when he was a young man her age. Simon often requested her to play for him. She complied with his requests by going through some of her newfound fingering techniques or some new selection that appealed to her.

Lili gave lessons three afternoons a week to interested students with enough serious discipline to play well. She was a demanding instructor and scolded half-hearted attitudes and complacent focus on the music or the instrument. She never charged a fee, but she let the students know, in no uncertain terms, that if they were not serious in their dedication to the music, then they were wasting each other's time. Promising students were rewarded for sincere efforts. Lili's musical contribution to the community was respected and admired by everyone who experienced her dedication and patience. Her graciousness and sincerity touched the rural community.

Sam became one of Wilson River's favorite young ladies. She had poise and confidence and was a model of good manners and civility. She grew into a serious child not easily given to frivolity, but she laughed and joked easily with close friends and family. Simon was devoted to her.

Starting with that first summer in Wilson River, Simon, Lili, and Sam frequently went on hiking expeditions such as when they climbed Mount Katahdin and slept overnight near the summit. The trips created a rich legacy and a lot of memories and photos that Lili maintained in a large scrapbook. A trip to Katahdin was a little more than they wanted to do on a long weekend, so their typical hike was shortened to include Boarstone Mountain. It established a tradition that became an annual affair with the family.

Simon's father and several other family members, all deceased, had built a log cabin on Little Wilson Stream several miles from their home at Wilson River. It was located on the Appalachian Trail, a hiking trail that started in the Smokey Mountains of Georgia and meandered through the Allegheny mountain chain that separated the eastern coastline from the interior of the country. The Trail terminated on the top of Mount Katahdin.

The first planned hiking expedition took place in July right after the black fly population had declined. They planned to spend three days on a portion of the Appalachian Trail that ran through the town. It was a wilderness adventure such as Lili and Sam had never experienced. It brought Simon into the realm of his everyday work world, where he was anxious to share the emotional experience with his family. Sam and Lili had studied the topographical maps of the area as preparation for the trip. It helped them get a "feel" for the area they were hiking, and the extended landscape beyond their vision.

They selected a day when it was warm, and the sky was clear with a few cumulous clouds on the western horizon. A soft westerly breeze swept the sweet smell of balsam fir and spruce across the land. They left the house and walked through the center of town where they picked up the trailhead for the Appalachian Trail. Simon carried the food for the next three days, his own personal things, and a sleeping bag. Lili and Sam carried their sleeping bags and an Army surplus canteen filled with water attached to their belts. All three of them had a supply of candy bars for energy on the trail. They had been conditioning themselves over the past few weeks by taking extended walks along the river for several miles past their home.

Their initial destination was a small isolated log cabin that had been built by Simon's father and other family members at the turn of the century as a place to gather for fishing and hunting outings. The cabin was a three hour hike from Wilson River along the trail leading to Boarstone Mountain, a rugged peak with sheer cliffs on the western and southern aspect. It

197

dominated the surrounding area with its majestic bulk. The cabin was located on Great Northern Paper Company land. The family paid a dollar a year for a one hundred-year lease with the understanding that it would be available to anyone who needed its protection from the elements. Employees of Great Northern used it occasionally.

The cabin's white cedar logs were bleached to a dull gray. It was situated close enough to Little Wilson Stream that a fish line could be thrown out one of the windows facing the water. Protection from prevailing westerly winds out of Canada was provided by a large ridge bordering the stream on the opposite side. Approximately twenty feet square, the cabin contained a single room with a set of triple bunks in the southeast corner. Opposite the bunks was a long built-in table with an assortment of rustic chairs made from small trees. In the opposite corner from the bunks was a small cast iron stove located to the right of the door. Simon and Samuel had purchased a reflector oven when they were young men and had left it in the cabin. Simon pointed to it with pride and boasted how delicious his biscuits were when baked on the stove with the oven. He volunteered to take on the duties of camp cook.

Suspended from the ceiling on thin wire was a large bedroll containing two mattresses and blankets. It was an effective and efficient way to store bedding so that rodents did not get to them. There was another short line holding a large notebook pad above the table. Excess foodstuff was stored in an earth cellar dug below frost line at the rear of the cabin. It was an ideal place to keep leftover canned goods without danger of scavenging animal intrusion or freezing from the severe winters. Heavy metal boxes contained matches, flour, sugar and rice in a moisture-free condition for years without danger of rodent damage.

They all agreed that their first day's goal would be to hike to the cabin and spend the rest of the day cleaning and airing it out. Sam put a fish line into the stream and caught two trout, one right after another. The fresh trout supplemented their supper of baked beans and biscuits. The well-battered wood box beside the stove was filled with well-seasoned firewood and kindling wood. It was a custom in the North Woods that a user replenished the wood that was used. Rarely was that custom ever broken.

Sam looked the cabin over closely and asked if she could sleep in the top bunk. From that location she could see the stream bubbling past, filling the cabin with its music. Simon told Lili and Sam that the rocks at the bottom of the stream provide the music. Remove the rocks and the water flows silently by. One of the first things Simon did was to set up and light two lamps he took from the outside earth cellar. The two windows did not provide enough light even on a sunny day. The interior of the camp was dim and uninviting without the illumination of the lamps.

The three of them spent their first evening reviewing entries in the large notebook Simon untied from the string above the table. It had notes written by Samuel and himself on an annual basis. The last entry for Simon and Samuel was Sunday, April 27, 1917. The next day they had left Wilson River for the war in Europe. Over the years, strangers and friends left thank you notes and comments on the successes or failures of their hunting and fishing expeditions at the camp. Simon treasured the small handwritten notes left by his mother, and the bold printing Samuel always used. One entry brought tears to Lili's eyes.

This is my first trip to the cabin without the twins. Sitting here at the table in the middle of the night, I feel that Samuel and Simon are with me. I wanted to take this trip by myself in memory of both of you, especially for Samuel who's never coming home. I'm having a hard time accepting that. I don't know how to go on without you, Samuel. I see your smiling face everywhere, in the top bunk, here at the table where you and Simon played cribbage for hours and outside where you chopped and split wood so often. I know that thousands of mothers are feeling the same pain with the loss of their sons, but in all honesty, it doesn't help much. Earlier this evening as I was resting on the bottom bunk in the darkness of the cabin, a beam of light came through the window by the table. It was so powerful that I got out of bed to see it clearer. A soft breeze touched my face, and I heard Samuel's voice saying in a hushed tone: 'I will always be with you', and the light disappeared. I cried for a long, long time. May God keep you safe Simon, for I don't know what I would do if I lost you, too. May our Lord take Samuel home to the light. Wait for me Son, for I'll follow you one day.

Maureen Hanley,
June 18, 1919

"I wish that I had tried to contact your mother. She must have been a very special lady," said Lili, drying her eyes. "You and Samuel were blessed. You grew up with people who lived close to Nature. My childhood memories pertain to life within the towns and cities. I feel a sense of sadness in reviewing these entries. It was a time that we can never recapture, and the values that sustained generations in that period of our history are lost, perhaps forever."

"I've often thought the same thing, Lili," replied Simon, shuffling a deck of cards. "Every time I've come to this camp with someone, we've played cribbage."

"I used to play with my father; he enjoyed it a lot."

"Could I challenge you to a game?" Simon smiled, placing a worn cribbage board in front of her. Pegs for the board were wooden match stems with the combustible portion broken off.

"I feel lucky and accept your challenge," Lili replied.

Sam had climbed into the top bunk and snuggled into her sleeping bag, tired from the long walk. The rhythmic flow of the brook and the gentle banter between Simon and her grandmother was relaxing. She fell asleep almost instantly.

Later in the evening, while Simon and Sam were sound asleep, Lili listened to the soft whir of the wind brushing through the tall spruce trees surrounding the wilderness cabin. It evoked a deep feeling of contentment in her heart. Once again, she thanked God for the gift of her beloved husband. He was a tower of strength. Nothing was impossible to him. His caring and gentle ways made her feel special. He had spun a web of love and security around her and Sam. Lili had never experienced such complete joy. The darkness of life in France was easily forgotten.

The next day, they left sleeping bags and most of their food at the log cabin and started on a hike to the top of Boarstone Mountain. Simon told them that they had time to make it to the top where they could eat their lunch in the majesty of one of the most spectacular panoramas he had ever witnessed. They arrived at the solid granite summit, hungry and ready for a rest. The view was beautiful beyond description. A brisk breeze swept the top, making it cool enough that jackets felt good.

Boarstone Mountain held three small ponds in its granite structure near the summit. Their crystal blue waters were cool and potable. The best view was to the east where Onawa Lake shimmered below in the bright rays of the sun. For miles around in every direction green spruce and fir forests blanketed the landscape, broken only by rivers and lakes scattered throughout the region. Mount Katahdin loomed in all of its magnificence in the northeast. Simon told them that it's the first place in the continental United States that the sun's rays touch every morning.

Simon told them a story about one of the times he and Samuel and several classmates climbed Boarstone when they were seniors in high school. There were six of them, and they had planned to spend the night at the summit or slightly below it to avoid the brisk winds. They had carefully planned the amount of food they would need and divided it evenly among the six hikers.

One of the classmates was a tall, rugged young Swede called Brownie. He was proud of his physical prowess and frequently boasted that he could lift more than any man in the group. Unknown to Brownie, Simon and the others had placed three rocks weighing about twenty pounds in his pack and quietly watched how he handled it.

The first stretch from Wilson River to the log cabin was uneventful, but there was a noticeable lack of boastfulness from Brownie. He was perspiring more than the rest of the gang and remained uncharacteristically quiet. The last half of the trip up the side of Boarstone was steep and exhausting to any climber regardless of physical conditioning. Frequent breaks were taken, and each time, Brownie was the first to sit down at the side of the trail. He was sweating profusely and tried to make light of it to the delight of the others. Their

201

happy-go-lucky cousin, Ken, commented in precise terms that they were all in pretty good shape to be handling the climb so well. Brownie half-heartily agreed, but did not brag about who was going to be the first to step on the survey bench marker at the summit.

Ken made it to the top first and pronounced himself the winner. The breeze at the top was refreshing to their perspiring young bodies. Brownie sat on a rock overlooking Mount Katahdin. He was starved and started to rummage through his pack for something to eat. That was when he discovered the rocks, and let out a howling roar in protest that echoed across the mountain range. He vowed to have revenge and started laughing at the trick played upon him by his friends. They all enjoyed a good laugh at Brownie's expense even though he vowed to get even...

They never climbed the mountain together again. Brownie was killed in action four years later. There was never a time when Simon climbed the mountain that he did not think of those days and felt sadness that so many good men had been lost to the world forever.

Chapter Twenty-Two

Four Years Later, June 25, 1950

Simon was in the shower getting ready for work when Ken pounded on the kitchen door and entered the house with a concerned look on his face.

"Hello, Lili, is Simon up yet?" he exclaimed excitedly. Lili knew that something unusual had happened. Ken always smiled. This morning he was seriously upset.

"What is it, Ken? Simon is in the shower."

"I just heard on the radio that Communist North Korea has invaded South Korea. President Truman has authorized General MacArthur to resist the invasion. I'm not sure what it means. Simon will be able to judge that..."

"I heard you, Ken," replied Simon, drying his head with a towel. He had a grave look on his face.

"Does this mean what I think it does, Simon?" demanded Lili, grasping his arm. She was getting a sick sinking feeling that her world was about to be threatened.

"It could, Lili. I'm not sure what's up. Turn the radio on. Don't worry. It'll take a lot before the nation has to call up its reserves."

That morning marked a drastic change in the lives of the Hanley family. Within hours, the Korean situation deteriorated. Simon had no doubts that he would be called. An anxious week passed. Simon was recalled to active duty with orders to report to Fort Devens in Massachusetts for extended duty. The unexpected had happened.

Lili's world tumbled around her. Her beloved husband was once again going to face the guns of war. It hurt so much, she could not cry. The news numbed and shocked her, creating an enormous emptiness that she tried to hide for Simon's sake. He said goodbye to her and Sam at the Dow Air

Force Base in Bangor. The picture of him standing tall and straight in his uniform, waving from the top of the boarding transom was locked in her heart. Sam was crying as she watched him salute and disappear inside the large military aircraft. She reached up to grasp her grandmother's hand for comfort, but Lili was powerless to control her own fears. They stood like granite statues, oblivious to the rest of the world, watching the plane lift off and disappear into the blue skies, leaving them alone.

"Promise me that you'll look after Grandmother," Simon had whispered softly in Sam's ear. "You and your grandmother are the two most precious beings in the world to me, and it's my duty as a soldier to protect the way of life that we cherish and love. I'll be back to go fishing with you soon, you'll see. I love you and your grandmother more than life itself, my dear child. If something should happen to me, remember the good times we had together. You're growing into a lovely young lady, and I'm so proud of you. Please promise me that you'll look after your grandmother."

"I promise, Uncle Si," Sam had answered. She was now eleven years old, not yet an adult, but more than a child. She knew and understood that combat was dangerous, and fear filled her heart. Tears flowed like two rivers down her cheeks. "I love you with all my heart, Uncle Si."

Simon embraced her for a long time and then turned to Lili. She was frightened and felt weak. He looked at her glazed eyes and wanted to scream that war had taken enough from him, but he remained calm, holding her in his arms. He wanted to be strong for them. She was fighting the reality that once again she was going to be left alone. A future without him was so frightening she could not imagine it. She started shaking all over, a little unsure if she could stand on her own. He sensed her grief and held her close.

"Have courage, Lili. I'll be back before long, and we'll pick up from there. Sam and I need you now more than ever. You're the strong one of the family, my dearest wife. I love you. My life started the day you fell into my arms. I'm so proud of you."

"Don't worry about us, my brave soldier husband. Do your duty the way you've always done, and when it's finished come back to our arms again. I don't believe that any soldier ever went off to war with as much love as Sam and I send with you. I promise to write often. I'll understand that you have important things to do. When you can write you know how much the letters will mean to us. Now go, Simon, before I fall apart completely, and I don't want you to see that take place. I love you, my darling."

"I love you, too, my Lili of the Valley," he whispered and walked away. He didn't look back until he climbed to the top of the boarding stairs.

Lili could not sleep that night. She thought of Simon and the frightening things he would have to face. She was also apprehensive about what was taking place within her own body!

***

War came to Korea with a vengeance. The South Korean Army was unprepared for the massive assault and turned to the United States for military assistance through the United Nations. America was as unprepared as South Korea, but decisions were made to rush all available assistance to the beleaguered peninsula and rectify their readiness status. Calling up the Reserves was one of them. Simon flew directly from Fort Devens to Tokyo to attend a conference at the Far East Command Headquarters where discussions were underway with allied commanders.

He was assigned to a regiment enroute to the Pusan perimeter, a last-ditch defensive position. The regiment was ordered to a temporary staging area adjacent to Pusan Harbor where Simon met up with them. Many of the men were World War II veterans. They would become a nucleus around which squads, platoons and companies could be built. Their equipment was fresh out of stockpiles from the last war. The regiment started to take shape the day Simon took command. The average rifleman did not like the strict discipline their new Colonel Hanley demanded of them. However, they were reassured that he was a combat veteran with common sense and should know what he was doing.

General MacArthur was planning his brilliant amphibious assault on Inchon, a port village on the western side of the peninsula near Seoul, the capital city. In conjunction with the assault from the sea, portions of the United Nations command tied up within the Pusan perimeter were ordered to break out

205

of the perimeter and drive northward. The breakout became the hammer that drove the enemy forces against the anvil of American forces capturing the city of Seoul.

Simon's regiment was the main hammer in the United Nation's arsenal. Previous to the planned attack he had scoured every depot and salvage yard in Japan for additional half-tracks for his force. He correctly predicted that his regiment would become the tip of the spear in the drive to the north. That meant he had to have more firepower than a conventional infantry regiment, and that firepower had to be mobile and faster than a tank regiment. Half-tracks with a quad mount of fifty-caliber machine guns were perfect for the job. If necessary, they could also give the force excellent anti-aircraft defense. He took one of the White half-tracks and equipped it with powerful radios for use as a mobile command post. The vehicle bristled with antennas. He preferred to be up front, pulling the regiment, than at the rear pushing it.

His orders were to drive north at all speed, bypassing enemy strongholds for mop-up units close to his rear. Simon felt comfortable with his mission and the men in his command. He was the right man for the job and led the way north towards Seoul in his command half-track, the third vehicle from the point. They broke out of the perimeter on the heels of a punishing artillery barrage.

The spectacular race to the north along a single road front came to be known in the press as Task Force Hanley. Simon rode his command vehicle controlling every aspect of his force. When necessary he massed his fire power to clear heavy roadblocks, and quickly pulled the column together after it was cleared. It was a virtuoso performance that drew a lot of press coverage. Lili and Sam proudly read about his exploits in the papers and were worried sick about the potential for disaster. Yet, they would not have expected anything less than his best. They knew their man and held their heads high, praying for his safety and quick return home.

After two weeks of heavy fighting, Task Force Hanley had smashed away all opposition before them. When heavy resistance was detected, the column halted and sent out flanking forces on each side, which either eliminated the threat or established a new route of advance. Simon was proud of the men's performance. They had written a new chapter in military history and dealt a devastating blow to the opposing North Korean forces. They had split the enemy command in half, facilitating their piecemeal destruction. The Task Force made contact with the Seventh Marine Regiment in the outskirts of Seoul, where he received orders to hold in place in a blocking stance along beside Marine lines. It was a welcome order. The force was exhausted and needed replenishment of food, medical supplies, and ammunition. Simon ordered every third man to sleep and instituted five-hour watch intervals so that the men could catch up on the rest they had been deprived of. Simon turned the command over to his executive officer and curled up in the rear of his mobile command post and fell asleep.

***

While Simon was conducting his famous march to Seoul, Lili wrote to him every day, keeping him up-to-date on daily events. In September, Sam had started in the sixth grade, which was now being taught by Miriam. News from home was welcome by Simon on the other side of the world, but it did not tell the complete story of what was happening to his beloved Lili. She did not tell him, and she forbade Miriam and everyone else that knew her from doing so. She did not want to detract Simon from the important job he was doing. She knew that the mission and his men required every bit of energy and strength he could muster, and she adamantly refused to needlessly alarm her husband.

Lili was in her early fifties and had started developing periods of extreme fatigue accompanied by frequent coughing spells and shortness of breath. She quite naturally passed them off as part of menopause, something every woman her age goes through. At first, she was not alarmed by the symptoms. During the year before Simon left for Korea, she had traces of the same symptoms and treated herself with large doses of aspirin, which seemed to help. She would not have thought any more of it until that one morning a few days after Simon had left for Korea. She was seized by a heavy coughing spell that brought up some sputum filled with blood.

She became alarmed and drove to Greenville to see a doctor at the hospital. He thoroughly examined her and had x-rays taken which confirmed his initial diagnosis, she had tuberculosis. She looked up at him in disbelief, held her breath at the dreaded pronouncement and fainted. The doctor and a nurse picked her up and placed her on a bed in a vacant room at the hospital. Then he called the Wilson River Elementary School and told the principal that Lili was being kept at the hospital overnight, and that someone should notify Sam. The Principal gave the message to Miriam in a private conversation in the corridor of the school. Miriam was sober and reflective when she told Sam that her grandmother was in the hospital at Greenville, and they could go to see her after school hours.

Sam was quiet and worried, uncertain of what to think. Concern for her grandmother was an inherent part of her life. She had promised Uncle Si to take care of her, and she took that promise seriously. Sam was no longer a child. Her calm demeanor and mature perceptiveness was a large part of her disposition. She had seen her grandmother's fatigue and malaise slowly develop, and had some reservations about the cause of her discomfort, privately worrying that they were symptoms of a more severe malady than she was being told.

No one knew Lili any better than Simon, and he was quick to believe that her chronic fatigue and hard breathing were menopause-related. A part of him grasped and clung to the simple explanation, emotionally incapable of thinking or accepting anything different than what Lili had told him. Sam had seen with a clarity, unique for an eleven-year-old child, that Lili was successful in sending her love away to war, free of worry for her welfare. Her general health deteriorated rapidly after Simon left. Sam had kept her observations to herself. After Miriam told her about her grandmother she went to the girl's restroom and sat on a bench near the door. Tears filled her eyes, and she started to cry, softly at first. The fears she had been suppressing for weeks now came rushing back. She was afraid for her grandmother, afraid for Uncle Si, and even more afraid of the unknown that was confronting her. Her secure world was crumbling, and she felt lost.

Miriam opened the door and looked in on her, directing another student away from the facility so that she and Sam could be alone for a while. Miriam had been a concerned and an admiring spectator, watching Sam progress over the past four years. Quick and alert, she had an inquiring mind and a wonderful sense of responsibility. Courtesy and compassion were a part of her interaction with friends and faculty at the school. Lili and Simon had done a wonderful job of instilling in Sam the values they lived by. It was refreshing to see a child like Sam with manners.

The violin had become an important part of her life. It had given her poise, self-confidence, and a wonderful sense of modesty that comes to those few individuals who have plunged into a field of endeavor and discovered, frequently to their dismay, that the volume of knowledge and skills that they possess is but a tiny fraction of that which is known. Sam had arrived at that point in playing the violin and interpreting the music she loved, and she was humbled by the immensity of what was unknown to her.

Miriam calmly sat down on the bench beside Sam and placed an arm around her. "Go ahead, Samantha, let it all out. You'll feel better afterwards. I'll take you to Greenville as soon as you feel ready to go. Miss Earl can watch over my class if you want to leave early."

Sam took the handkerchief Miriam offered and dried her eyes. "Thank you, Miss Olson. I'm ready to leave now if you can."

"Come, child, we'll go see your grandmother. You're going to have to be brave for her, Samantha."

"I'll try," Sam said, suppressing a mounting hysteria.

The drive to Greenville seemed an eternity for both of them. The fall foliage had just gone past its peak color, but it was still beautiful. They were preoccupied with thoughts of Lili and the immediate future. The tapestry of color surrounding the green waters of Moosehead Lake that presented itself to them as they came over Indian Hill was enough to momentarily calm their anxieties. Then Miriam pulled her Studebaker coupe off to the side of the road so that they could sit quietly a few minutes and let the majesty of the scene inspire and strengthen them. The sun was slowly sinking towards the west, sending off oblique rays that reflected against the sparkling water, giving the lake's surface a brilliance that had depth and substance.

Miriam watched it for a while, and pulled back on the road. "I know that you're anxious to see your grandmother."

Lili was held in a quarantined room so that Miriam and Sam could not sit with her or embrace her. Tuberculosis was very communicable, especially any of the infected sputum that might be on a handkerchief, glass, or eating utensil. Lili lay in the white hospital bed looking small, fragile, and very much alone. Miriam's heart went out to her. They had become close friends. It was evident that Lili was seriously ill. Dark circles showed under her eyes. She had lost that sparkle that had always been a part of her. Now she gave the impression that fighting was just too exhausting. Fear and desperation filled her sad eyes. Lili's appearance haunted Miriam for a long time.

Miriam and Sam waved through the viewing glass. Lili returned their wave with a sad smile and trembling lips. It had been a few days since they had seen each other, and Miriam didn't recall that she looked that bad, but she had noticed that Lili was using more and more facial makeup. Ordinarily she never used anything except a small amount of lipstick. Marion surmised that Lili had been hiding her illness from the ones she loved for quite some time.

Dr. Benjamin Choate escorted Miriam and Sam into his office. He was a small-framed man with thick glasses.

"I want to speak to you. We've kept Mrs. Hanley in isolation because she's ill and needs treatment beyond our facilities here in Greenville," he announced.

Miriam understood his reluctance to discuss Lili's illness to a child and said: "Dr. Choate, this is Samantha Hanley, Lili's granddaughter. Her husband is a soldier in Korea and is in heavy combat as we speak. I'm a friend of the family and Samantha's sixth grade teacher."

"I see, Miss Olson. I'm a believer in telling the patient and their family the truth. Only then can they be prepared to cope with the consequences placed upon us by the diseases we have to fight."

"Is Lili gravely ill?" asked Miriam with tight lips.

"Yes, she is ill. She has tuberculosis and is in need of treatment that only a sanitarium can provide," Dr. Choate replied honestly. "She needs prolonged bed rest in a facility with a lot of sunlight and ventilation. Isolation is a must for the tubercles are highly infectious. She also needs a high protein and calorie diet."

"What is the prognosis, Dr. Choate?" Miriam asked. She thought she already knew the answer, but she wanted to hear it directly from the doctor.

"I refuse to tell you that she will get better, but I've seen miracles take place that defy medical science..."

"I understand," interrupted Miriam. She saw a puzzled look on Sam's face and did not think it necessary to have the grim facts spelled out for her at that time. The heartsick potential of the pronouncement and the ensuing affect on the family devastated Miriam. The grief was going to tear a warm loving family apart. She reached out to embrace Samantha.

Samantha was in tears. She understood. Her worst fears were now a reality. Her first thoughts were of her beloved grandmother lying alone and afraid in the white hospital bed down the hallway. Even at her young and inexperienced age, Sam knew that if anything was to happen to her grandmother, she was afraid that her strong gentle Uncle Si would become a broken man. The gravity of the situation ahead of the family moved Miriam to tears. She felt the tenseness in Sam's lithe body.

"Come, Samantha," said Miriam, looking down into Sam's watery eyes. "Let's go and see your grandmother. Remember, we must be strong for her. For years she has been strong and protective of those whom she loved. Now she needs us to be there for her. No matter how bad we feel, your grandmother is feeling worse, even though she'll try to hide that fact from us."

"I will, Miss Olson, but I'm scared for her. I wish it could be like it was before Uncle Si went away..."

"I know, Sweetheart, I know," consoled Miriam, trying to control her own fears and run-a-way imagination.

A heavy darkness hung over the future. A short time ago it all looked so bright and promising. Miriam was angry with her God and questioned the wisdom of visiting such a dreaded disease upon Lili at this time in the family's life. She clung to the remote possibility that the doctor's diagnosis might be in error, and Lili was going to be all right, but, alas, when she looked into Lili's large beseeching eyes, she knew that the original prognosis was correct.

Miriam and Sam stayed by the window until Lili closed her eyes and fell asleep. The attending nurse told them that

Lili had been given a sedative to assist her breathing and that she would be resting for the remainder of the night. As they were about to leave the hospital, Dr. Choates called for them.

"I'm sorry to bother you again. We're placing Mrs. Hanley in the Tuberculosis Sanitarium at Fairfield, Maine, first thing in the morning. You may visit there with her under much better controlled conditions. Is there any way that her husband can be contacted so that he can get a leave to visit her?"

"I'll see to it that he's notified as soon as possible of her situation, Doctor Choates. When he can be relieved of his command is up to the Army, but I promise to convey your message one way or another," answered Miriam, already thinking of the best way to make demands for Simon's immediate relief. "Thank you, Doctor Choates for your candid opinions. Please tell Lili that I will care for Samantha and that she should not worry about that."

"It'll be my pleasure, Miss Olson. I'm sorry to have to have been the messenger of such bad news. I understand what is ahead for all of you, and my prayers are with you."

"Thank you. Come, Samantha, let's go home."

"Where is Grandmother being taken, Miss Olson?" cried Sam, reluctant to leave the hospital.

"She's going to a place where we can visit as often as you want. They're going to make your grandmother more comfortable and treat her disease with all of the latest advancements in medicine."

"Will she ever get better?" It was a question Sam had been screaming to ask, hoping that it would be yes and fearful that it would be no.

Miriam flinched from the question and searched for a way to answer Sam truthfully without inflicting more pain. "You're a young lady now, my dear, and you've got to be very strong. The honest answer to your question is 'no'. The possibility of her getting better is very remote; yet, Doctor Choates admits that medical science does not have all the answers. We'll pray for your grandmother and try to be brave so that we can accept God's will, no matter which way it turns.

"I'd like for you to move in with me. There's plenty of room for you and Jeb. We can swing around to your house and pick up some clothes and personal things for you. What do you think, Samantha?" questioned Miriam, looking at her withdrawing to the far corner of the seat.

"I don't want to leave the house. I just want Grandmother to be there," Sam cried in anguish. Her most haunting fear was that she was going to be left alone.

"I know, dear child, I'd want that, too, if I were you..."

The ride to Wilson River was filled with raw emotions. Tears flowed freely. They were numbed with shock and wondered how they were ever going to cope with the days ahead of them...

Chapter Twenty-Three

Colonel Simon Hanley had just returned to the regimental Command Post from a routine check of his three battalions. The regiment was positioned northeast of Seoul, a portion of the broad front that was driving the North Koreans toward the thirty-eighth parallel. The frantic charge from Pusan to Seoul had taken its toll on him and his command. For the past few days he never had a chance for the luxury of sleeping on his folding cot under a tarp slung between two half-tracks. It was a welcome relief after several days of catching a few winks sitting in the hard seat of his mobile command half-track while it was negotiating the rough Korean roads. Simon had just stepped out of his Jeep when his executive officer frantically motioned for him to come to the radio center on the half-track that was half-buried in an embankment. Simon took the phone.

"Hello, Colonel Hanley here."

"Colonel, this is General Walker. I haven't had a chance to congratulate you in person over the remarkable performance of your flying wedge formation that linked the Eighth Army with Seoul. Task Force Hanley has made us all proud."

"Thank you, Sir. I had a good regiment, and I'm proud of them, too."

"Colonel, I just received orders to send you back to the states. A helicopter is on its way to your Command Post with a Colonel Kelly on board. You are to turn your command over to Kelly. The helicopter will take you to Wonsan airfield where you're authorized to commandeer a seat on the next flight to Japan."

"What's all of this about, General?" asked Simon, wondering if he had done something wrong.

"I can't tell you, Colonel, because I don't know, but I can tell you that the request for you to be sent home came from the highest authority at Far East Command in Tokyo. Look upon it as a reward for your history-making task force. You've earned a break, Colonel. You're going home, and I wish I was going with you."

"Thank you, Sir. Things are relatively quiet on the front at all three battalions, so this is an ideal time for a command transfer," Simon replied. His mind examined potential reasons behind his removal, and none of them made him feel elated.

"My orderly just passed me a note which says that the genesis for the order came from retired General Grady," informed General Walker. "He's an old friend of mine. The verbal authority I've given you will be confirmed in written orders carried by Colonel Kelly. When you get back to the States, have a steak for me. Good luck, Colonel."

"I'll be glad to, Sir."

Three days later, Simon landed at Dow Air Force Base in Bangor. His cousin Ken was waiting for him behind the security chain fence. Simon did not have a chance to place a call to Lili. Things had been happening so fast there just wasn't time! He was troubled and wondered about his unusual departure from a combat zone. Simon looked everywhere for some sign of Lili and was instantly filled with fear when he saw Ken alone. The sober look on Ken's face was enough to confirm his worst fears... something had happened to his Lili! The ugly thoughts that filled his mind were unthinkable. He ran through the security gate to confront Ken.

"Ken, is it Lili...? Is it Lili...?" he cried out. Simon saw the sorrow on Ken's face, and felt as if he had been physically assaulted.

"Yes, Simon..." Ken wrenched Simon to him in a powerful bear hug. Time stood still. Simon heard the words as if they were being spoken to a stranger. "She had tuberculosis, Simon. She died yesterday..."

"No, no... not my Lili..."

Ken's powerful arms kept Simon from crumbling to the ground. Blood drained from his face... Cries of disbelief and pain found muffled expression as Simon buried his face on Ken's shoulder. As a combat veteran of three wars, Simon had lived with death for a large part of his adult life. It was an integral part of what he did as a soldier. He deeply felt the loss of men in his command. That sorrow was always accompanied by the lasting possibility that decisions he had made were responsible for their deaths. He was constantly reviewing his decision-making process because it was a reflection of his ability to lead men in combat.

But deaths on the battlefield were different. They were not unexpected. It was combatant against combatant, and one had to triumph over the other. Keith's death had tortured Simon for years and the emptiness never went away. Lili's death was different in every way. She had become his life, his reason for living. She gave meaning to his existence and brought joy and peace to his soul. He was not given any warning that disaster of such a magnitude was about to be visited upon him. He was in a trance, partially aware of what was around him, yet oblivious to everything except the message of Lili's death.

Maybe it was just a bad dream, and he would wake up soon and hold her once again the way he did. He was denied the opportunity to say good-bye and to thank Lili for making his life so content and meaningful. Simon desperately needed to thank her for a thousand little things they had shared in that short time they lived as husband and wife. He didn't know if he could go on without her.

Ken was able to direct and partially carry Simon towards the 1949 Nash Statesman that he and Lili had been so excited about when they purchased it a year ago. Simon was in shock. He was having trouble understanding what had happened and how he could come to grips with such a cruel reality. Without that partial emotional shutdown he was experiencing, complete chaos and madness would have resulted. With some difficulty, Ken was able to get him into the passenger seat and close the door.

"I'd give anything if I didn't have to be the one to bring you such bad news, Simon," Ken cried helplessly. He headed the Nash towards Wilson River.

"Why didn't I know about it?" Simon demanded harshly.

"Lili became ill just days after you left for Korea, Simon. Even before that she was having a difficult time trying to hide the fatigue and cough that rapidly became worse," Ken described.

"Why didn't she tell me? I could have gotten a deferment until she got better…"

216

"Simon, I believe in my heart that Lili knew what was ahead for her and kept it to herself for a long time. You know the quiet courage she had. It was typical of her. I believe she did it so that you could answer the recall to duty the way a soldier is expected to do. Nobody knows for sure just why she kept it to herself."

"She should have shared it with me so that it would not have been such a heavy burden for her. The fact that she carried such knowledge alone makes me prouder than ever of her, but it also makes me angry that she did not let me help. It was my right and my duty to be with her..."

"The doctor in Greenville placed her in the tuberculosis Sanitarium at Fairfield. She was very ill, and her condition deteriorated rapidly. The doctor told Miriam that Lili ultimately died from pneumonia. I'm so sorry, Simon." Ken finally broke down and wept too. "It's been such a sad time for everybody that knew her. You should know," continued Ken, "Miriam started burning up the phone lines to Washington when she learned that Lili was being placed in a Sanitarium. She was determined to find someone with authority to have you sent home as soon as possible so that you could be with Lili at the end of her illness. I'm sorry, Simon. That end came sooner than any of us expected. Sam is staying with Miriam."

"Oh my God, poor Sam," Simon screamed. In his grief he had forgotten about her. "How could God do this to such a precious child? Why...?"

"Only He knows, Si. Only He knows..."

"Where's Lili now?" Simon had trouble asking the question.

"She's at the funeral home at Wilson River. It was her wish that she be buried within twenty-four hours after her death according to Jewish tradition. They're waiting for us at the funeral home now. We did not know for sure if you would be on the flight to Bangor. I took a chance on meeting it anyway. The committal service will take place at the lots the two of you picked out on the hillside cemetery at Wilson River."

Simon was quiet for the rest of the trip. His mind was a total blank. It was as if he was drugged and in a state of suspended animation. He was having trouble thinking about the chronology of events preceding Lili's death. His heart turned to thoughts of Sam whose young life had been filled with cruel losses and he knew that he had to be strong for her. Sam's grandmother was the one person in the world that she loved and needed the most. He could not imagine what his precious Sam was going through. She needed him now as much as he needed her. Simon prayed for the strength to be there for Sam as he had promised.

Sam and Miriam met Ken and Simon in the parking lot of the funeral home. It was a tearful reunion. Sam clung desperately to Simon. It had been over four months since he had seen Sam. She had grown taller. She looked more than ever like Lili. He held her effortlessly in his arms, feeling helpless to comfort her. He couldn't even do that for himself, how was he expected to do it for Sam? He had promised to protect her from harm, and now she was facing the most traumatic experience of a lifetime, and he was powerless to prevent it. They wept in each other's arms for several minutes. He could feel the throbbing convulsive cries wrack her young body, angry that his God had allowed such sorrow to be heaped on such an innocent human being.

Miriam stood silently by, sharing their grief. Off to one side of the parking lot the ominous black hearse was waiting to take Lili to the lot she and Simon had selected.

Miriam placed a sympathetic arm around Simon and announced in a low voice filled with emotion, "You and Sam can go in to be alone with Lili. I don't know what to say. She was your wife, and I know how much the two of you meant to each other. I can't imagine the depth of your pain, but I want you to know that Lili became my best friend, and I cherish the memories I have of her. Come inside Simon... this is your time to say good-bye." Miriam walked Sam and Simon to the funeral home entrance and opened the door for them.

An hour later, the modest casket was placed in the black hearse for a final journey to the hillside cemetery. The hearse led a long convoy of people who had been touched by Lili's generosity and unselfishness. Simon was in his own private world of torment, unmindful of things around him. He was still holding Sam in his arms, blinded by tears.

A local Rabbi read several prayers over Lili's casket at the grave. He paused to look at the group of mourners around her. "We are saying good-bye to Lili Hanley, a dear friend. She left us a rich legacy of unselfish loyalty and self-sacrifice. She gave of herself and asked for nothing in return. She deserved an easier life than she had, but she was one of those rare individuals who had the moral courage to make difficult choices and the discipline to accept the consequences attached to the choices.

"We owe her memory the best that is in us, and those who knew the softness and tenderness of her heart would agree that she would want and appreciate that kind of memorial and tribute to her. She was with us here in Maine for such a short time, but she will live on forever in our hearts and memories. Rest in Peace, Lili Hanley, and may God be with you forever more."

It was mid November, and the wind that swept across the open field of stones had a chill that went through the heaviest of clothing. Slowly those who came to say good-bye to Lili paused at the casket to pay their last respects before leaving the cemetery. Simon and Sam stood like granite statues staring at the casket until everyone had left the cemetery. Sam shivered from the cold. Simon looked down at her and saw his twin brother Samuel and his precious Lili in her face. She looked lost and forlorn as she turned to him.

"You aren't going to leave me, are you, Uncle Si?" she asked in a soft tremulous voice.

"No, Sam. I'll never leave you. You're cold, come, it's time for us to go home."

Ken drove Sam and Simon back home, and escorted them into the living room, and left them alone. Miriam had followed them in her coupe. After Ken left, she placed a manila envelope on the living room table next to the couch where Simon was sitting with glazed eyes, staring at the fire in the fireplace which Ken's wife had prepared for them.

"I'm leaving these for you, Simon. I know that words and offers of help are meaningless to you and Sam at this time, but you're not alone. If I can help, please call me. The neighbors and friends have left a lot of food in the kitchen. Both of you should try to eat something if you can. I'll say goodnight to you, Sam. Take care of Uncle Si." Miriam embraced both of them and quietly left.

Later that night, after Simon was assured that Sam was sleeping soundly, he opened the large envelope containing some of her personal toiletry items, an address book and stationary supplies. A letter addressed to Simon fell out on the table. His heart started to pound as he opened the envelope with trembling fingers.

My Dearest Husband,

I'm writing what may be my last letter to you. For several days I have been too weak to hold a pencil. I know that my time is limited, and I want to tell you how much I have loved you, my dear gentle Simon. The few years we've spent together have been the high-water mark of my life.

Forgive me for dashing all of the hopes and dreams we had for the future. I accept God's will, but it's so unfair that we can't share our love a little longer. I was hoping to watch Samantha grow into womanhood. Now, you'll have to do that for me...

I understand how difficult this letter and the previous notices you have received of my demise will be, my love. If I had the power I would change things, but... I know that my time is near.

I will always be with you and Sam in the brightest days and the darkest nights. Think of me when the cool breeze from the river passes your cheek and when the heavens are alive with bright stars of far away planets. Do not mourn my death. Think of me as waiting for you so that we can share eternity together.

I have loved you so very much, my dear Simon. I wish that I could feel your strong arms around me one more time. Remember me, and the things we shared, with a smile and a thankful heart.

I never told you before, but that first time I played "Danny Boy" for you and Miriam was a sad time for me. I had a strong premonition then that our time was going to be limited, and that you would return from a war and find my grave, as the song poignantly foretold. That vision has haunted me for the past few years, and, alas, it was a true prophecy...

My love for you is eternal.

Your loving wife,
Lili

THE END

Other Historical Romance Novels

BY
Clifton LaBree

A Song for Lisa   A Historical Romance

This is the story of a young American woman captured by the Japanese in the Philippines, 1941. Like most prisoners, she was brutalized and sadistically treated with a cruel disregard for human life. Three years later, Lisa and her companions had reached the low point of starvation and abuse .....

Lake of Three Sorrows   A Historical Romance

A warm spiritually uplifting story of courage, commitment, and sacrifice. This is the story of Dale Cooper, a battle-weary American soldier who served in two world wars.

Flickering Flame (Colonial Series Book One)

A historical novel, about the Cullen family who settled in Portsmouth, New Hampshire, and their participation in events prior to the French and Indian War. Freedom and opportunity were on the march, but it extracted a heavy price. Frontier settlers were ruthlessly killed and butchered by rampaging Indians lead by French officers and Jesuit priests who frequently incited them to greater levels of inhumanity...

Raising the Torch (Colonial Series Book Two)

A continuation of the saga from Flickering Flame, Colonial Series book one, of the Cullen family in Colonial Portsmouth. This is a moving story of love and sacrifice when a small colony had the audacity to fight for independence from their motherland...

Non-Fiction Books

By

Clifton LaBree

New Hampshire's General John Stark, Live Free or Die: Death Is Not the Greatest of Evils

Publisher - Fading Shadows Imprint

A fresh look at one of America's staunchest defenders of liberty and freedom. John Stark was a courageous New Hampshire citizen-soldier who fought in both, the French and Indian War, and the Revolutionary War. His pursuit of leadership excellence on the battlefield distinguished him as one of the most successful combat commanders of the war, and one of the least appreciated.

His selflessness, modest life style, and devotion to the cause of freedom are an inspiration that time has not diminished. He remains today the embodiment of the frugal, independent, and cantankerous New Hampshire Yankee.

Gentle Warrior, General Oliver Prince Smith, USMC

Published by - Kent State University Press. Kent, Ohio, 2001

The Story of one of the United States Marine Corps best General Officer. His flawless performance in Korea is a story that needed to be told.

FADING SHADOWS IMPRINT

Fading Shadows Imprint was established to bring to the public books of historical events and portraits of people enduring tragic circumstances of by-gone days. Hopefully, they will generate a deep appreciation and respect for the exceptionalness of the United States of America, and an appreciation for the sacrifice and selflessness of those who valiantly served for liberty and freedom.

The characters are fictional, but the historical events and dates have been seriously researched and are factually presented. Some books feature incidents during the French and Indian Wars as well as the War for Independence.

World Wars I and II are eras rich in stories that beg to be told. I've tried to pay tribute to the collective courage and heroism, often unheralded, that has defined Americans in every engagement. It was a time when the immortality of dreams and aspirations were defended by the blood of young men and women. There is a beautiful monument and cemetery in a small French village where thousands of white crosses and Stars-of-David are set in perfect alignment, honoring thousands of American soldiers who gave their last full measure. A large granite slab bearing mute witness to their sacrifice has the following words chiseled in stone: TIME WILL NOT DIM THE GLORY OF THEIR DEEDS. Another monument reads: VIRTUE AND COURAGE ARE THEIR OWN MONUMENT AND REWARD. Those simple words define the American soldier from the dark days of the Revolutionary War to the present. They are an American treasure, unique in the history of the world.

Every generation has its own signature and characteristics that uniquely define them. The World War II generation is defined by the immortality of the ideals and truth they gallantly defended.

The United States has freely given precious blood and treasure to defend the rights of man to be free, and we have never asked for anything in return. No other nation on the planet has sacrificed so much for the noble virtues of liberty and freedom. We hope that the selections offered by Fading Shadows Imprint will touch your hearts and generate a deeper appreciation and love for our country.